SHE WAS BEAUTIFUL.

Dana was beautiful. Her green eyes stood out in startling contrast against her tanned face, and her dark hair tumbled everywhere, brushing her cheeks and her slender shoulders. Morgan felt a surge of intense need.

He leaned forward and traced a finger down the curve of her cheekbone. "I'm sorry it distresses you, but I don't control the weather."

Her eyes widened in question, whether from his touch or his comment, Morgan couldn't say. She parted her full mouth, wrapped her hand around his finger. "I really must leave today, Morgan."

"I know you think so." He pulled back his hand. Only four more days remained. If he could keep her here . . . win her love.

"Does that mean you won't let me leave?" she asked.

The question pricked a tender spot Morgan thought had died long ago. His desire vanished instantly. For a moment there, feeling the human male's affection, the human male's need for a woman, he also felt his humanity return. Now all she'd left him was a wolf's instinctive need. . . .

Shadow
on the
Moon

Connie Flynn

A TOPAZ BOOK

TOPAZ
Published by the Penguin Group
Penguin Books USA Inc., 375 Hudson Street,
New York, New York 10014, U.S.A.
Penguin Books Ltd, 27 Wrights Lane,
London W8 5TZ, England
Penguin Books Australia Ltd, Ringwood,
Victoria, Australia
Penguin Books Canada Ltd, 10 Alcorn Avenue,
Toronto, Ontario, Canada M4V 3B2
Penguin Books (N.Z.) Ltd, 182–190 Wairau Road,
Auckland 10, New Zealand

Penguin Books Ltd, Registered Offices:
Harmondsworth, Middlesex, England

First published by Topaz, an imprint of Dutton Signet,
a division of Penguin Books USA Inc.

First Printing, March, 1997
10 9 8 7 6 5 4 3 2 1

 REGISTERED TRADEMARK—MARCA REGISTRADA

Printed in the United States of America

To Mike, Roxanne, Bryan, Brandon and Brittany.
This one's for you.

Prologue

Yeafanay cawfanay naylanay may.
Yeafanay cawfanay naylanay may.

Twisted roots clung to the rocky, wind-tortured soil, producing gnarled trunks and starved branches that struggled to sustain their sparse leaves. Equally malnourished bushes fought the trees for the meager nutrients the ground provided, and the round, silver moon bathed everything in pale, ghostly light.

Morgan stood in the center of the barren clearing, watching his companion with a degree of professional detachment. She was swaying to and fro, solemnly chanting gibberish and scratching a large circle on the crusty earth around him with a tree branch.

Very Gothic, Morgan thought, grinning. *Lily has outdone herself this time.*

"A man-wolf shall be born this day," Lily sang, completing the ring and discarding the stick with a flourish. With equal drama, she slipped off her simple woolen coat, revealing a gown so obviously staged for the occasion that Morgan's grin erupted into laughter.

"Don't treat this lightly, Dr. Morgan Wilder," she said, regarding him sternly with her dark eyes.

"Put your coat back on, Lily. You're risking hypothermia." A chuckle still rumbled in his throat.

Then, as if to prove his point, the frosty wind picked up. He drew his coat close to his chest. "It's freezing up here."

"I am not cold." Twirling slowly, she gave a toss of her long white hair. Her black gauzy robe lifted, spun around her shoeless feet. "Indeed, my blood runs hot. My wolf spirit is strong."

With another twirl, she lifted her arms, reaching for the moon. "As is the way of the wolf, my darling Morgan, tonight you become my lifetime mate and soar above mortal concerns. Strong, fleet of foot, invincible. The forest and the alleys will be ours. We'll share everything. Our bed, our rank, our offspring . . ." She stopped, held him firm in her dark gaze. "The blood we spill."

Morgan's chuckle died on the wind. Not that

Lily hadn't always been unorthodox, but tonight she almost acted . . . possessed.

"Don't tell me we're going to do that old blood brother ceremony," Morgan said cynically. He was cold and hungry and getting angry. "I'm disappointed, Lily. I thought you were going to dispel my skepticism about these night creatures. Do you think dragging me to these ugly mountains and dancing around in your dressing gown will do that? I have to say, this is rather kooky, even for you."

"There are forces at work in this world you do not understand."

For the space of an insane heartbeat, he almost believed. Of course, the tortured, barren plateau practically personified evil. And the dark wind whipping malevolently around his ears seemed to whisper Lily's truths.

But grotesque settings don't a werewolf make.

Just as Morgan was congratulating himself on so skillfully handling his anxiety, a chorus of howls rose from the treetops of the black forest below, held as one long note, then wobbled and died. Another chorus immediately followed.

And another.

"Did you hear that, Lily? Come on, we're getting out of here." He flew out of the circle, intent on returning to the little car they'd rented in

Paris, which was now parked more than half a mile away.

"Morgan! No!" Lily rushed forward and shoved him toward the ring. Morgan grabbed her hands, stumbled backwards. When they hit the circle's perimeter, Lily jerked away as if she'd hit a force field.

With a long, purposeful step, Morgan breached the circle again, then gripped Lily's arm. "Get your coat," he ordered. "Don't argue."

"It's too late. . . . The forces . . ." Lily peered over her shoulder. Morgan followed her gaze.

"Dear God!" he bellowed.

Eyes, glowing darkly red. Enormous heads. Massive, dangerous jaws, parted to reveal gleaming fangs.

One by one, they filed into the clearing.

With a gasp, Lily pushed Morgan back in the ring.

"What are you—" Morgan sputtered. "Are you crazy? Run, Lily. Now! Those wolves will tear us apart."

But she was deaf to his voice. Throwing back her head, she lifted her arms to the moon. The air whipped her flimsy robe and snowy tresses, swirling them around her in a frenzy.

Morgan's blood froze as he saw the pack of wolves part and circle in opposite directions around the ring. Seven of them, he noted through the haze of fear in his mind, and they blocked all hope of escape. They surrounded the circle, sat down, and stared at Lily, obviously waiting.

But for what?

"Yeafanay cawfanay naylanay may," crooned Lily.

Why hadn't the wolves attacked her? he wondered, then forgot the question as his knees grew weak and began to throb.

"Yeafanay cawfanay naylanay may."

Lily paused. Each wolf raised its head and a great unified howl lifted up, echoing off the rocks, filling the sky. As the last echo faded into the black night, Lily again began to chant.

*"Lady moon in her great fullness squares
dark Pluto now.
Yet fickle Lady waits for none
and soon moves on.*

*Oh, Phantoms of the Dark Beneath rise up
and heed my cry."*

Pain shimmied through Morgan's body, piercing, unbearable pain. His legs buckled. Staggering backwards, he cried out and crumpled

11

to his knees. Through all this, Lily continued her litany.

> *"Bring fang and claw and strength beyond*
> *what mortals know.*
> *Bestow these gifts upon your servant now,*
> *that he may roam the earth*
> *as wolf and man, as man and wolf.*
> *Forevermore."*

With each word, Morgan's agony grew more intense. His legs and arms burned with the fires of hell and he clawed at them, wanting to pull them out as he would some grievous tooth. His jaw shifted and needles pierced every inch of his skin. A thousand knives jabbed at his head.

> *"Rush, Great Phantom, rush, yeah, rush.*
> *Race, Great Phantom, race, yeah, race.*
> *The Lady rolls on, time grows short."*

Lily's voice rose with the wailing wind that beat at Morgan's agonized body like a razor-sharp whip.

> *"Heed us now. Heed us now.*
> *Time grows short. Heed us now."*

Barely aware of the cruel rocks slicing his

burning skin, Morgan writhed on the hard ground, battling the misery of his own flesh. His mind filled with jumbled, crazy questions. How had Lily's fingernails grown so long? Or her teeth so sharp and shiny?

"Lily," he cried from the depths of his pain, but only a grunt emerged.

> *"Yeafanay cawfanay naylanay may.*
> *Yeafanay cawfanay naylanay may.*
> *A man-wolf is born this day!'*

Morgan heard nothing more. Lost in a whirlwind of agony, he thrashed inside the ring. Anguished sounds exploded in his throat. Torment was his whole world now. He was lost in it.

Dying. There was no other explanation. He was dying. And because it hurt too much, he closed his eyes in futility and rolled into a ball, adrift in his own wretched whimpers.

Time passed. He sensed movement around him, but refused to open his eyes. Why were they tormenting him? Why didn't they kill him now? Eyes still closed, he lifted his head awkwardly. It felt heavy and stiff, but the thousand knives were gone. He brought a hand to his brow, felt fur. A peculiar yelp escaped his mouth.

His eyes snapped open and he stared in un-speakable horror.

Where hands once were, he saw hair and claws—large, powerful claws that could rip a throat apart. A crazed laugh bubbled in his throat, but when he opened his mouth only a groan emerged.

"Your alchemization is complete, Morgan," Lily said from above him. "You are one of us now."

She stood in the perimeter of his vision, a sil-houette against the dark woods. Behind her, a bat darted for the trees and he could see each rib of its small wings, see its tiny feet drawn close to its body. It was all so clear, he'd swear the sun was shining. Surely his eyes were play-ing tricks. He focused on Lily, who now bent to stroke his head. Red glinted off her ebony eyes.

Her touch repulsed him. Instinctively, he turned his head, snapped at her hand. He caught a tuft of fur.

She laughed. "Ah, you are angry. But you will grow accustomed to this new life."

The pain must have driven him insane, thought Morgan. Reality, illusion, had blurred. Just like it had for poor Boris, who had spurred him into this loathsome wild-goose chase.

He scrambled clumsily to his feet and wobbled in the air, the weight of his body dragging him down on all fours. He wanted to speak of his bewilderment, to tell Lily that her murky robe now looked like a coat of silver-white hair, that her teeth had grown long and sharp. But he could utter only a series of whines.

"Your skepticism is refuted." Lily's mouth widened into a beastly smile. "You are mine now, my darling Morgan. For many, many glorious lifetimes."

"*No-o-o-o!*"

And elsewhere, by those brave enough to live in the perilous mountains, were heard the echoes of a night beast's agonized howl.

(

Chapter One

Dana Gibbs clicked on the cab light of her four-by-four vehicle to check out the crude map a buddy in the Arizona Fish and Game department had sneaked to her. It seemed she was lost. Although she'd found the referenced mile marker with no trouble at all, the map unfortunately didn't show the Forest Service route number, nor was there any indication that two roads forked with the main highway.

She scowled up at the dark Arizona sky, taking it rather personally that the weather report hadn't mentioned snow, then checked her watch. It wasn't even five o'clock, but the sun had long ago disappeared into layers of blustering clouds. She felt pretty blustery herself.

From the onset of this grueling drive through the narrow, twisting roads of the primitive Blue

Range, her mood had been glum. She'd driven all night from Albuquerque to offer her help on this expedition, only to meet a reception as chilly as this unexpected March storm.

Captain Will Schumacher of the Arizona Highway Patrol had given her a fishy look, as if she were somehow personally responsible for the recent slaughters.

"Thank you, Dr. Gibbs," he'd said dryly. "But every jurisdiction in the state is wanting to horn in on Mission Lobo. We have enough radicals on the team. We don't need another one."

She'd swallowed the insult without retort, although at no little cost to herself, and tried to tell the chubby and pompous man that the carnage couldn't be the work of wolves. Not even bothering to mention that the Mexican wolf had been extinct in the wild for decades, she brought up the obvious. Contrary to fairy tales, wolves didn't mutilate their prey by ripping off limbs and tearing out entrails. They killed it, then ate it.

Also, there was the question of the infant boy. A forest ranger had found the baby wailing from cold and hunger amid the torn remains of its parents. If, by remote possibility, wolves had been responsible for the carnage, why would they have spared the weakest victim?

None of it made sense.

She went on to explain that she wouldn't even have come if it wasn't for the sightings. But three separate groups of backpackers had reported seeing a large canine deep in Ebony Canyon. Since few people were skilled enough to hike so far back into rugged country, Dana gave some credence to their reports. Those men and women understood the wilderness, knew animal tracks and spoor, and were not given to panic attacks.

Still, even the best of her limited persuasive skills got her nowhere, so Dana decided to strike out on her own, despite the captain's chilly reception. The idea of finding a truly feral pack that had experienced little or no contact with man thrilled her. Though she knew it was a long shot, she had to check it out for herself. Something she couldn't do sitting in her Ranger, trying to figure out which way to go.

She shut off the dome light, pulled up her parka hood, and stepped from the Ranger.

Snowfall was still light, but a capricious wind periodically whipped the flakes into whirlwinds. The highway was deserted. She hadn't passed or been passed by anyone for over an hour. Of course, sensible people were home in front of warm fires, not standing at the fork of a remote road shivering in the wind.

The waning sun cast soft, hazy light from

somewhere behind the thunderheads, which combined with the falling snow to create a fog that made Dana think of the mists of Avalon. She stuck her tongue out playfully, caught a soft crystal and let it melt in her mouth.

She loved the wilderness. Loved the pine smell, the murmuring sounds that soothed her soul, loved feasting her eyes on the unspoiled beauty. Warm fire or no, she'd rather be here any day of the week.

She sniffed the crisp air, a habit she'd developed from long years of working with wolves. They did it to check the terrain for prey or predators. Since she lacked their keen olfactory nerves, it served no such purpose for her, as her father often told her. He usually finished by saying she spent so much time with her animals she was beginning to act like them.

A gust of wind blew under the edge of her parka. She tightened the drawstring, then started walking toward the intersecting roads. They were a four-wheeler's nightmare—unpaved, splotched with ice, and barely wide enough to allow two cars to pass without scraping sides. Judging by the deep ruts, a snowplow had been through recently, leaving cliffs of snow on the sides of each road.

Dana approached the fork where the roads met the highway and squinted through the gathering low fog. Maybe the north road. After all, she was headed in that direction. Faulty logic, she had to admit, but if the choice turned out badly, she could always backtrack.

So what if she ended up camping here all night? Her Ranger was well equipped. Her main concern was that Mission Lobo would start their search without her.

Of course, the unit would have to contend with the storm, too. Besides, despite the excited skip of her heart every time she thought of it, she would undoubtedly learn that there weren't any wolves. Her best guess was that some fly-by-night zoo owner had released a captive animal into the wild after learning how expensive they were to feed. Maybe a bear, or even some large jungle cat.

Perhaps a delay wouldn't hurt. She could sure use a solid night's sleep. Between meeting with bureaucrats and nursing an Arctic white wolf who was struggling through an Albuquerque hot spell, she'd had few opportunities to close her eyes over the last several days.

She was beginning to feel the effects. Not that she minded spending time with Sharky. He was a sweet animal, devoted to his mate, and he'd be gone soon enough. New Mexico was too hot. When winter ended, a facility in Alaska would take him in. . . .

Dana felt a familiar pang of loss. She hated giving up even one of her animals. With a shake of her head, she went back to choosing a road. Even the lure of a long, solid block of sleep and the knowledge that she'd probably come up empty-handed on this excursion couldn't mitigate her excitement. She had to be there on the front line. If wolves did exist in Ebony Canyon, they needed someone to protect them from the trigger-happy officers under Schumacher's command.

North it was.

She headed back to the Ranger.

While she'd been woolgathering, the sky had blackened and the wind was now a steady blow, pelting her with frozen snowflakes. It rattled the branches of the bare ash and cypress and sent macabre whistles through the needles of the evergreens. The sound reminded Dana of the thin scream of a dying rabbit and sent prickles through her body.

Abruptly, she stopped walking. Something was out there, behind the bending pines and whipping branches.

Watching her . . .

She studied the dense forest, searching for movement. All was still, but she'd learned to respect those sudden prickles of her skin. Once, when she'd felt much this way, she'd turned a corner of a trail to find a bear raging against a swarm of bees. The prickles had saved her life.

She lowered her head against the wind and quickened her pace toward the Ranger. Just as she reached for the door handle, a howl resounded over the highest treetops. Achingly mournful, it carried a message of pain, loss, death.

Dana felt the sorrow to her bones. Grotesque images of flying limbs and spurting blood flashed through her mind. Her shivers turned into flesh-racking shudders. Her knees buckled. She grabbed for the handle, jumped inside the ranger, and shakily activated the locks.

Just a coyote, she told herself as she turned on the engine with trembling fingers, unnerved by her intense reaction. She'd grown up in some of the country's most rugged areas and felt safer backpacking alone through deserted canyons than she did on most city streets. True, she'd felt fear before, but not limb-numbing terror such as this.

Her hands were still shaking when she engaged the four-wheel drive and jammed the Ranger into gear. The four-by-four creaked and swayed as she entered the road, jarring her in her seat. She clenched her teeth, focused on avoiding the worst ruts, and soon forgot the fearsome howl.

Several bumpy miles later, Dana rounded a sharp S-turn and pulled to a full stop. The road had already deteriorated into a narrow cow path, and now an enormous wall of snow had swallowed it.

Tapping her fingers against the steering wheel, she sighed loudly, and backed up, hoping for enough room to turn around in. She then angled the Ranger to the right, gingerly rolling back until she felt the tire hit the ridge of a drainage ditch bordering the road. Next, she pulled forward as far as possible until she reached the opposite side. She repeated the procedure several times, carefully avoiding the boggy ditch, which she knew would suck her four-by-four right in.

With considerable effort, she finally had the Ranger at a suitable angle to the line of the road. From here, she turned the steering wheel as far as it would go, then stomped on the gas, counting on weight and momentum to carry her out. But she'd misjudged the slickness of the road. The tires tried to grab, but failed. The vehicle fishtailed and skidded toward the ditch.

Whomp. Thump. Thump. The right front wheel scaled the edge of the ditch, jolting the Ranger to a stop.

"Dammit!" Dana pressed her lips together, slammed the gears in reverse, and floorboarded the gas pedal. The wheels spun impotently and she released the gas.

Throwing open the door, she stomped through the mud, dug out a lantern from the rear, and went to inspect the damage. Her back tires sat on a sheet of ice. The front passenger wheel was mired in the ditch. Cursing herself for having decided she didn't need chains because the western storm season had passed, she swung the lantern around, seeking something to wedge under the stuck wheel. The light fell on a branch, thick with pine needles, several yards inside the forest.

Dana hopped across the ditch.

The lantern splashed light on the underbrush. Birds flapped their wings and flew from dark shadows. Various creatures scurried and squeaked on the ground. Finding the normality of the sounds reassuring, Dana hurried toward the branch, confident she'd soon be out of her predicament.

A howl shattered her serenity. The night creatures instantly hushed and only an undulating echo broke the silence.

Dana froze midstep. Her nerve endings vibrated, and for a moment her foot remained suspended in air. Angry at her loss of control, she stamped the foot down and exhaled heavily.

Her breath misted in the lantern's wake, creating a heavy fog. The light quivered in her trembling hand.

Battling an urge to dash for the Ranger, Dana made herself creep toward the branch. As soon as it came within reach, she snatched it up and sprinted toward the road, nearly tumbling when her foot caught the top of a dark stone.

Finally, she reached the Ranger and hastily bent to wedge the bough beneath the mired wheel. When it was securely in place, she climbed inside. By now, her body was stiff from cold and tension. She struggled to remain clear-headed as she looked over her shoulder and applied gentle pressure to the gas pedal.

The Ranger didn't budge. Dana upped the pressure. Nothing happened. As she steadied herself for one more try, the terrible wail came again. So loud, so close, it seemed just outside her door. She spun toward the windshield. She'd forgotten the lantern! And in the perimeter of its spilled light, a blurred shape moved with superhuman speed.

Dana slammed down on the gas pedal.

The Ranger lurched—once, twice, then again. She let up, stomped down again. The vehicle shuddered, broke loose, and careened back at drag racing speed.

Dana instinctively hit the brakes, all the while knowing it was the wrong thing to do. Brakes squealed, tires screeched. The Ranger zigzagged, then spun. She battled the steering wheel, trying to force it in the direction of the skid, but it defied her control. Behind her, the wall of snow loomed larger and larger until it filled her rear-view mirror.

Like a great white shark, the wall opened up and sucked in the four-by-four like a minnow until it jerked to a halt against the skeleton of solid earth. The jolt threw Dana against the steering wheel, propelled her up and into the windshield, then rebounded her back into the seat, where she slumped like a rag doll.

Her head roared with pain. The coppery taste of blood filled her mouth. Her vision grew fuzzy. Within the beams of the headlights, ever-green branches swayed and dark, unnameable shadows danced. Blinking, she tried to bring the sights into focus. She felt light-headed and giddy.

As a strangled moan escaped her lips, her world quaked. She watched numbly as snow slid down the windshield. At first the avalanche only covered the hood, then, gaining momentum, it dumped huge chunks of snow on the roof, where they clattered, bounced off the glass, and slid down the fenders. Dana screamed.

Then the windows were filled with white. All

was deadly quiet. The only light inside the car came from the dimly glowing instrument panel.

Who will protect my wolves? Dana wondered as she passed into unconsciousness.

And from the shadows of the forest, a pair of gold-green eyes witnessed her misfortune.

❨

Chapter Two

Beneath a towering pine stirred a man as huge and solid as the tree trunk that sheltered him. A long wool overcoat hung to his knees over heavy leggings that were tucked into bulky, serviceable boots, and his face was hidden in the abyss of a deep hood. Each item was of a nondescript dark color, not quite black or navy blue or gray, allowing him to melt into the shadows.

What had possessed him to come this close to a major road so early in the evening? He knew better. But he'd heard the screams so often of late, could barely abide them, and a night such as this was made for death. *They* would be out, seeking lost travelers, and he felt somehow compelled to stop them.

He'd been observing the female for some time, had seen her purposeful and confident movements. Had seen her become first alarmed, then panicked, causing her to react so unwisely. Was she even now trying to claw her way out like a snared rabbit? Surely, she was every bit as defenseless, every bit as doomed. Without help, she wouldn't last till dawn.

Her vehicle had been so fully engulfed by the snowbank that only the hood and grille remained exposed. The beam of its headlights, still vibrating from aftershock, quivered on the road's frozen surface and made the falling snow look like a shimmering curtain. The front passenger wheel spun on its axle, several inches off the ground. Otherwise, he detected no movement.

Nearby, an owl hooted a warning. A rodent squealed, then scrambled through the forest carpet. The night fell into deep stillness, save for the purr of the engine and the *whup-whup-whup* of the airborne tire. He strained to hear, anticipating what was to come. Soon a rustle arose from the underbrush. A soulful wail followed.

Why did those creatures howl so incessantly?

Knowing it was a question without an answer, he calmly turned toward a tangle of brush and thickets. Within the dusky shadows, two sets of watchful eyes glinted red in the light from the woman's abandoned lantern. He returned their gazes with a hard stare, but they held their ground. Slowly, his lip curled in threat.

"Back off," he snarled.

The eyes retreated, leaving another squealing rodent in their wake.

He nonchalantly turned his back and sprinted easily over the wood and stone obstacles littering his path to the road. With one athletic leap, he scaled the ditch and landed nearly fifteen feet away beside the vehicle's spinning wheel.

His hood fell back, the wind tugged at his shaggy hair, and snowflakes struck his brow and nose. The cold troubled him little; he was well fortified against it, but he didn't want to frighten the poor woman to death.

Smiling with black humor, he reached into his overcoat, pulled out a ski mask, and slipped it over his head. Next, he examined the damage to her vehicle. Over a foot of snow covered the cab. The snow would act as insulation and undoubtedly would keep her warm, but the running engine would soon eat up her oxygen. She was still alive though, very alive. He could smell her in there, the spicy scent of warm flesh, the tang of hot, rushing blood. Could hear the strong pulse in her veins.

He dug into the snow bare-handed, heedless of the scratches he put in the paint, effortlessly deflecting the myriad new chunks dislodged by his movements. When he'd cleared all the snow from the driver's window, he leaned over and made out the woman's motionless silhouette through the condensation on the glass.

Unconscious.

This came as no surprise. He'd seen her strike the windshield, seen her forehead turn crimson, knew she probably had a concussion.

Doomed. Without his help, the others would finish her off before dawn. A guttural protest escaped his lips.

He must walk away. The risk was too great.

Yet it had been written. On such a night, a maiden would come. . . .

With a resigned sigh, he stepped back from the window and hurled away the remaining snow. When he was done, he pulled the door open and reached to shut off the engine and lights. They offended his sensitive ears and eyes.

He looked down at the slumped form. Blood was clotting in her dark, curly hair and the beginnings of a bruise already stained her forehead, yet he still saw how striking she was. High, well-defined cheekbones. Smooth, golden skin. A slender, well-developed body. A dislodged comb hung in her hair, letting her curls fall forward, which gave her a tumbled, morning-after look.

His heartbeat quickened and he realized then how long it had been since he'd touched a mortal woman. Fingers trembling, he moved a hand toward her fragile throat.

The wound still bled, the fresh blood trickling slowly down her face in tiny streams. He inhaled the tart odor and instantly salivated.

He jerked his hand back.

Do no harm. The ingrained dictum sprang to his mind and lodged there. He tried to dismiss it. Surely it didn't mean he also had to prevent harm. This wasn't his doing. How could he be blamed, when the female had foolishly driven down an unmarked dead-end road and bogged her truck?

A laughterlike sound traveled through the night. He glanced up, sniffed the air. Was he even now being mocked by his indecision? Watched, to see if he'd leave the unconscious female so they could fulfill their dark needs? Or worse, far worse, use her to fulfill his own?

He looked up the storm-darkened path, seeing things that would escape a mortal's eye. A doe stepped out of a stand of trees, nibbled on some half-frozen grass, withdrew. A squirrel poked up its head beside a tree. A hawk swept down and the squirrel retreated.

Maybe if he covered her with warm blankets, rangers would dig her out in the morning. In a few days she'd be sharing her adventure with all her friends.

Right, he thought dryly. Why would the Forest Service check a dead-end road during what appeared to be the worst snowstorm in decades? He looked up. Nor could a helicopter see her— not through the dense pine overhang.

He was her only refuge. Shuddering from the effort of quelling his instincts, he reached over her slumped figure and picked up a duffel bag from the storage area behind her seat. She was a mortal woman, after all, and he had not yet forgotten that they needed fresh clothes and other necessities.

He hesitated for another heartbeat, again tempted to leave the female to her fate. His gaze drifted aimlessly, taking in the provision-packed interior, moving to the space he'd cleared on the windshield and onto the patches of lantern light reflecting off the red hood.

Red. The color brought memories of flickering firelight. Long talks with White Hawk, old tales from ancient tribes, that all aligned with the promises in The Book.

Was she the one?

Absurd. The Book contained nothing but legend—old wives' tales to pacify wretched creatures like himself. With an impatient jerk, he turned, bent, and lifted the female from the seat as easily as if she was a doll. A moan passed her lips. He froze. But she merely wriggled deeper into his arms and collapsed against him like a dozing kitten.

Holding her firmly against his massive chest, he broke into a rhythmic lope and started the long trek up the stormy mountain. And all the while a subtle question of which he was barely aware repeated itself.

Was she the one?

Dana's head hurt. Bad. So bad, she hardly noticed the lesser aches in the rest of her body. Thoughts wandered through her fuzzy mind; she stirred and turned. Dreams . . . bizarre, disturbing dreams. A white tomb enclosing her. Dancing lights full of ominous shapes. Something black and hideous bending over her. Claws touching her neck. Then . . .

Someone carrying her, holding her gently against their warmth, a reassuring voice.

She heard the snap of resin, smelled mesquite. Her eyelids fluttered open. Above her, an oddly familiar ceiling of golden logs glowed in the light. A man bent over a weathered stone fireplace.

"Dad?" she mumbled. "Dad? Did Mother come back?"

The man got up, crossed the room, a blur in Dana's foggy vision.

"Dad?" she cried again, lifting her head.

Large, gentle hands touched her shoulder. "It's okay, Dana. Lie back down."

Her eyelids fell closed and she drifted off to dream again.

The next time she stirred, her images were crisper. The wrong road. The stuck tire. The crash.

The howls.

She awoke with a start. Gingerly, she levered onto her elbows and looked around. She was alone in a spacious log cabin that gave her the sensation of stepping back in time, into the cabin in which she'd grown up. Wind whistled in the eaves. Across the room a fire leaped in the hearth of a stone fireplace. To one side she saw a rough-hewed padded rocker and ottoman. Wood flanked the other side. In the center of the room was a crude wooden table with a couple of chairs tucked underneath.

Where was she? How far from Mission Lobo base camp?

Who had brought her here?

A door opened and she cautiously turned her head. A man in a flannel shirt and loose denim jeans stepped into the room. His body filled the door, top to bottom, side to side. A wild bush of black wavy hair fell over his shoulders, and his thick eyebrows were separated only by a scarlike crease. Two deep grooves bracketed his nose, and the rest of his face was hidden beneath a ragged beard. His overall appearance made Dana think of the legendary logger, Paul Bunyon.

"How are you feeling, Dana?" he asked, chasing away that image. This was no lumberjack's voice. It was smooth and cultured, hinting at a privileged Eastern education.

"Okay, I guess." Dana tentatively touched her aching head. Someone had neatly bandaged it. "Did you do this?"

"As well as I could."

She saw now that he held a metal basin and some medicinal supplies. He crossed the room in two long strides and put them on a table beside the bed. His shoulders cast her in complete shadow and his hands were as large as the iron frying pan her mother once used. A brotherly pat on the back could send her flying across the room—not an easy task, since she was no featherweight herself. She supposed she should be apprehensive, but all she could think was—

"My wolves," she said, abruptly swinging her feet to the floor.

A mistake. She grabbed her head and leaned forward.

"Don't move so suddenly," he directed, shifting to her side.

"But . . . but, my wolves. I have to . . ."

"Wolves?" He smiled, his face transforming as if a light had come on behind it. The crease between his eyebrows disappeared, the brackets softened. For the first time, Dana noticed his eyes. Gold, flecked with dancing lights of green. Soft, gentle, immensely sad. But he'd asked a question, and she must answer it and immediately get his help. The pain in her head was a nuisance, of course, but nothing she couldn't ignore.

"I'm here for Mission Lobo, just in case there really are wolves. I have serious doubts, because the killings aren't consist—"

"You've lost me. What are you talking about?" His smile vanished, leaving Dana to wonder if she'd imagined the transformation.

"Are you a hermit or—" She stopped abruptly. He was obviously a friendly man who'd come to her aid. Not that she'd needed it. She would have woken up eventually, dug out the Ranger. Nevertheless, she had to quit biting the hand that fed her, or in this case, pulled her from danger.

"I'm sorry. I get so involved I forget the whole world doesn't revolve around my profession. The bang on my head didn't help, either.

Anyway, people have been killed in the Blue Range and they're blaming it on a pack of wild wolves. I'm a biologist and I've come to disprove those claims."

He frowned skeptically. "There are no wolves up here. People have big imaginations. Some say pterodactyls still fly through the canyons."

"I'm not getting through to you, am I?"

"I know you have someplace to go, but I also know you're in no condition to go there." He put a hand on her shoulder. "I'll help you to the bathroom."

"It's okay. I can do it." Annoyed by his dismissal, she struggled to her feet, despite the protests of her bruised muscles. But her head wouldn't be ignored. Her vision blurred and she groped blindly for the headboard.

"Don't push yourself." He put a supporting arm around her back. "You took a nasty bump."

This time Dana didn't argue. His shirt felt soft against her cheek, and his scent—a merging of pine needles and smoking firewood—comforted her.

"You're supposed to take it easy the first time you get up after a concussion," he chided gently. "I'll walk you around the room until you get your legs back."

"I have a concussion?"

She got no answer. Instead, he nestled her

firmly under his arm and urged her into a first step. She was five ten herself, but he towered over her, easily holding the weight of her body. His warm breath brushed her hair, and his chest rose and fell evenly against her shoulders. She settled into the shelter of his arm and took one tentative step after another, suddenly feeling safer and more secure than she'd felt in a long while.

By the second trip around the tiny room, her feelings of dependency started getting uncomfortable.

"I think I can manage now." She pulled away and began walking alone.

He stood nearby, watching. When she stopped, he said, "You have a strong will, Dana."

"Thank— Say, how do you know my name?"

"I brought one of your bags up." He gestured to the foot of the daybed.

"Oh, you read the tag." Her legs were feeling a little wobbly, so she backed up, sat on the bed, and plucked at the sleeve of her thermal undershirt. Suddenly, she remembered she hadn't been wearing it when the accident happened. This giant of a man had stripped her down, seen her half-naked.

Looking up uneasily, she said, "By any chance do you have a name, too?"

She hoped he would reward her with a smile and was disappointed when it didn't come.

"Morgan. Morgan Wilder."

"So where am I, Morgan?"

"You're in my home."

"I kind of figured that one out. Where is it?"

"Strong willed," he said. "Bright. What a woman."

Although his tone was light, the lines near his mouth had deepened and Dana didn't quite know how to respond. She'd never been good at that kind of thing. To her, people were a little unfathomable. You didn't know what was going on behind their eyes when they said things. Not like the wolf. That creature was direct. Every sound, every movement had meaning.

"You didn't answer my question." Obviously he didn't understand this wasn't just idle curiosity. "Where are we?"

"Up some distance from the road."

"How did you get me here?"

"I have my ways." He pointed to a narrow door near a stack of open pantry shelves. "You still need the bathroom?"

"An indoor outhouse?" She involuntarily wrinkled her nose.

"Better than actually going outside." His face softened as though her reaction had mildly

41

amused him. "I have a few conveniences. One of them is indoor plumbing. You need help?"

"No, no, I'm fine." She got up unsteadily and kept an eye on him as she reached for the doorknob.

"Not that door!" Morgan's eyebrows met in a line as sharp as his tone.

Startled, Dana saw that her hand was wrapped around the doorknob of the room from which he'd entered. The door had large, heavy crossbeams fortified with metal plating.

"My bedroom," he said, more gently. "I, uh, I have a thing about my privacy."

"Sorry," she mumbled, wondering at his sharp response. But she ended up admiring the small bathroom, which had a pale solar light. It featured a small bathtub and a toilet with a water tank hung quite close to the ceiling. Obviously a cistern on the roof fed both the tub and toilet.

After taking care of her business, she planned to check out her head injury. Somehow she couldn't believe it was as bad as Morgan said. Unfortunately, there was no mirror, which went a long way toward explaining his unkempt appearance.

Well, chances are she didn't look so hot herself after all that. Not that it was important. The vital thing was to get Morgan to understand that she had to leave immediately.

When she came out of the bathroom, he was waiting for her.

"Some ground rules." He spoke so abruptly, Dana snapped her head around to stare at him.

"About what?" she asked, trying to act as if the sharp movement hadn't hurt.

"Looks like you'll be here for a few days at least."

"No, oh, no. I'm leaving tomorrow."

"Naturally, you'd be better off in a hospital, but we'll never get out of here in this storm."

Dana had almost forgotten the storm. In her pain and disorientation, she'd virtually blocked out the noise. Now she could hear nothing else. It beat at the walls and roof, rattled the windows. Fierce, angry sounds.

"What time is it?" she asked abruptly.

"The sun went down a little while ago."

"Then I've only been asleep a few hours or so. I haven't lost that much time."

"Try twenty-four hours or so." Morgan raised his thick eyebrows. "This is another day. I roused you, walked you around the room a few times, but you never really came to."

"It was you. . . ." Soft hands touching her, the gentle murmuring voice, sometimes close, sometimes distant. "You took care of me all night?"

He nodded.

"I thought I was dreaming." The depth of his kindness nearly brought tears to her eyes and made her realize the extent of her injuries. If not for him, she could have died. "How can I thank you?"

He regarded her intently for a second. "Now you see why you can't leave. This storm could last all week, but even if it doesn't, you're in no condition to travel."

"Not all week," Dana shook her head, and immediately regretted the action. "I can't stay! The mission— I should have been there last night."

"Dana. There are no wolves."

"You can't say that for sure," she replied hotly. "Maybe there are. Maybe a pack's survived up here all these years. You don't know. If they have, they need my protection."

"No one can outguess the weather," he replied, plainly dismissing her concerns. "I'll take you out as soon as your health and the weather permits. In the meantime, I want the rules clear. You have full reign in this room. Help yourself to food, add logs to the fire, whatever you need."

"I'm leaving in the morning, Morgan. No—"

"Don't go outside after dark."

"—matter how hard—"

"It's for your own safety. This is not a civilized national park. It's a wild forest land. There are dangers out there you can't imagine."

"—it's snowing."

Morgan waved his hands toward the bedroom with a grace unusual for a man his size. "Please respect my privacy and stay out of my room. My taste in music is rather unusual, so you may hear strange sounds at night. Ignore them. They mean nothing."

"Didn't you hear me? I'm leaving in the morning."

"Yes, I heard, but you can talk forever and it won't change anything. There are already drifts over twelve feet high out there, and you're still weak as a lamb."

Dana slammed her hands on her hips. "Don't tell me about snow! I grew up in the backwoods of Montana. No Arizona snowstorm could compare to that."

"Oh?" Morgan walked to the window and lifted the shade. "Come here, Dana."

She didn't know why she obeyed so meekly, but she did, and what she saw outside shocked her.

A maelstrom of black and white. Nothing but swirling blizzard. The wind howled. The cabin walls creaked and moaned. The roof shuddered. An icy draft swept down the chimney, creating a shiver in the licking flames.

Dana felt the chill to her marrow. Turning away without uttering a word, she went to the daybed and climbed beneath a warm blanket, suddenly grateful to be inside this sturdy shelter. Her head throbbed, her every muscle ached, and Morgan was right. The storm was a bad one, and she wasn't in any condition to go out in it.

At least not soon.

(

Chapter Three

"Unit thirteen-twelve calling Base Camp Lobo," called Charlie Lonetree into the speaker of the staticky CB.

"Give it up, man." Deek Kowalski swiveled his seat and gestured at the radio. "They can't hear you, for crissake. There's too much weather."

"Yeah, well, I'm trying to get an okay to go in."

Deek glanced skeptically out the windshield. A foot or more of snow surrounded their well-equipped van. "I'm guessing even four-wheel drive won't move us till the plow gets here. Why worry? We got plenty of fuel and a week's worth of food." He leaned over, pulled a bag of Cheetos out of a cupboard and began ripping it open. "Want some?"

Charlie shook his head. "What I'd like is to get some miles between us and Ebony Canyon."

Deeked hooted and slapped his knees.

"You don't believe those old legends, do you, man?"

"Shit, no. But the snow's heavier at this elevation. Sooner we get down, sooner we'll move out of it."

"You can't pull one over on me. You half think it's true."

Charlie ignored him and peered out the snow-battered windshield, thinking he saw man-shaped shadows darting among the swirls of white. Imagination. Spooks from tales told by the grandfathers. He didn't even do the sweat lodges anymore, much less practice the old ways.

Deek was still laughing, the son of a bitch.

"Dooweep, dooweep, dooweep." Deek waggled his fingers ominously, then clutched his chest. "Help! Bigfoot's coming! Watch out! There's the ghost of Geronimo! Whoops! Here's a tyrannosaurus rex looking for supper!"

"Knock it off, asshole." Charlie snatched the speaker back up. "Unit thirteen-twelve calling Base Camp Lobo."

"Hey," Deek exclaimed, apparently losing interest in giving Charlie a bad time. "The storm's easing up."

"Yeah?" Charlie glanced up from the radio. Sure enough, the snowfall had ebbed to drifting flakes, and the wind had slowed. "The CB's still not getting through."

"Chill out, man." Deek shoved out the Cheetos bag. "Sure you don't want any?"

"Maybe later." Charlie slammed down the speaker, then moved the driver's seat forward and turned on the ignition. "I'm going to try to get us out of here."

As Charlie shifted into gear, Deek suddenly fanned the air around his face. Charlie pinched his nose and turned accusingly toward his partner.

"Sorry." Deek got up and headed for the chemical toilet in the back.

"Not there, man. These are close quarters. You'd better go outside, or we'll be living with the aftereffects for the entire ride."

Deek glanced out the window, then back to the curtained-off potty area, clearly torn between two bad choices. "Even worse." His voice held resignation. "It's my guess we won't be getting out of this snow, which means we'd have to put up with it all night." He sighed heavily. "I'll probably freeze my butt off, but . . . okay. Where's the paper?"

"Under the backseat." Charlie shut down the engine.

A few minutes later, Deek, armed with a roll of Charmin and a Baggie, opened the side door. A blast of frigid air rushed into the van.

"You got a *Playboy* anywhere in case this takes a while?" he joked, clicking on his flashlight as he stepped outside.

"Just hurry," Charlie grumbled. "And shut the freaking door. We're losing heat."

"Yes, sir!" Deek gave him a mock salute, then started for the back of the van. In seconds, all Charlie could see was the light, and pretty soon even that disappeared.

"Has it been storming ever since—"

"It's gotten worse."

Morgan seemed restless. He prowled the room like a big cat, his mane of hair crackling with static, until he finally stopped to glance at Dana.

"How's your head?"

"It aches a little."

"I thought so."

He came to the bed and picked up the basin, which he carried to a free-standing sink and filled with water from a pump. Next, he lifted a brewing kettle from a stove that Dana assumed was propane powered, although she couldn't see the tank. As he poured steaming water into the basin, she took in the remainder of her surroundings.

In an exposed area beneath the sink were some rags and a collection of cleaning supplies. Next to it stood a refrigerator, with a fuel tank attached.

The room had two windows. Several solar light fixtures, still glowing dully, dotted the walls between them. But if the storm didn't abate soon, Dana knew they'd be using candles.

Living by candlelight in a small cabin with a giant of a man. Now that was a thought. Not a particularly comforting one. Before he'd snapped at her, she'd felt right at home. But his surliness, combined with the remoteness of the area, and the idea that he'd undressed her while she was unconscious, undermined her feelings of comfort.

He approached with the steaming water. Instinctively adopting the submissive behavior she'd learned from her wolves, Dana pressed against the wall, only vaguely aware that the movement exposed her vulnerable neck and stomach.

"I frighten you." He set the basin on the table.

"No . . . no," Dana hastily reassured him, lowering her eyes to avoid any hint of challenge. "I'm still sore . . . I . . . well, you know what I mean."

"You're disoriented, too. It's natural after a head injury." He picked up the penlight he'd left on the table, sat down on a wooden chair and flicked it on.

"Hold still." He lifted one of her eyelids. "I want to check your pupils."

He aimed the light into Dana's eye and she flinched.

"Hold still!"

"You're shining a floodlight in my eye!"

"I see you're one of those cranky patients." He let go of her lid and began the procedure on her other eye.

"Are you a doctor?"

"It doesn't take a medical degree to see you might have a concussion. You took a nasty blow."

"It's not a concussion. I'm sure of it." As if in protest, her head throbbed again. "Okay. How bad is it?"

He clicked off the penlight, put it down, and looked at her thoughtfully. His eyes reminded her of a stag she'd once seen cornered by a pack of wolves. It had regarded them, not with terror, but with resignation to its terrible fate. Feeling suddenly uncomfortable, she glanced away.

"Your pupils are no longer dilated, but you were unresponsive for quite a while." He poured disinfectant onto a cotton ball, then lifted the bandage from her forehead and moved the cotton toward the gash beneath. "This may sting a bit."

"I wasn't able to get much sleep during the last few days," Dana offered, steeling herself against the bite of the antiseptic. "Maybe that's the reason I was out so long."

"Looks like you're going to live." Morgan resettled her bandage. "Hungry?"

Dana nodded.

"I'll fix you something to eat." He went back to the kitchen and turned a burner on under a porcelain saucepan, then began nervously pacing in front of the stove.

A bit unsettled by his restlessness, Dana began examining the cabin again. It was built almost like a fort. All the doors were set in frames over a foot in width and reinforced by heavy crossbeams. Oddly, only the bedroom door had steel plates, and Dana wondered why. Wouldn't it make more sense to fortify the front door?

She got up and began circling the room, touching this and that—the corner of the sturdy dining table, a chair, the refrigerator, a bookcase—wanting to make it all familiar, in some sense make it hers. As she passed the kitchen, Morgan shoved a bowl toward her.

"Porridge," he said as he handed it over.

"Not very exciting, but it's easy to digest and sticks to your ribs."

Dana peered down. "You have milk and sugar?"

"Will goat's milk do?"

Dana smiled. "I haven't had goat's milk in years."

"Appetite good. The patient's recovering." Morgan's remarkable smile emerged.

Dana met his smile, but it faded immediately. He stared thoughtfully for the space of a breath, then opened the refrigerator and pulled out a pitcher of milk. Dana poured it on the porridge along with several teaspoons of brown sugar found in a bowl on the table, then sat down and dug in, surprised to discover how hungry she was.

"That was good," she informed Morgan after she'd cleaned out the bowl.

"Want more?"

Dana shook her head, watching Morgan with curiosity as he continued prowling the room. When he circled the table for the third time, he picked up her empty bowl and carried it to the sink. Then he moved to the open pantry and picked up a bottle.

"Tylenol," he said, placing it on the table. "Take a couple if it hurts too bad. But no aspirin. It exacerbates hemorrhaging." He paused for a moment, then began pacing the room again. "You seem healthy enough, but you were out of it long enough that I'm concerned."

"Like I said, I've been skimping on sleep."

He eyed her thoughtfully, stopping at a bookcase where he picked up a slim volume. "I'd rather err on the side of caution."

Dana touched her forehead. The bandage was tidy and secure. A real professional job. "You sure you're not a doctor?"

"Did I say I wasn't?"

Dana sighed. Why must he always be so obscure?

"I'm a psychiatrist—that is, I was." He let out a bitter laugh. "I switched from internal medicine after I found out I fainted at the sight of blood."

"I guess I'm lucky you stayed conscious long enough to treat me." Dana smiled, wanting very much to ease the tension between them.

"Are you?" he'd completed yet another circle and now stood in front of her, looking down. "You may come to think differently, Dana."

Her smile faded. "Is that supposed to mean something?"

"No. Nothing in particular." He turned to the metal bedroom door and, after palming the knob, looked back at her. "I won't be out again tonight. If you get hungry, help yourself. The wood's a bit low, but should last the night."

"Thanks."

"Remember." He opened the door slowly. "My music's a bit odd. Pay no attention."

How odd could a man's music be? Dana wondered as the door closed with an ominous click.

She got up then, roaming aimlessly around the room. Without Morgan taking up so much space, she saw the cabin was bigger than she'd thought. Still, she felt trapped. She hated storms and the way they kept one boxed up, sometimes for days and days. On the other hand, this was Arizona, where storms usually blew over rapidly. And at least she was warm and dry and under a doctor's care.

Her wanderings took her into the kitchen nook. The pan that contained the oatmeal was neatly covered on the stove. On the burner next to it, another covered pot simmered over a low flame. Dana lifted the lid, saw chunks of meat bubbling in a thick broth, inhaled the sent of rosemary and sage. Maybe she'd have some later, if she got hungry again.

She replaced the lid and wandered toward the pegged rack where her parka hung alongside Morgan's winter wear. He certainly lived a simple existence, almost Quaker-like. He could also be surly enough. Although, considering he was burdened with an injured and unwelcome houseguest, she supposed he was treating her pretty decently. For heaven's sake, she couldn't have lasted twenty-four hours unconscious in that Ranger. When was she going to admit he'd saved her life?

A vague saying floated to the forefront of her thoughts. Something about saving someone from death and thereafter being responsible for them all their life. The way Morgan hovered over her made her think he might believe something of that sort. Well, she'd discourage that line of thinking. Somewhere out there, a highway patrol team was waiting for a break in the storm so they could go out and sharpshoot some wolves.

If they existed. She couldn't pinpoint what lay behind her unscientific conviction that the wolves were out there, being badly maligned by both government officials and the press. Everything she knew about the wolf told her that no pack could exist for this long without being discovered. Yet her instincts urged her to be there, make sure, protect those animals. And she couldn't do that languishing in a mountain cabin. Action was required, not introspection.

It was then that she noticed several pairs of snowshoes stacked neatly beneath the rack. There were some traditional webbed shoes, but also two slim, modern metal sets. She picked up one of the sets and grabbed her boots, which were stored alongside Morgan's, then sat on a low stool near the door. After lacing up her boots, she fiddled with the adjustments on the snowshoes, eventually managing a perfect fit. Then she took them off and hid them behind the webbed shoes.

She then went to her duffel bag, to see what in fact she'd packed in there. More long underwear, a set of nylon leggings, some thick socks. With the snowshoes to aid her, she could make the hike by herself. No matter what Morgan said, the minute the weather broke, she'd hoof it down the mountain.

The decision made her feel more in control, but she remained restless. She wandered about, threw another log on the fire, stoked it, and continued to roam. Finally she stopped in front of the tall bookcase where Morgan had picked up the book he'd taken into his room with him.

Fascinating reading, Dana thought. One section was filled from top to bottom with novels of all kinds. A host of survivalist books, on subjects ranging from planting organic gardens to using solar power, were crammed into another group of shelves. There were medical books and magazines and a section devoted to psychiatry.

Strangely—she was usually more interested in

the behavior of animals than that of men—this drew her attention. She saw books by Freud and Jung and other names she didn't recognize. Several had ominous titles: *The Divided Self, Sanity, Madness and the Family, The Wolf-Man—Sixty Years Later.* Leather slipcases held various publications. She picked up a case labeled *American Journal of Psychiatry* and took out an issue. It had been addressed to Morgan at a post office in Alpine, Arizona, and was over two years old.

So he hadn't given up his devotion to psychiatry entirely. She wondered why he had left the field. She was about to pick up another magazine case when a small leather volume caught her eye. The spine was badly chipped and she couldn't make out the title, so she opened it to the flyleaf. *The Lycanthropy Reader: The Wer-wolf in Moderne Times.* Underneath was a publication date of 1826.

Certainly a subject off the beaten track. She carried it to her bed and curled up to read.

As she flipped to the first page, she heard a horrible moan. She bounced up like she'd been shot from a cannon, cringing from the ache her sudden motion caused. Several more moans and cries followed. She rushed to the window, sure the sounds had come from outside, and stared through the streaked pane. It was black out there, a dark swirling morass. Nothing could be seen, and with all that wailing wind, she was sure nothing could be heard.

But still the moans and groans continued.

Heart pounding, Dana raced to Morgan's door and lifted her fist. Just as she was about to knock, she realized the grotesque noises came from there.

Morgan's music.

How odd could a man's music be? She grinned wryly, thinking she'd never heard anything odder—or more unsettling.

Feeling a sudden need for protection, she returned to the bed and cocooned herself in its layer of blankets. After a moment, she picked up the book.

The wer-wolf, it opened, *is the bane of all mankind. Caught in a blood frenzy akin to that of the loathsome shark, this vile mixture of man and wolf is driven to kill and maim by forces beyond its control. The urge is most irresistible on the eve of the full of the moon. . . .*

With a raging storm outside, a fire blazing in the hearth, and the theme of the Marquis de Sade playing in the next room, Dana certainly couldn't have picked more fitting reading material.

A short while later, still clutching the book, she fell into an uneasy sleep.

☾

Chapter Four

Morgan stood outside the window and watched the firelight kiss the curves of the female's sleeping face. The flesh-splitting agony of alchemization had passed, as it always did upon assuming beast form. He felt strong now, relaxed yet alert, able to shift from werewolf to wolf, wolf to werewolf, in the blink of an eye. He was presently in the werewolf man-shape. Although it was less agile, it was much more powerful and felt more familiar.

His thick winter undercoat protected him from the swirling wind and snow, and his eyes, ears, and nose were keen. Night sounds, storm sounds, surrounded him, and he noted each and every sound distinctly, like a musician hears each instrument in an orchestra. Now he heard the female stir and he pricked up his ears, absorbing the slow, regular thump of her heart as it propelled rich blood deep into her body, then brought it up, close to the skin. He saw the tiny pulse in her exposed neck. Fragile, so fragile. How easily his sharp canines could—

The wind began to ebb; the snowfall lightened. The smells inside drifted to his nose. He sniffed, caught the familiar aromas of smoke and venison. Beneath them were newer scents, feminine scents—thick and musky, laced with the sweetness of soap and lotion. His pulse quickened.

How would it feel to hold her in his powerful arms, bend back her slender body, slice that smooth throat and feel her hot blood?

The impulse brought back every agonized moment of the last five years. Before Dana's arrival he'd almost forgot his loneliness. Time had ceased to exist the moment he arrived in remote Ebony Canyon. Often it seemed Lily had bestowed this curse on him just yestereve. At other times, it seemed a cruel eternity ago.

After Lily had worked her magic on that barren mountain, he'd ignored her directions to stay by her side and fled, covering ground with a speed that amazed him. Immune to cold, assailed by sights and sounds and scents he'd never known existed, he'd streaked through the icy night, between twisted trees and angry brambles, over rock and boulder, leaping, nearly flying, driven by dire and irresistible impulses he little understood, both savoring and despising his new form. He wanted blood, living flesh. He yearned to use his new and terrible teeth and claws.

The next morning he'd shivered awake near the base of the mountain, naked, his hands and face covered with blood, unable to remember where he'd gone, what he'd done. Lily was there, in human form, staring down at him with those huge dark eyes. She covered him with a thick fur robe, then took his hands and lifted him up.

"Come," she said. "I'll teach you control."

She led him to the little rental car, drove him back to Paris. He stayed with her nearly half a year. During that time, he learned to shape-shift at will, rather than allowing it to come unbidden upon him. But searing pain continued to accompany his alchemization.

"It's because you resist your new nature," Lily told him.

Morgan knew she was right and also knew he wouldn't change. He never wanted to surrender his last remnants of humanity.

Never, he vowed. Never.

Finally he left her. She'd tried to stop him, invoking Lupine Law.

"I am an alpha female, Morgan. I've claimed you as my mate and you cannot refuse."

"Oh, but I can, Lily. I can."

He boarded a plane to New York, ran from her as if his life depended on it.

Morgan's muzzle contracted into a wolfish grin. *As if his life depended on it.*

The last thing he needed worry about. He'd acquired what most humans only dreamed of. A lifetime of several hundred years. Heaven on earth, some would say.

If only they knew it was actually hell.

The female sleeping inside his cabin made his hell even worse. He'd relished touching her as he tended her wounds, listening to her breathe, feeling the smooth texture of her skin. A warm, living human woman from the race that once was his. A woman to redeem him.

Dana Gibbs?

Such a common name for such an uncommon woman. Although she appeared vulnerable and helpless, huddled on the narrow bed, he knew differently. If ever an alpha female existed, she was Dana. Passionate, opinionated, independent, fighting for her own. Her head surely ached like hell when she first came out of her coma, but all she thought about was protecting her wolves.

Wasn't that ironic?

Morgan looked up in despair, wanting to pray to a God he no longer believed existed. The clouds had broken, leaving fuzzy holes through which peeked a pale ghost moon. To unschooled eyes, it would seem full. Yet it was not. Madness was still five days away. Time enough? Perhaps. But then again . . .

Morgan howled in helpless protest.

The woman inside tossed beneath the blankets. For a little while longer, Morgan watched her sleep, then changed to wolf form, whirled, and ran across the deep snow into the forest.

It wasn't long before Charlie wished he had that *Playboy* himself. How much time did a man need to take a dump? God, he wished they'd never sent him to this freaking mountain. He'd seen one of those bodies, and whatever did that was—something else, that's what. Maybe something the grandfathers spoke of.

An unpleasant vibration swept through his body and Charlie picked up the speaker, trying to hail the base camp again. He got no response.

The humming generator and buzzing radio masked any outside sound. Charlie glanced out the windshield. Although the moon was again tucked behind clouds, he could see that it still wasn't snowing, and he desperately wanted to try to leave.

But where the hell was Deek?

Charlie waited another ten minutes or so, afraid the snow would start again at any minute. Finally, and reluctantly, he pulled on his parka and boots, grabbed another flashlight, and opened the door on a night as cold as death. Animals scurried away in the wake of his beam. His breath vaporized, then vanished into the black night. Wind rushed in his ears.

He found a path framed by snow-laden trees and moved forward, feeling as if he were stepping into some dark mouth.

"Deek?" He searched for his friend's telltale beam, saw no light except his own, so he kept on walking. The night seemed eerily quiet. No sounds except the crunch of his feet on the underbrush. When his flashlight fell on a sudden drop-off that ended the trail, he stopped short.

Oh, Great Spirit!

What if Deek had fallen? Between the wind and the noisy equipment in the van, Charlie wouldn't have heard him scream. He moved forward cautiously and swept his beam beyond the rim. It fell on a cluster of blackened stalagmitelike formations.

He leaned over the ledge and saw a clearing about a hundred feet down. To his left was a narrow footpath. Surely Deek wouldn't have climbed down there just to take a dump. He cupped his hands over his mouth and called Deek's name. He was about to turn away when he saw a narrow beam of light streaking along the rocky path below.

Deek's flashlight? Why hadn't that damn fool just found himself a tree like normal folks? Sighing, and heart pounding harder than he wanted to admit, Charlie headed toward the footpath. Just as he'd taken his first step down, a scream cut through the silent night.

Charlie scuttled back, smacked into a tangle of brush and fell. Ignoring the prickly thorns, he doused his flashlight and scrambled deeper into the underbrush.

A sickening gurgle, much like that of a clogged drain, followed the scream. Charlie folded against the earth, clapped his hands against the sides of his head. Sweat beaded on his forehead and formed into icy crystals that stung his skin. Fighting a wave of nausea and the nearly overwhelming need to urinate, he forced himself to sit up.

Where was Deek?

Berating himself for cowardice, he urged his quaking body on and crawled from his hiding place. When he rose, he drew his sidearm.

Just a hawk killing a rabbit, he told himself over the blood drumming in his ears.

But rabbits were nocturnal.

A mouse, then.

Must be a helluva mouse to scream that loud.

Charlie's blood raced faster, pounding his eardrums.

A giant killer mouse, waiting to have him for dinner.

A maniacal laugh bubbled in his throat and he cut it off sharply, terrified of being heard by who-knew-what. He couldn't see the hands in front of his face, it was so dark. Maybe he'd just hightail it back to the van. It *was* just a dying mouse; Deek was fine, would return any second. No question about it. But this was all his fault. If he hadn't insisted on Deek going outdoors . . .

Christ, he never knew a man's breath could be so loud! He forced himself to calm down. Soon he became aware of other sounds around him, sounds not his own. The trees moved overhead, humming like living entities. The Winged Ones and Four-leggeds hooted, scurried, whistled, and crept among the Stone People. Damn the grandfathers for filling his mind with supernatural nonsense.

He forced one rigid foot forward, then another, and marched like a wooden soldier back to the footpath. Unwilling to risk using his flashlight, he followed the narrow beam of light on the path and prayed the moon would reappear. When he reached the clearing, he hesitated, swinging his pistol in front of him.

"Deek?" His call came out as a squeak.

A single step would take him out in the open, unprotected. Coiled with tension, he squeezed the handle of his pistol hard, ready to pull the trigger, shoot at anything that moved.

Then the thunderhead slid off the moon. Large and close, it flooded the clearing with silvery light. But soon it would hide again, and that knowledge impelled Charlie to action.

He entered the clearing and scanned it quickly. Large and circular, it was dotted with black Stone People and bordered on two sides by high granite walls. Clusters of frost-deadened weeds shimmered silver in the wind, and stands of whispering trees surrounded the remaining sides.

At the center of a wide, barren ring that appeared man-made was a stone fire pit with logs and kindling scattered haphazardly around it. A place for picnics, thought Charlie. For playing baseball and romping with children and dogs.

At ten thousand feet? Few would hike this far for a family outing.

Maybe Deek had stumbled on the clearing and decided to check it out. That was just like the bastard, to explore a new campsite during a break in the worst storm in a decade. The thought comforted Charlie and he found the courage to call his friend's name again.

The flashlight didn't move.

"Stop horsing around, Deek."

A sudden wind gust swept the clearing,

sparking a flickering tongue of white-orange inside the pit. The fire burst to life, filling the shadows with light.

Charlie's stomach lurched. A low moan escaped his throat.

"Deek?" he whimpered, trying to tear his eyes away from what he saw.

What he'd thought to be logs were . . .

Body parts. An arm, a leg, another leg. Dark stains, colorless in the weak light, smeared the earth.

Charlie's weapon slipped away. His legs collapsed. He fell forward with arms outstretched, flattening his palms against the earth like a pagan paying homage to the moon. Spasms tore his body and he dumped out the remains of his supper, idiotically grateful he hadn't eaten any Cheetos. Wave after retching wave swept through him, and he clutched the brittle grass, vainly attempting to control himself.

Eventually, the spasms passed. Charlie lay very quiet. The acrid, dying smell of winter filled his lungs. He felt the dry texture of lifeless grass against his wind-chilled cheek.

Finally he became acutely aware of his own danger. He lifted his head, seeking his fallen weapon, saw it at the edge of the fire ring. Feeling safer and suddenly angry, he sat up, swiped a fist across his mouth before planting it on the ground to lever himself up.

What was he hanging on to? He slowly uncurled his fist, saw a fabric scrap crushed in his hand. Dully, he turned the scrap over, unsurprised when he saw an Arizona state seal with the words Fish and Game Department embroidered in the center.

Deek's uniform patch. Ripped away, neat and clean.

Charlie welcomed the numbness that fell upon him as he stared. Now he felt only a basic instinct to survive. His senses heightened, he became keenly alert.

Something was coming.

The fire sputtered, flared, sputtered again, sending up spirals of smoke as it died. The moon slithered quietly into a bank of clouds. A low, steady rustle came from the woods.

The hair on Charlie's body bristled. He froze in place, listening with fear-honed ears as the noise intensified like notes in a terrible symphony.

"Oh, Grandfather Sky," Charlie whispered. "Send all our relations—"

Suddenly the notes crescendoed with a cymballike crash. Brush and branches rattled, hapless rodents squealed, birds flew off with a clatter. The sound grew louder and closer, louder and closer, until it roared like an approaching freight train.

"—the Stone People, the Standing People, the Four-leggeds and Winged Ones."

The forest wall exploded and the night grew quiet again, save for the thuds of running feet.

"Call them to aid me now in my time of peril."

Charlie dove for his gun, scrambled up and streaked for cover at the base of the footpath.

"Help me, Grandfather Sky."

He whirled, dropped to one knee, fired at the dark, amorphous shape—was it man or animal? Then, like the Four-leggeds he'd invoked, he crawled up the rocky path. At a sharp turn, he spun and fired again.

A wail—half yelp, half howl—followed the crack of the pistol.

Nearly mad with terror, Charlie lurched to his feet and ran, fighting the force of gravity, stumbling as loose rock slipped beneath his feet. The savage roar behind forced him on.

Then his foot hit empty air. Brambles tore at his coat, nicked his face. Pebbles rained down. An owl screeched in warning; a wolf howled its rage.

Charlie's scream mingled with their cries and echoed over the treetops in a baleful death song.

((

Chapter Five

Unlike its dark relative the vampyre, the wer-wolf is not immortal. Indeed, he is long-lived, several lifetimes by human standards, yet he can be slain. Does the hunter need silver bullets? This author laughs. Nay. A simple shotgun. An ax. A knife. Any of these tools may suffice.

Dear God, Dana thought. With this kind of nonsense being written, no wonder people once feared wolves. Still, she found it hard to tear her eyes from the page.

The stout-hearted hunter must assure that the beast expires while the wolf curse is upon it. To shoot or hack or stab the heathen as it alchemizes will not do. No! Once the purity of the human soul begins returning—

"Humph," scoffed Dana.

—once the purity of the human soul begins re-

turning, the wounds heal as if by magic hand. Nay, stout hunter, nay. Slay the beast as wolf, not as man.

Dana's eyes raced over the page. For a moment, she got caught up in the dramatic language, the passionate belief of the author.

Then cut off its ears and paws, pry loose its devil fangs, bury the remains in hallowed ground. . . .

Enough!

Dana slammed down the book and climbed off the bed. Her short nap had refreshed her, but she had no idea what time it was. Why didn't Morgan have any clocks? She glanced at the watch on her wrist, hoping it too had revived. But behind its shattered crystal, the hands were still stopped at the moment of the accident. For all she knew, it could be daytime behind the storm-dark sky.

Storm? She listened for sounds and heard the low hum of the wind. Underneath was a repetitive sound that reminded her of drums beating.

Thunder, she decided, rumbling far away. But the eaves no longer groaned and the fire was strong and straight inside the hearth. She dashed to the window and looked out to see a cloud of snow billowing in the moonlight.

She glanced at Morgan's door. His music had stopped while she was asleep, and by now he'd undoubtedly nodded off.

She hesitated. He'd asked little of her, just that

she stay inside at night. Not an unreasonable request, considering that half a dozen people had been killed in this area in the past few months. But Morgan seemed to know nothing about that, so his dire warnings and reluctance to let her leave were puzzling. Of course, he also didn't understand how important her work was, and she couldn't blame him for not wanting to take her out in such violent weather.

It was probably too much to ask that the storm had passed entirely. The distant thunder suggested it hadn't. But maybe by sunrise or even midday it would be gone. It couldn't hurt if she just stepped out for a minute and got the lay of the land.

She looked over at the dwindling fuel supply. Less than half a dozen logs remained. At the rate the fire was eating them, they wouldn't last until morning. Well, she knew how to fetch logs with the best of them. She'd use that as her excuse. Maybe when Morgan saw what she'd done, he wouldn't be angry that she'd disregarded his request.

The idea excited her. She hurried to get the waterproof leggings, then searched Morgan's pantry shelves for something to light her way. She found a Coleman lantern with plenty of fuel inside.

By the time she'd pulled on her boots, she

was skittish as a wolf cub. She lit the lantern and went to the front door. As she swung it inward, a pile of snow collapsed onto the cabin floor.

"Damn!"

Impatiently tossing chunks back onto the stoop, she cursed again when she saw rivulets forming on the floor, knowing she'd have to waste even more time mopping up water.

As she went for the mop, a horrendous squeal came from somewhere in the wild forest outside. Not that such pitiful sounds weren't common in the wilderness, but bad weather tended to keep predators and prey alike in their lairs. Dana peered out the open doors but saw nothing, and now the only sound came from pine needles whispering in the wind. Even the thunder had stopped.

Shrugging, she began mopping up the melted snow.

Not long after, she stood on a long covered porch, the lantern hanging from one arm and a shovel in her hands. The air felt crisp and wonderful as it nipped her bare cheeks, and she realized she'd been feeling as cooped up as a hothouse flower.

A huge yellow moon reflected brightly off the rolling snow and she could see for quite a distance. Off to her left were a couple of sheds, one of which looked like it held wood. Beyond were several structures that she couldn't quite make out, and even further out, the landscape seemed to stretch endlessly. To her right, and circling around until it met the never-ending meadow, was the thick forest.

She wasn't certain which way led to the bottom. By the position of the moon, she judged the meadow to be somewhere to the west. But which way led to her four-by-four?

With a shake of her head, she scooped snow off the top step leading from the porch. She wouldn't be getting any definite answers in the dark of night, so she might as well head for the sheds and bring in some wood. At least she was free for a while.

Morgan plowed through the churning snow, his four powerful legs barely touching down before he leaped again. To one side was the icy crest of Ebony Canyon. To the other, the golden rectangles of his cabin windows were becoming near.

He halted and licked away the last remains of blood from his mouth, then similarly cleansed his paws. How he hated this humiliating task. Almost as much as the impulse that drove him to run at night, every night, seeking a victim to satisfy his lust.

When he finished washing, he alchemized from wolf to werewolf shape. Soon he'd be behind the cabin, where he would pick up his clothes and shift to human form. Had he not brought the female to his den, he would have gone to stand in front of the warming fire before shedding his werewolf form.

Why had he brought her here? His common sense told him she wasn't the one. To find her at the base of the mountain, so close to the time of the Shadow of Venus was simply too coincidental. And she'd be nothing but trouble. The others would come, try to take her from him.

He felt a sudden stiffening of his guard hairs. Were they here now? Turning, he sniffed. Seconds later, something black streaked across the snow. A pale blur of white-on-white followed. Soon he heard a soft thud behind him, and he turned.

An unusually large wolf, made all the more remarkable by its pure white coat, was regarding him with the open curiosity of a family pet. He recognized the feigned friendliness, knew it concealed a menace made even more deadly because it was hidden.

"I told you to back off," he growled in warning, lifting his eyes to include a darker wolf slinking at the white one's flanks.

The larger wolf shook its great head, then

crouched. Its muzzle shrank, its body and legs elongated. Soon, a womanly form stood before him. But this was no ordinary woman. Her curving body was covered in silver-white hair and her long, nimble hands bore claws.

"Give us the human female, Morgan." She spoke the Lupine language in a throaty rumble and bared her sharp fangs.

"Stay away from her, Lily," Morgan replied, also speaking Lupinese.

"Are you headed to romp with those cur you keep?" She reached out a long hand and drew her claws across his furred throat. Her dark eyes narrowed.

Those claws could open his throat in seconds, but Morgan felt no fear. She was strong and deadly, but he knew she wouldn't hurt him. He grasped her wrist, allowing his own claws to dig into the tender pads of her palm. She gave no sign she felt any pain and repeated her demand.

"Give her to us."

At her words, the darker wolf darted forward and stood at her side.

"The woman's mine." Morgan bared his teeth. He hadn't planned to say those words, but now he'd taken a stand. To back down would show weakness, something a lone wolf couldn't afford to do.

"Jorje is hungry." Lily gazed sympathetically at her companion "He hasn't had a human kill in days."

Emboldened, the creature looked up at Morgan and growled. A small lift of Morgan's lips sent it cowering back.

"He doesn't yet have your courage." Lily bent and gave the wolfling a languorous stroke. Then she straightened and tore her wrist from Morgan's grip. "I promised him the female and he shall have her."

"No!" Morgan bristled his coat and scraped the snow, sending a fresh spray of powder into the swirling snow.

Lily smiled cynically.

"Look at you. So determined to remain one of them." She jerked a disparaging hand toward the cabin where the female slept, then leaned forward until her nose nearly touched Morgan's.

"You are a werewolf now, Morgan. A hunter, like us." She sidled around, rump outthrust in sexual invitation. "You can't escape. Why do you have such trouble grasping that fact?"

With a rattlerlike motion, Morgan dipped his head and nipped her thigh. She scurried back with a *ki-yi-yi*. Jorje cringed and whimpered.

Lily whirled, glaring first at Jorje, then at Morgan.

"Give it up, Lily. It's not going to happen."

Morgan directed a scathing glance at Jorje. "Mate with your lapdog instead."

"How little you understand the ways of our species. What's so important about this female anyway? Humans are prey, that is all." In an abrupt about-face, she laughed, the musical tinkle at odds with her fierce expression. "Oh, Morgan, you *are* a fool. Do you think she's the one told of in The Book? Do not believe everything you read."

Although surprised, Morgan wrinkled his nose to convey disagreement. He'd never underestimated Lily's cunning, but how had she guessed so quickly? Moreover, he suspected she was right. The Book was written by a fearful man, living in a fearful place. And yet . . .

What had drawn him to that ruined dead-end road at exactly that time? The Book told of—

Before he could give it more thought, Lily sniffed and glanced over his shoulder. Morgan followed her gaze and saw a glow moving away from his cabin.

He felt a surge of rage. Dana had disobeyed his command. This a female never did! Then remembering she was human, not wolf, he sighed. Keeping her at his cabin would be even harder than he'd thought.

Lily inclined her head toward Jorje. The wolfling crept forward. Morgan crouched, inflating his hackles to their limits. With a snarl, he spread his arms and blocked their path.

"This is my territory, Lily. Return to the dark, cheerless woods of Europe and leave me be. You're not wanted here."

Lily put her hands at her waist, jutting out one hip in a provocative human gesture that Morgan had once found irresistible. She regarded him thoughtfully.

"The puny door of your puny dwelling offers her no protection," she growled.

"No, but I do. And so does Lupine Law."

Showing fang, Lily bristled her coat like porcupine quills. Jorje weakly lifted the hair on his dark shoulders, but still held back. Morgan could see Lily was considering her options. True, the pair could rush him, but Jorje was immature, vulnerable to the dominance of an older male. Although they might initially overtake Morgan, he could take out the smaller wolf with one swipe of his powerful jaws. And unlike them, Morgan was not tightly bound by the Law.

Lily obviously reached the same conclusion. "Very well. You may have her. For now." She patted the dark wolf on its head. "Come along, Jorje. We'll find you another."

With that, she smiled. Her body shifted, wavered, and with a small glad whimper she returned to creature form as easily as taking a breath. She nudged Jorje, and the pair leapt toward the rim of the canyon. Morgan followed them with his eyes until they disappeared.

Yeafanay cawfanay naylanay may. The Song of Hades filled his mind, bringing back the night he'd been consigned to hell in vivid detail, yet also bringing renewed hope. A ritual from The Book had made him what he was. Could everything else its pages foretold also be true?

Years ago, when he first came to Ebony Canyon, he'd taken the section on the Shadow of Venus out of The Book and studied it carefully, almost committing it to memory. It was packed with chants and rituals all based on astrology. Before his transformation, he would have considered it all hogwash.

But in the beginning he'd been willing to try anything to escape his curse. He'd taught himself how to erect and read astrological charts and had even pinpointed the planetary aspects the maiden must possess to successfully perform the ceremony.

As time passed, his hope waned. Now he had little faith the ceremony would work. Of course, until now there hadn't been a maiden.

She must love him, so said the text. With an abiding devotion that eclipsed fear and death. Since using his hypnotic powers was expressly forbidden, why would Dana, or any woman, love him? He'd become a hermit. Most days, even in human form, he looked and lived like the creature he'd become. A creature not unlike the ones Dana had fiercely sworn to protect.

No, not at all unlike.

And subtly, very subtly, Dana behaved like the animals she loved. As soon as she'd become alert, she'd scanned the small cabin, searching for danger like wolves in the wild. Later, she'd roamed the room, touching objects as if marking her territory. But most notably, she'd shrunk in size when he'd frightened her, looking away, baring her belly like the submissive female he knew she wasn't.

This one was no stranger to the way of the wolf. And from her display of devotion, he knew she loved them. Could her love spill over to that abomination of nature, the werewolf?

To him?

He looked up sadly at the waxing moon. Slim wisps of clouds streaked its mottled surface. It appears so harmless, so insignificant in the ways of man. Morgan knew differently. Even now it sped on toward that fated night.

In the meantime, he thought, as he lowered his gaze to the glowing lamplight inching toward the woodshed, he needed to discipline her, teach her exactly who was the dominant one of this pair.

Her life depended on it. Or, at least, his did.

The going was slow. As Dana shoveled her way to the shed, she sank nearly to her hips several times, and wished she'd had the foresight to don the snowshoes. But too late now. She needed to get that wood stacked inside before Morgan woke up.

She felt a bit edgier than she'd expected. Darkness and night sounds didn't normally disturb her. But the lingering memory of the eerie howls she'd heard just before the crash still nagged at her. Besides, it was the absence of sound that bothered her most. Not unusual in the wake of a blizzard, but nevertheless, the cries of a few night birds would have gone a long way toward making her feel more secure.

The loss of time wasn't helping, either. If she didn't get back before Morgan woke, he'd be angry that she'd ignored his warnings. She could better face that anger if she succeeded in her task.

And she would be in a better position to ask Morgan to take her back to her Ranger. He had no excuse now. The sky was beginning to lighten and clear. By morning the storm would have passed.

Soon she reached the shed, which was actually more of a lean-to. Settling the lantern on the roof, she looked around and spied a sled leaning against a wall. She kicked it down on its runners, then started brushing snow off the wood and stacking it on the sled. The ceaseless wind kept blowing fresh snow across the patch she'd shoveled, but she took satisfaction in knowing it wasn't quite as deep anymore, which meant she wouldn't be sinking to her knees.

As she piled on yet another stack of wood, she heard a rumble.

Low and throaty.

She turned slowly.

Had something darted behind the corner of the cabin?

She lowered her head, looked up, moved her eyes left to right. All was quiet around her. Moonlight streamed on the expanse of empty billowing white.

Letting out a quick laugh, she realized she was behaving just like Sheila, the first wolf she'd raised from a pup. Her dad was right. She had begun to act like them.

When had she come to fear things that went bump in the night? It was only a tree branch scraping the roof, not a banshee. With another laugh, she straightened the wood on the sled, then turned for another load.

The rumble came again.

Dana paused, searching for its source. This definitely wasn't a scraping branch. Gingerly inching around, she picked up the shovel and angled it across her body, then scanned the snow as she turned.

Her heart gave a wild leap when she saw the large white canine loping along the horizon.

Was it a wolf?

What else could it be, up here, so far back in the wilderness? She froze, not wanting to frighten it away, and fervently wished she had a camera. It was closing in on her now, but she knew the minute it caught her human scent it would turn tail and disappear to wherever it came from.

Could it really be true? Had her instincts been correct?

She waited in excited apprehension as the animal rapidly narrowed the distance between them.

( )

Chapter Six

Morgan quickly climbed into his clothes, shivering and feeling a pang of regret. He rued his wolf curse, true, but to his everlasting shame he also savored its invincibility, and always hated the nip of the cold after he'd returned to human form.

With an irate jerk, he tightened the fastenings on his parka and turned from the chilling breeze to the cause of his annoyance. He regretted the impulsive growls he let escape when he'd seen her out in the open, easy prey for the white bitch and her groveling servant. What kind of woman was Dana Gibbs? The ones he'd known during his New York life wouldn't have dreamed of going out in the wilderness on a dark, blustery night. Hell, many of them didn't go out in the city at night, nor risk their precious fingernails digging snow and loading wood. But this one was oblivious to the danger around her.

Immediately, his psychiatric training rose to defend her. Dana wasn't a New York business-woman. She was a scientist who was used to wild country. From her point of view, what did she have to fear? Werewolves? They would hardly be in her frame of reference.

His rationalizations only served to fuel his annoyance. He didn't think in those terms these days. What good was psychological insight to a hermit? He could view her behavior any way he wanted, but one fact remained. He'd made a mistake bringing her up here.

So why didn't he take her back? If she could shovel snow and load wood, she could make the hike just fine.

With a final tug on the drawstring of his parka, Morgan shook off that question and rounded the cabin to deal with his errant houseguest.

His heart stopped the instant he cleared the corner.

"Dear God, no!"

Dana was rolling on the ground with a large white creature, who was emitting guttural noises that chilled Morgan's blood. His joints immediately started to ache and swell. His eyes blurred, and he knew there was little time before he became temporarily immobilized. Using all his willpower, he forced the changes back and broke into a run.

In the next instant, he realized there was a complete lack of fear in Dana's squeals. Then he saw why.

"Aphrodite!" he cried angrily, feeling the frailer human emotions now. The creaks of his joints subsided. The dog jerked away from Dana, who sat up and tried to drag her back, laughing all the while.

Morgan stopped and stared.

How long was it since he'd heard a woman's laughter? And what a rich, full-bodied laugh she had. It came from deep within and held a joy he'd forgotten existed. He almost doubled up from the sudden pain of his loneliness.

"Aphrodite! Come!" he commanded harshly.

The dog cringed and slunk toward him.

"We were just roughhousing," Dana said indignantly. "Why are you treating her like that?"

By that time, Aphrodite was at his side, looking full of remorse. Morgan's anger ebbed, but he still had a headache, and the light from the lantern irritated his eyes so much he could barely see Dana. He squinted through the glow, trying to find some excuse that didn't include admitting he had thought Lily was attacking her.

"She escaped from her pen and she knows better." His words came out gruffer than he'd intended, but the explanation apparently mollified her.

"I know what you mean. I have a couple of wolves that do that. Smart little devils."

She rocked lithely to her feet and brushed the snow from her clothes.

"Go inside," said Morgan, in a more gentle tone. "You didn't dress for this cold. I'll put Aphrodite away."

"Why don't we take her with us?"

"To the cabin?"

Dana returned Morgan's hard stare without hesitation. What was with him, anyway? So the dog got out. It wasn't like she'd be annoying the neighbors. A big dog needed plenty of exercise. And that matted coat could use a good brushing. A warm fire wouldn't hurt, either.

She told Morgan so.

"Aphrodite lives in the pen with the rest of the team, Dana," Morgan replied coldly, leaning down to take the dog's collar. "She's a working dog, not a house pet."

"Doing what?" Dana waved her hands at the empty space around them. "Herding all the sheep out here?"

"They carry supplies I bring up by sled. How do you think I get the fuel and food?"

"Oh? Well, uh, I did wonder."

Morgan nodded and started forward, leading Aphrodite with him.

"What is she? A wolf hybrid? She sure—"

"Dana, look at your legs. You've got to be chilled."

She glanced down. Snow was caked on her jeans. Now that Morgan mentioned it, yes, she had to admit she was cold, although she hadn't noticed until he brought it up. He had a way of making her notice unpleasantness. Now, Aphrodite, there was a creature who appreciated simple pleasures.

"You took a big risk coming out here with that concussion," he continued in a scolding tone. "And that roll in the snow didn't help any, either. Go inside and put on some dry clothes."

"Let me go with you to see the other dogs." She trudged over and gave Aphrodite a pat that was rewarded by a lick on the cheek. She glanced up, laughing. "A hybrid. Right?"

"Dana!"

"All right, all right." She bent down for the rope attached to the front of the sled. "Just let me get the wood."

"Go. I'll bring it."

"Morgan, I'm not an invalid."

"Please, Dana." He brushed his gloved hand through his bushy hair and looked so distraught that Dana felt a pang of sympathy. She'd pushed him pretty far and she knew he thought he was looking out for her welfare. Maybe she'd better stop arguing.

"Okay." She dropped the rope and headed back for the cabin, leaving the lantern for Morgan. The moon gave plenty of light for a simple walk on a shoveled path. Every now and then she let out a laugh of pure joy.

She dawdled so much, Morgan wanted to scowl, but all he could do was drink in her laughter. She was so vital, so glad to be alive.

He wanted to keep her that way. No easy job when she ignored his simplest request. What was so hard about staying inside at night?

When she finally entered the cabin, he let go of Aphrodite's collar and waded through the snow toward the fences that protected the kennel. Snow was piled high against them. He'd have to clear them before going in, which was just as well. He needed time to cool down before speaking with Dana again.

The dog loped easily beside him, sinking then rising in the blowing flakes, sniffing now and again, veering off course. Each time she did, Morgan called her back and thought of how badly he now needed her.

She'd been part of the first pair, brought up for companionship, or so he'd told himself. But when he began breeding them, he knew that hadn't been his true purpose.

Seven dogs, said The Book. Not six, nor eight. Seven. All unusually large; all named after ancient deities. It had taken three years to breed them, with failures taken into the little village of Alpine and handed over to eager kids who had no idea what kind of monster gave them away. For the past year, he'd worked with them until they could sit still in a circle for hours.

Lily had never attempted to harm them. According to The Book she couldn't. The protective power of the numeral seven kept them safe. But should even one dog die . . .

The rest wouldn't live another night.

Captain Will Schumacher of the Arizona Highway Patrol was glaring at his communication officer. "Try them again," he barked, as if the unresponsiveness was the fault of the officer.

"Unit thirteen-twelve, this is Mission Lobo. Come in." The man waited a few seconds, then looked up. "They still don't answer sir."

"I know! Don't you think I have ears?" Schumacher whipped his head around to scowl at a group of officers gathered behind him. "Damn fools wandering off like that. Just like those wildlife people. And if that wasn't bad enough, there's this." He waved a piece of paper impatiently. "I told that wolf professor not to come. Now I learn she's lost out here somewhere. As if we didn't have enough on our plate. Well, they're not getting in our way. Hear? I want teams out looking for wolves, not idiots who don't have enough sense to come out of a storm."

"Captain Schumacher?" A man wearing aviator-style glasses stepped from the crowd. Schumacher's gaze lingered malevolently on the Fish and Game Department emblem decorating the pocket of the man's vest, which covered a non-regulation hunting jacket. Everything about the wildlife people grated on Schumacher's nerves, but the ones who ignored code annoyed him most of all.

"What do you want, Fishman?" Schumacher snapped, glad to find a target for his ire.

The man appeared oblivious to Schumacher's insult. Instead he planted his feet under his disgustingly fit hiker's body and said, "Maybe we should rethink our priorities. I doubt Charlie and Deek would wander off without notifying us, and that concerns me. As for Dr. Gibbs, she's one of the foremost wolf biologists in the country. She was instrumental in the reintroduction of the red wolf and—"

"I *know* who the hell she is!" Schumacher looked up at the dome of the tent. "Why doesn't anyone ever tell me something I don't already know?"

"What's more," Fishman continued, as though Schumacher hadn't even spoken, "she's used to the wilderness and has probably pulled off to wait out the storm. As far as the wolves go, it's the opinion of my department that they don't exist."

"Don't *exist*? Then what do you suppose killed those people?"

"There are any number of explanations that don't involve wolves. Regardless, I think our priority should be to search for the missing men."

"Did anyone ask what you thought?"

"Yes, Captain. The governor did."

That stopped Schumacher in his tracks. He couldn't remember Fishman's real name, but he did remember that the man's opinions were backed up by a strong reputation in his field. Much as the captain hated wasting what little time the break in the storm gave them, he couldn't ignore someone so well connected.

At that moment, another officer rushed into the tent. "The copter's coming, sir."

"Good. At least something's working around here." Without another word, Schumacher followed the messenger out the tent door.

Less than half an hour later, yielding to the

wildlife officer's advice, he had assembled a squad to search for the missing Fish and Game van.

"Move, move," he ordered. "Hurry up."

The men loaded a small arsenal of handguns and semiautomatic weapons into the back of the helicopter, then scrambled for their seats. As Schumacher began boarding, his communicator ran out of the tent.

"Did you contact thirteen-twelve?" Schumacher asked, wanting any reason to abort the manhunt.

"No, sir," answered the young officer. "But someone sighted Dr. Gibbs."

"Humph. The least of my worries. So what's the word?"

"Her Ranger was spotted heading south on the Coronado Trail." He gave the captain the number of the closest mile marker.

"Send out a unit." It didn't set well with him to dispatch badly needed officers. But what could he do?

The lieutenant nodded and Schumacher climbed into the helicopter. With a buzz of blades, they were airborne.

By chopper, the distance to the van's last known location was short. Soon the captain was ordering the pilot to duck down between the trees, merely scowling whenever the man said a move was too dangerous. Schumacher didn't much care for chopper pilots; they were a rebellious breed. Yet in matters of safety he had to defer to them. In one apparently "safe" dip, they spotted the Fish and Game van.

"Take us down," Schumacher shouted into his communication headphone.

"As soon as I find a clearing."

Schumacher bobbed his head and mimicked the pilot's words, but the man had shut off his headphones and the captain's voice was lost in the whir of engines and blades.

"There," the pilot said, having deigned to re-establish communication. He pointed to a field of black rock towers. "It's a hike back up to the road, but there's plenty of room to land."

After second-guessing the pilot for a while, Schumacher gave the order to land. Although the man was only doing his job, Schumacher was ready to discipline the bastard by the time they touched down. He wasn't used to helicopters, and the rapidly approaching earth filled with all those eerie black outcroppings had scared a year of life out of him. Someone ought to pay.

Before he could voice displeasure, his men were out of their seat belts, and he was forced to disembark so they could toss down the weapons.

"All this for a few *canis lupus*," mumbled Fishman, who'd somehow copped a seat on the flight. Schumacher shot him a quelling look, receiving a shrug in return.

The captain tightened the fastenings on his jacket and pulled the muffs of his cap over his ears. The day was darkening again. A chill wind swept along the ground, lifting loose leaves and branches toward the sky, biting at his legs.

"We have to make it quick," the pilot advised, "else we'll run into some weather."

Schumacher picked up a rifle from the pile, ordered his men to go through the maze of rocks, then followed at a safe distance. The windswept clearing was bare of snow except for drifts hanging around the bases of the black towers and the edges of the forest. To him, the ugly growths looked like dark fingers preparing to curl around him and squeeze out his life. When they approached a particularly close pair, he hesitated a moment.

Then he heard a low groan.

Chapter Seven

The romp with Aphrodite had thoroughly lifted Dana's spirits. True, she'd been disappointed when she realized she hadn't encountered a wolf, but rolling in the snow with the frisky dog had more than made up for it. She was still elated when she stripped off her soggy clothes, slipped on a thermal shirt and sweatpants, and settled beneath warm blankets.

Waiting for Morgan's inevitable return soon became unbearable. She felt unaccountably guilty for having ignored his demand that she remain indoors, the last thing she should be feeling. Or was it? After all, he had pulled her out of a wrecked vehicle and probably saved her life. Perhaps he did have a right to be angry, since his request did stem from the best of motives.

But she was determined not to cower.

She fiddled with the binding on her blanket, rearranged the fit of her pants, wiggled to get more comfortable. When she finally spied the werewolf book on the bedside table, she picked it up. As silly and far-fetched as the book was, it always held her attention.

The wer-wolf's strength is prodigious. With a single sweep of its deadly claws it can vanquish foe and prey alike. Thus, dear hunter, you are forewarned. Keep your distance until prepared to strike. Be wary. You will get but one chance.

The text went on to describe the werewolf's uncanny speed, the density and keenness of claws that could cut glass, teeth like razors, hair like wire, skin thick as an elephant's and immune to all but the sharpest weapons.

Its Achilles' heel, my friend, lies in its underbelly. Soft and tender as a newborn lamb's, a single arrow or flick of the hunter's blade will send the beast to its doom.

The hair on Dana's arms bristled. This was fiction, pure fiction, yet she felt sympathetic toward this poor mythical creature so hated by mankind that someone felt compelled to write an entire volume on how to destroy it. For a moment, she let her imagination soar.

If such a mutant existed, what would happen if she encountered one? Clearly it could speak. Did it hate its human counterparts as deeply as they hated it? Would it immediately attempt to destroy her, or could she ask the questions she always wanted to ask wolves?

Was their lifelong mating motivated by unswerving love or simply a social device that aided survival? Did their thick coats keep them warm on frigid winter nights or did they feel the cold as deeply as man? Was each wolf happy with its position in their rigid social structure or did the omega wolves secretly resent their betters? Her mind swelled with possibilities so consuming that she jumped when the front door banged open and let in a weak stream of sunlight.

Without giving Dana so much as a glance, Morgan shouldered his way into the cabin and stalked over to a rough mat. He shook the snow off his clothes, hung his wool jacket on a peg, then somehow managed to condense his frame enough to occupy the low stool Dana had used earlier. After stripping off the rest of his snow-damp outer garb, he stood up and shoved his bare feet into a pair of thick fleece slippers.

Dana giggled.

"Is something funny?" he asked sternly.

"Those look like a couple of unshorn ewes."

Although she knew it pushed her luck, she couldn't hold back a second giggle. He looked down, and she waited for the biting retort she knew would come. To her surprise, Morgan's face broke into that luminous smile.

All the grudges she bore against him vanished in its light.

"They keep me warm." Then an unexpected sound came out of his mouth. Laughter.

He saw her stunned expression, and laughed even harder.

"That's something I never expected to hear," she said bluntly.

"Nor I."

Pain flashed suddenly in his eyes, stabbing at Dana's heart. What tragedy had caused this man such unending heartache? She wanted to ask, but he turned abruptly toward the fireplace.

"The wood's on the porch," he said. "I'll bring it in later."

"I planned to have it all stacked before you woke up," Dana replied in a rueful tone.

"That wasn't necessary." He threw the remaining logs on the fire. It flared. The resin snapped, the room grew lighter, warmer. But Morgan had turned cold again. Grimly he approached her bed, folded himself on the chair beside it.

"I instructed you to stay inside at night, Dana."

She would be firm, she'd told herself, but instead she cringed like Aphrodite, contrite about offending him. Damned if she'd apologize, though. She was her own woman. Free to come and go as she pleased.

"I'm free to do as—"

"There are dangers out there you've never dreamed of." He placed his wrist across her arm. Oddly, the gesture reminded Dana of her wolves. From them, of course, it would be a friendly act. From Morgan, it felt like a rebuke.

"Look," she said weakly, sliding away from him. "You know nothing about me." She sprang up and looked down. Feeling less intimidated on her feet, her voice grew stronger. "I grew up in the backwoods of Montana. You want cold? I'll tell you—"

"You already have told me," he interjected quietly.

"Okay," she continued. "Then let me tell you about hikes into wilderness so thick we had to hack our way through. You know what's back there? Grizzlies and wild boar so vicious they'd sooner slice you to ribbons than let you pass. Don't tell me about danger, mister. I know all abut it."

"This is Ebony Canyon, Dana."

She stopped, regarding him intently for a second. Surely he didn't . . . "Don't tell me you believe those ridiculous tales?"

An odd expression crossed his face. Was he hiding something or was he feeling chastened?

God, she missed her wolves. A person could always tell what was going on with them.

"Is that it?" she demanded. "You actually give credence to those legends?"

"Of course not." He shook his head, sending his mane flying. At that instant, he seemed as feral as Blue, the wild wolf given over to her care about a year before.

"What, then?"

She placed a hand over a throb at her temple, which Morgan instantly noticed. He shot to his feet and lifted her bandage.

"You've reinjured yourself. Another good reason not to go out at night."

"I hate being cooped up," Dana said, by way of explanation. His hands were still cool and felt good against the ache.

"No fresh blood." He resettled the swathe of cloth. "Let me look at your eyes again."

"Oh, Lord, not the flashlight."

He shook his head. "Just checking for dilation."

Dana exaggerated the widening of her eyes, disappointed when she got no response from Morgan.

"The pupils look fine. I think we can remove the dressing, make do with a simple Band-Aid." His expression grew vague and he lifted a strand of her hair. "Too bad, though. You look like an Indian princess. All you need are a few beads."

A surge of self-consciousness swept over Dana. She hadn't combed her hair since she'd left Phoenix, and the unruly curls were as tangled as Aphrodite's coat.

She touched his hand. "Don't. I'm a mess."

"It's beautiful," he said softly. "Wild. Untamed. When were you born?"

Although taken a bit by surprise, Dana answered without questioning why he asked. "December tenth."

"So you're a Sagittarius," he murmured. "Born midmorning, I'd guess, say about ten?"

"Ten twenty-three, actually. How did you know? Are you into astrology? I thought psychiatrists scoffed at that kind of thing."

He blinked several times, as if he'd been in a fugue, and let her hair drop.

"I dabble a bit." He picked up a pair of scissors from the bedside table, shuffled through the medical supplies until he came up with a wide adhesive strip, then gently pushed Dana down on the bed.

"Look up," he directed. When Dana complied, he began clipping off the bandage. A few seconds later it fell in her lap.

"That's a lot of blood," she said, grimacing.

"I'm glad you noticed. Maybe you'll stop thinking you're indestructible."

He grabbed the bottle of disinfectant,

swabbed some on the cut, then peeled the backings off the adhesive strip. Dana rolled her eyes up, trying to watch Morgan as he worked. His touch, so gentle and caring when he tended her wounds, was at such odds with his frequent surliness, she sometimes felt there were two Morgan Wilders.

When he was done, he stepped back, inspected his work, and scowled again.

"You could get hurt a lot worse than this, Dana," he said gently. "Trust me when I tell you to stay inside after dark."

"So the werewolves don't get me?"

"What did you say?" He jerked his head sharply and stared into her eyes.

"The werewolves." She pointed to the book lying on the covers.

"Oh. You've been reading The Book." A weak grin tugged at the corners of his mouth. "Actually, I'm more concerned about vampires."

"Me, too," she responded, with a return smile. "I've always hated bats." Wondering if this was the time to bring up her departure, she decided it was as good as any. "You don't need to worry, Morgan. The blizzard is over. When the sun comes up, you can take me back to my truck. I'll be out of your hair for good."

And into the hair of all those government officials, if she had her way.

"There's a fresh storm coming."

She gave him an incredulous stare. "You can't know that."

"Yes, I smell it. It's coming." A rueful look crossed his face the minute the words were out.

Dana shook her head, wondering if he was teasing. "Come on, Morgan. Only animals can smell the weather, and there's even some question about that. You saw it out there. The sky is clearing. A great day's coming."

"How about, my lumbago's acting up?"

"Look." She pointed to the window, where morning rays peeked through. "Let's get my things together, hitch up the dogs, and go now. If you're right about the storm, you'll be back before it starts."

Morgan got up, went into the cooking area, and started pumping water into a tin coffeepot.

"Did you hear what I said, Morgan?"

His hand paused over the pump and he turned to look at her sadly.

"Yes, I heard." He pulled a can of coffee from one of the open shelves.

"Well, you seem to be ignoring me."

He carefully measured the grounds into the pot's basket.

"Morgan!"

With less care, he dumped in a couple more scoops, then turned to look at her.

"There are skyscraper-high drifts out there, Dana. The trails are blocked. Even dogs can't travel over that kind of snow." He put the pot on the stove and lit a burner under it. "Let's see what tomorrow brings."

Dana groaned. "But . . . No, that won't work. By then the highway patrol will be out sharp-shooting wolves. They need me, Morgan."

"Don't you think those cops can take care of themselves?"

"Not the cops! The wolves!"

Morgan had been acting as if his future hung on whether the coffee perked, but now he left the stove and walked over to her.

"When are you going to get it?" He scowled down at her. "There are no wolves."

"No, yes." God, she wished he wouldn't hang above her that way. "You're probably right. It's a wild-goose chase. But wouldn't it be incredible if there was a pack up here?"

"Incredible?" He shrugged. "Okay. If it stays clear today, we'll try tomorrow. But I warn you, it may be the day after."

"That's too late!" Dana stomped her foot, then felt instantly foolish when Morgan raised his thick eyebrows.

"That's too late," she repeated weakly.

"It's the best I can do."

Morgan headed back toward the brewing coffee. The aroma filled the cabin, and he felt an urgent need to drink some. Normally he slept during the morning hours, but he didn't dare leave Dana alone. The minute he closed that bedroom door, she'd hightail it for her vehicle.

She had huddled back under her blankets, and he felt a pang of sympathy. Like him, she was driven. Yet her motives came from concern for another creature. His, by contrast, came from obedience to sordid forces, and fulfilled nothing but his own dark needs. He stayed by the stove, keeping her in the edge of his vision, and noticed that her hand unconsciously dropped to *The Lycanthropy Reader*. It hadn't occurred to him that she might find it on his shelves among the mass of other books there, and he wasn't sure how he felt about her reading it.

Maybe he should remove it sometime when she wasn't paying attention. On the other hand, this woman was a scientist. She probably viewed The Book as an entertaining fantasy. But when the inevitable moment came when he revealed his true self, her unwitting education might make it easier for her to accept the incredible and unbelievable sights of her own eyes.

By the time the coffee deepened to a full-bodied brew, he had decided no harm could come if she continued reading. He reached for a couple of enamel cups. "Would you like some?" he asked.

She nodded glumly. "Just black."

A few minutes later, he carried the coffee to the bed, handed hers over, and sat in the chair. She circled her hands around the cup, rubbing them back and forth, apparently for warmth. When she lifted her arms to take a sip, the thin, waffled fabric of her thermal shirt tightened around her high breasts and revealed the nubs of her cold-hardened nipples.

Lord, she was beautiful. Her green eyes stood out in startling contrast against her tanned face, and her dark hair tumbled everywhere, brushing her cheeks and her slender shoulders. Her legs were folded around her body with the gracefulness only a slim, toned woman could achieve. Morgan felt a surge of intense lust. He hadn't touched a mortal woman in that way since before the night of his transformation, and need was suddenly strong in him.

He dared not let this happen. To risk this woman, when he'd just found her . . .

But he leaned forward, regardless, and traced a finger down the curve of her cheekbone. The skin beneath was smooth and firm.

"I'm sorry it distresses you, but I don't control the weather."

Her eyes widened in question, whether from his touch or his comment, Morgan couldn't say. She parted her full mouth, wrapped her hand around his finger. He felt an erection push against his zipper, aching to be released.

"I really must leave today, Morgan."

"I know you think so." He pulled back his hand, took a swallow of coffee, and wondered if she knew he exaggerated the difficulties of getting back to her vehicle. She was, after all, familiar with rugged country. But only four more days remained. If he could keep her here . . . win her love . . .

"Does that mean you won't let me leave?" she asked accusingly, narrowing her eyes.

The question pricked a tender spot Morgan thought had callused over long ago. His lust vanished instantly. For a moment there, feeling the human male's affection, the human male's need for a woman, he'd also felt his humanity return. Now all she'd left him was a wolf's instinctive need to hide its wound.

"Let you leave?" He rose from the chair and glared down at her, gratified when she flinched subtly. "I have nothing to do with the weather. But if you want to blame me, feel free. What do I care?"

He stomped to the stove and refilled his cup. As he watched the steaming brew spill out of the pot, he realized with a start that this was no way to win a woman's love.

☾
Chapter Eight

"Oh, sweet Jesus!"

Several of Schumacher's officers were emptying their guts on the ground. Others swore or cried out in shock. The captain's own stomach jumped wildly and he struggled to keep his breakfast down.

He nearly lost the battle when he saw the hand with the gold ring still encircling one finger. Tearing his eyes away, he retched when he saw another object, tasted bile.

Dear God, that was a man's thigh!

"Deek," moaned a man doubled up near the edge of the clearing.

It was the Fishman. Schumacher walked woodenly toward him, carefully keeping his eyes level, avoiding the carnage around him. When he reached the wildlife officer, he glanced down scathingly.

113

"Can't even hold on to your guts long enough to do your job, can you?" Then he caught sight of a large roundish object and his stomach lurched again. He whirled away in horror.

"It's Deek," choked out the wildlife man. "Deek."

"Shut up!" commanded Schumacher. Bad enough to see a dismembered hand or leg. But a man's head—all frozen like that—with his terrorized eyes wide open in a blood-drained face. Jesus, what had done this?

"Did you hear something?" asked the helicopter pilot, who'd remained unnervingly composed.

Probably a Vietnam vet who'd seen worse, thought the captain. He shook his head. He heard nothing but the revolting heaves and gasps of his crew.

"Over there," the man insisted, pointing to a cleft in a cliff.

Fishman sat up and wiped his face with his sleeve. "Charlie. Maybe Charlie made it."

"Check it out," Schumacher ordered, feeling an intense desire to regain control. "Get up and go with him, Fishman. If the other guy bought it, too, you can identify the remains."

"Not sure my stomach can handle that." Fishman got up anyway, but before he followed the pilot, he said, "By the way, my name's Rutherford."

Schumacher felt a moment of grudging respect. Not many men would chance finding a second friend in that condition. He knew he should turn to his other men, provide leadership, but instead he continued watching the two men. As they neared the opening, he finally heard something.

"He-el-lp . . ."

Weak, very weak, but someone was alive inside that crevasse.

"Stretcher," Schumacher called out loudly. The entire team headed for the copter, leaving him alone among the rock fingers, which he almost feared would suddenly come alive. A fire pit in the center of the clearing gaped at him like an open hungry mouth. He smelled death in the air, heard the shrill whine of the wind and the whir of the distant helicopter, hated how they dulled a man's hearing.

Something evil had done this. And it was still out there. Waiting. Watching. Was it even now—

"Captain," shouted the pilot. "Over here."

Schumacher broke into a lope and came across the men a few yards into the cleft, which he saw was actually a path to the top.

"He's down there." Rutherford pointed to a

narrow drop-off in the path, where a man was wedged into a crack far below.

"His ankle's trapped."

Schumacher turned to the pilot to do what he did best, give orders. "Go hurry up the others."

"Yes, sir." The pilot pointed at the sky. "Good advice. If that storm hits, we'll be trapped here."

The look of sheer terror on the man's previously implacable face was unmistakable and mirrored Schumacher's own.

"Then tell them to move their asses," he barked, nearly jumping when his command echoed off the rocks around him.

The pilot took off.

Schumacher looked around, hunting for one more thing to control, and saw nothing but bloodstained earth and body parts. He shuddered violently, then called after the retreating pilot. "Have someone stuff those . . . those remains into a carcass bag."

"Not remains," corrected the trapped man in a voice low with pain and anger. "That's Deek. Deek Kowalski. He was my buddy. And some goddam monster tore him to shreds."

Schumacher swallowed his anger. It would not look good to berate an injured man. Puffing up to his full five feet and almost seven inches of height, he forced a sympathetic tone he was sure would soothe. "Don't worry, son, we'll find those killer wolves and wipe them off the face of this earth. Count on it."

"Yeah," Charlie replied scornfully. Then, to Schumacher's shock, he let out a maniacal laugh. He was still laughing when the men loaded him into the helicopter.

"Would you like to help feed the dogs?"

Dana turned from the sink and smiled hesitantly, clutching an enamel bowl she'd been drying. While brooding about Morgan's stubborn refusal to take her back to her car, she'd decided he was one of those dour, depressed types. But ever since their disagreement he'd acted almost cheerful, whistling occasionally as he dished up some of the ever-present porridge and fried some bacon he'd pulled out of his propane-powered refrigerator.

She'd been hungrier than she'd thought, and she ate quite a bit, then offered to clean up afterward, all the while wondering what had brought about this change in Morgan. Here he was, surprising her again.

"You mean it?"

"You aren't a prisoner here, Dana." He glanced at the window, which showed a bright morning already fading. "But if you want to go, hurry. The storm I warned you about is coming."

Dana put away the bowl and hurried to the fireplace for the clothes she'd left there to dry.

As she headed to the bathroom, Morgan said, "Those are still damp."

"I'll live. They're all I have."

He studiously eyed her long frame, which made her suddenly aware of her thin thermal shirt. She folded her arms over her breasts. A grin tugged at Morgan's mouth but failed to break through.

"Maybe I can help you out." He went into his bedroom and came out a few minutes later with a down jumpsuit.

"Try this."

Dana pulled the suit on and zipped up.

"Hardly a fashion statement," Morgan said. "But it should do."

"No biggie. I've never been much for fashion."

Then she glanced down and did a double take. The suit puffed out around her ankles and wrists and hung in loose folds down her body. She looked like a walking sleeping bag.

"Wow! If I wore this in public, I'd get arrested for sure."

"Sorry. There's no assortment of sizes."

Morgan grinned as Dana waddled to her boots. When she shoved aside the excess fabric in order to sit on the stool, he gave out a chuckle. Dana instantly felt foolish, and a flush came to her cheeks.

"For what it's worth," he said, "I think you look kind of cute."

Although Dana questioned his judgment, his remark made her feel better. She picked up a boot and began tugging it on. "At least I won't get cold, which I'm sure will keep Dr. Wilder happy."

"Glad you're thinking of me." His grin widened, and he bent to pick up a set of the metal snowshoes. "These will make the going easier than it was last night. Hmm, I could swear there was another pair in here."

Dana looked up warily as he searched, knowing he was seeking the pair she'd hidden. Now that she'd overcome the shock of his mood change, she rather liked his smiles, liked hearing him laugh. If he noticed the adjustments she'd made to the snowshoe settings, he would realize what she had in mind, and his dour side would undoubtedly return.

"Why do you have so many?" she asked, hoping to distract him.

"Oh, trying this, trying that . . . Here they are."

Dana's heart skipped a beat as he examined them.

"How about that? These might fit you just like

they are." He bent and slid them across the wood floor. "Try them."

Dana latched them on, giving out a surprised exclamation when they turned out to be a perfect fit. He looked quite pleased, obviously fooled by her reaction.

"That's a nice set. With those straight edges you won't be tripping over your feet." He grinned again. "Too bad I can't say the same for the snowsuit."

Dana was so relieved she hadn't been found out that she gave a giddy laugh.

"Strong willed. Bright. Laughs at my jokes. What a woman."

"Do you have a checklist?" she teased.

"I used to, back when . . ." He gave his attention to inspecting the other set of metal snowshoes, clueing Dana that the subject was closed. She stood up to get her parka and gloves.

"Don't walk on the floor with those," he said a bit sharply. Then his tone softened. "It scratches the wood."

"Yeah." She leaned over, unlatched them, and stepped out. "My dad used to say the same thing. I was always forgetting."

"In Minnesota?"

"Montana."

"Right. Montana."

The refrigerator generator began to hum.

Water drip-drip-dripped as it fell into a pan from the slightly open pump. Dana looked at Morgan. He looked at her.

They both looked away.

"You ready?" She made a big deal over pulling on her gloves.

"Soon as I get the pail." He pulled a huge galvanized bucket from a spot between the stove and the sink.

"What do you feed them?" She was having difficulty meeting his eye. "Must be hard getting dog food this far up."

"Venison. I have a smokehouse outside." His gaze wandered around the room, studiously avoiding her.

"Yeah? Hey, that's great."

"It works."

Morgan tucked both sets of snowshoes under his arm, grabbed the bucket, then opened the door. Dana followed him down the steps, and as they secured their latches, she thought of the odd moment before, glad it had passed so quickly. She'd never met a more mercurial man. Not that she'd spent much time in close quarters with any man but her father, who'd been as steady as a rock; but even with her limited experience, she knew Morgan was unusually moody.

She remained silent as they moved over the virgin snow, breaking the quiet day with the shuffle of their snowshoes, which were nearly lost beneath the windswept powder. Everything looked different in the daylight, and Dana now saw that Morgan's cabin was tucked into a semi-circular nook of dense junipers, pines, and bare-leafed birch.

The rising sun behind them kissed the tips of the trees and danced in a swirling expanse of snow that went off to the west. The white ground undulated like a restless sea and at first seemed to go on forever, but as Dana lifted her gaze, her eyes came to rest on a sudden drop-off. Pointing in that direction, she looked at Morgan.

"What's over there?"

They had just reached a small building with smoke coming from a small metal flume, and Morgan reached for the latch before answering. "Ebony Canyon."

"We're on the rim of the canyon?"

He nodded, pulling at the smokehouse door.

"Good Lord, Morgan. That's over fifteen miles from where I crashed. How on earth did you get me up here?"

He nodded his head toward the dog pens. "By sled. I was out with the dogs."

"In the midst of a storm?"

Steam billowed around Morgan, carrying the tang of smoldering mesquite. He ducked his head inside, saying something Dana couldn't quite make out.

"What?"

"It wasn't storming when I left." A disembodied hand holding a slab of meat emerged from the steam. "Here. Make yourself useful."

Dana dropped the meat into the bucket, then accepted another one. As he handed out one chunk after another, she mulled over what he'd just told her. Somehow he had brought her from the edge of the highway to an elevation of over ten thousand feet. With the help of his dogs, of course, or so he said. But . . .

Had he packed her onto the sled like so much baggage or taken a more caveman approach and slung her over his massive shoulders? And why would a man who claimed he could smell a storm decide to take his dogs out shortly before one started? The inconsistency bothered her. Was Morgan hiding something with all his avowed concern for her safety?

Still holding out her hand, still passing meat into the bucket, she unconsciously shook her head in denial. True, Morgan could be gruff sometimes, but most of the time he'd been courteous and respectful. If he had an ulterior motive, it wasn't readily apparent.

Just then, Morgan's head reappeared. He shut the door on the steamy smokehouse, then sniffed the air like one of Dana's wolves. She felt an instant pang of homesickness.

"I hope the weather holds until we're done." He swung the heavy bucket onto his shoulder as easily as if it contained Styrofoam.

Dana scowled up at the sky, which remained bright and blue, and remembered why she'd left Montana. A mass of dark clouds to the northwest seemed light years away, yet she knew they'd be above them in no time at all. Lord, she hated snowstorms.

"Guess you were right," she said, somewhat grudgingly.

"Come on." He turned for the kennel. "We still have some time."

As they approached, Dana saw shelters of varying sizes inside the chain-link pen. Several dogs loped up and down a long, narrow run affixed to one end of the kennel. Just then, one of them stopped and howled, sending the entire pack racing for the gate.

Dana's homesickness came back in an overwhelming wave. How were the Alaskan wolf and his mate faring? Was Blue eating properly? He never really trusted anyone but her.

"Please, Morgan. Take me down the mountain. If we leave now, we'll beat the storm."

He turned slowly toward her, leaving his hand poised over the latch. The first thing Dana saw was his eyes, which had suddenly become aching gold-green pools. Somehow she had hurt him. Although she knew she wasn't the first to wound him, she still regretted doing it. Again, she wondered what had scarred this man so badly.

She reached up and stroked his wild beard.

Dana's gloved touch shot through Morgan's body like a glass of warm brandy, and he dropped his hand from the latch and stepped closer. Her emerald eyes regarded him with so much compassion, he couldn't tear his gaze away.

He'd been alone so long, had grown used to prowling the night in kinship with the beasts of the forest, grown accustomed to the lack of human companionship. Now . . .

Could he forget about the Shadow of Venus, and just keep her here as his companion? Then, eventually, reveal his true self? Perhaps she would come to love all sides of him and bring light and joy to his miserable existence.

"How long have you been here?" Her voice held unusual gentleness, as if she sensed his desolation.

"Almost five years." *So very long.* With a shock, he realized he'd been kidding himself. Here was a rare opportunity to reclaim his humanity, one that wouldn't reappear for another seven years. If reclaiming his humanity meant putting her at risk, then so be it. Fate had brought her. Fate would protect her. And if it didn't?

What choices did he have? He just had to make her understand.

He tilted his head, resting it against the curve of her palm. How sweet was her simple touch, how soothing, yet it filled him with such agony.

Had to make her . . .

"Were you always alone?"

"I go down for supplies every now and then."

Understand.

"How wonderful!" She dropped her hand, tried to whirl, nearly tripped over her snowshoes. Shocked, Morgan just stared.

Reclaiming her balance, she spread her arms wide and cried, "All of this is yours. No crowds. No utility lines or noisy cars. I envy you, Morgan. Oh, I envy you." She looked at him earnestly, eyes alive with excitement. "But I can't stay. I need to find those wolves."

"There aren't . . ." He turned away, began unlatching the gate.

"I know. Probably not. But don't you see, Morgan? I can't take that risk. I have to leave. Now!" The tone of her voice softened. "Please."

He kept his back to her, not wanting to see her spoken plea reflected in her eyes. The steps leading to the ritual—the revealing, the bonding—were treacherous, far too treacherous. If he cared for her at all, and he knew he already did, he should immediately remove her from danger. Take her far away from Lily and Jorje. Far away from him.

"Please, Morgan."

She touched his shoulder. Another sweet shudder coursed through his body. He gazed over the north stand of trees, measuring his next words, unsure what they would be. His answer came from the distant sky.

"It's too late. The storm's already coming."

Then he opened the gate. Dana had yet to learn it, but her role in his redemption had been cast.

Chapter Nine

"Tomorrow, then," Dana said dully, glaring up at the thickening clouds. The wind was whistling a baleful warning and whipping snow across the ground. She rubbed her ears briskly, then transferred her glare to Morgan.

"I hate you for being right." But her resigned smile told him she didn't mean it.

Morgan smiled back, relieved the weather had ended their debate and absorbed her anger. Winning her affections would be much easier if she didn't view him as her jailer.

"Come meet the rest of my dogs. That should cheer you up."

"Some," she grumbled. "But I refuse to cheer up much."

The dogs were now crashing at the fence in their eagerness to eat. Morgan told Dana to follow and stepped into the pen, holding a piece of meat. As his large black lead dog moved forward, he saw Dana assume an uncharacteristically meek posture.

"This is Zeus," he told her. "Aphrodite's mate."

Zeus gobbled down the first hunk of venison and Morgan reached in for another.

"Over there"—Morgan pointed to the right, where the rest of the pack waited—"are Odin and his mate, Freya. These are Shakti and Persephone, and the little gray runt is Fenris."

"Do you always hand-feed them?" Dana asked.

"What else do I have to do with my time?"

Zeus finished eating, gave Morgan a couple of affectionate licks, then backed away. Aphrodite came forward, and Morgan lifted out another hunk of food and let her lap it from his flattened palm. Dana noticed the white female giving her a sideways glance, which she took as an invitation.

"Mind if I take a turn?" she asked.

"Watch your hand. She's a greedy thing."

"She reminds me of my Alaskan wolf, although she's a lot bigger." The dog turned toward her and she gave her a pat on the head, which was quite easy since the large dog came nearly to her waist. Dana squatted beside Morgan, made a few caninelike noises, and scratched the soft fur under Aphrodite's chin. Now that she'd received the seal of approval from their lead female, the other dogs crept closer.

"She likes you," Morgan said. "I'm surprised. As you may have guessed, the dogs aren't accustomed to strangers."

"She recognizes a kindred spirit." Dana took her glove off and stowed it in a pocket, then reached for some meat, coming out with a tattered piece of liver which Aphrodite immediately gobbled. The next piece Dana pulled out appeared to be part of a flank and was equally ragged. "This meat looks torn apart," she remarked. "What kind of knife do you use?"

"I'm not much of a butcher. I faint at the sight of blood, remember?"

"Then how do you bring yourself to hunt?" *And with what*? She hadn't noticed guns in the cabin.

"I don't. I buy meat from the Indians."

"Indians. Up here? I thought that was—"

At that moment Aphrodite whirled to snarl at Persephone, who'd been sidling up to Zeus. The weaker dog cringed, then slunk forward with a whined apology. Aphrodite gave her a quick glance, then haughtily looked away. A canine rebuke, given, received. Incident now over.

"Amazing!" Dana lost interest in hearing about Indians. "They behave just like my captive pairs. How much wolf is in these dogs?"

"About sixty percent."

"They're so big." A hearty diet accounted for some of the size, but even the runt would be considered big for a wolf.

"There's Great Dane in them. I was looking for both size and docility. Fenris is a bit of a throwback, but he has so much heart, I kept him."

Aphrodite took one more piece of meat. This contained a bone, which she carried to a corner of the pen, then lay down and began gnawing on it. Odin came up and gave Dana's hand a nudge. She pulled out another scrap of meat and put it on her palm. The precaution wasn't necessary. Unlike his white leader, Odin nibbled delicately.

"Looks like the whole pack's honored you with their acceptance, Dana."

Dana smiled, warmed by the team's approval, then rocked back to ease her thigh muscles. Thunder clapped in the distance. She looked up to see scudding anvil-shaped clouds. Morgan followed her gaze.

"Won't be long now," he said. "It's probably already snowing in the west."

Dana simply scratched Odin's ruff, determined to enjoy the rest of her brief freedom without fretting over the weather. A few minutes passed, and she noticed the thunder was still rumbling.

"What's that?"

Morgan shrugged. "Echoes, maybe?"

Not sure she agreed, Dana continued listening. The rumbles grew closer and louder. Then she saw a dark swirl against the darker sky. The shape rose above the canyon wall like a giant dragonfly, its rotor spinning and spewing sound.

"No. No, it isn't!" she passed the meat to Morgan, shot to her feet, and pointed at the fin-like tail clearing the rim. "It's a helicopter! Can't you see it, Morgan?"

No, oh, no, no, no! Morgan screamed inside.

His attempt to reach his feet was seriously hampered by Odin's eagerness to reach the food. In the few seconds it took to settle the dog down, the helicopter grew to more than a swirl. Its nose pointed westward, away from them, and Morgan prayed the occupants didn't look back, because Dana had already backed out of the pen. Now she was trying her best to run in the snowshoes, frantically waving her arms at the ascending chopper.

Morgan saw her lips move, but her shouts were lost in the roar of engine and whirling blades. His heart leapt to his throat. Any second, the copter might dip, turn east. And if it did, there was no way they could miss seeing Dana.

He felt the familiar prickle; bones shifted, oh, so subtly. His initial dread changed to terror. He must stop her. To have her so close, then for her to be taken away . . . But first he must control his fear. . . .

Pushing Odin aside, he dumped out the remaining meat and raced from the pen, slamming the gate behind him. Already his boots and snowshoes were biting at his widening feet. His joints creaked and groaned. He tore off his footwear, then raced after Dana, who was virtually skating through the blowing snow, waving wildly, moving ever nearer to the iced-over edge of the canyon.

"Dana!" Morgan cried. "Don't!"

She couldn't hear him, and her eyes remained fixed on the retreating aircraft. Suddenly, the helicopter dipped and turned a circle. She turned back to him, talking, but he heard no sound.

The alchemization accelerated; his pain became almost unbearable. He could barely see her features now. Soon his vision would haze over completely. He'd fall to the ground. Hair would cover his face, his splaying hands and feet. With agonizing effort, he forced the process back and staggered on toward Dana.

Then, with a skier's grace, she thrust out her hips. The metal shoes skimmed forward, carrying her to within feet of the unstable snowbank edging the canyon.

At that moment, the helicopter swept upward.

"Come back!" she screamed, her desperate wail reaching Morgan's now agonizingly sensitive ears.

She jumped clumsily into the air, waving her arms like windmill blades, and wavered there for a second. Then losing her balance, she tumbled to the earth.

The helicopter rapidly diminished in size, disappearing behind a mass of dark clouds.

Foggily, Morgan saw Dana bury her face in her hands, heard her sobs. His heart gave a jump of hope. If she stayed where she was, he could reach her before—

She dropped her hands, gave an angry toss of her head, and shoved against the bank.

"Don't move, Dana! The ledge!"

The crusty snow gave with a loud crack. The edge crumbled slowly toward the abyss, pulling Dana with it.

"Daaa-naa!"

She clawed at the snow behind her. Futilely. The avalanche continued moving, carrying her close, close, closer to the drop-off.

With a roar, Morgan leapt forward, ignoring

the screams of his alchemizing joints. Just as the ledge gave way, he swept Dana up like a child's toy.

An instant later they were yards from the danger, though snow and rock still fell, clattering and echoing against the canyon wall. Powder blew relentlessly around their legs. Wind whipped at their clothes and skin. But all Morgan cared about was Dana, who clung helplessly to his neck.

"Dana, Dana," he murmured into her hair, breathing in the live scent of her, listening hard for the beat of her blood. "I thought—oh, God— I thought I'd lost you."

She nodded furiously against his chest. "I . . . I wasn't paying at-t-tention. The . . . the helicopter. Oh, Morgan, they didn't . . . didn't even see me."

Now that the threat had passed, Morgan's body began to relax, taking his pain and fear with it. He disentangled her hands from his neck and stared into her heartbroken eyes.

"I don't understand you, Dana. You almost fell into that canyon, but you're more concerned about the helicopter."

"Didn't you see those marking?" Tears streaked down her face, but her sobs abruptly ceased, leaving behind obvious frustration and anger. "That was a highway patrol chopper.

They're hunting for the wolves without me." She tried to whirl away, but her snowshoes caught in the snow, scattering powder almost to their shoulders and revealing Morgan's bare feet.

She stared down at them with a horrified expression. "Oh, Morgan! You're getting frostbitten."

She squatted, grabbing an ankle with her gloved hand. The warm touch shot straight to Morgan's bone and he flinched.

"Oh, God, I've been so silly. I'm sorry, Morgan. I'm sorry. I know better. I do. I should never have gone to that ledge. We both could have been killed."

"You almost were," he said harshly. "Get up. I'll be fine by morning."

"Not unless we treat this." She scrunched the hand from which she'd earlier removed the glove into her sleeve and grabbed Morgan's other ankle.

It hurt like hell.

"I said I'll be fine!" He jerked free, ignoring the surprised and wounded expression that flickered across her face. "As soon as I put my boots back on."

"Why did you take them off?" Her emotions already hidden, she rose haughtily to her feet.

"So I could get to you before you fell!"

"Are you saying it's **my** fault you ran barefoot through the snow? Why on earth would you do that?"

"To reach you in time," he snarled. "Now if you don't mind, I need my boots."

Full of fury, disappointment, hurt feelings, and myriad other bewildering emotions, Dana glared into his angry eyes. For just a crazy minute there, when he'd held her in his arms, trembling as if he'd recovered something of immense value, she'd almost thought he cared. Now he acted like she was his cross to bear, a silly creature, barely worth the effort he'd expended.

"I didn't ask you to play hero, Morgan. What makes you think I couldn't have gotten out of there myself?"

A scornful expression crossed his face and he gazed off in the direction of the pen.

"Don't ignore me. You don't know what I could have done."

To her surprise, he answered with a sorrowful groan. Dana turned to follow his gaze and her heart sank to her toes.

The dogs were gone.

☾

Chapter Ten

The seeming invincibility of the wer-wolf comes from the alchemization process. When this craven beast is wounded in either human or wolfish form, the act of transformation brings instant healing. Thus, all traces of former action is lost. What this means, brave hunter, is one never knows who is the beast among us. The deadly and cowardly creature that slinks into the woods with your bullet in its flank at night may yet walk with you hale and hearty come the morn.

Dana lifted her eyes from the page, beginning to think she'd be spending the rest of her life huddled under the blankets of the narrow bed she now called home. Wind again battered the eaves, snow beat against the windows, and she missed New Mexico like crazy.

Although she saw it pained him to do so, Morgan had insisted on pulling on his boots without her help, and when she offered to help find the dogs, he gruffly ordered her to carry wood inside so they wouldn't freeze during the storm. Although still angry, she had seen the wisdom of his suggestion. Besides, Morgan wouldn't have failed to secure the latch if she hadn't been chasing the helicopter.

Alternating between bitterness and remorse, and heartbroken at failing to catch the attention of the helicopter, she'd done as he asked. After she'd stacked the wood and fed the fire, she'd wandered around the cabin at loose ends until she finally picked up the book.

Likewise, a beast injured while in human form heals instantly after passing through the fires of alchemization. The neighbor limping at noontide from a stubbed toe will move freely and easily ere the night passes. Watch for these clues, so as not to be taken unawares. Many a dismayed hunter upon finally slaying the beast has soon gazed upon the face of a loved one. A husband, a wife, a lover, a friend. Yeah, even a parent or child.

The door burst open, bringing Morgan and a flurry of snow. Dana's hand flew to her heart. He dropped his snowshoes beneath the pegged rack and seemed not to notice that he'd frightened her.

"Did you find them?" Dana asked, after recovering from her start.

He headed for the mat without answering, his boots thudding ominously with each step. Snowflakes still clung to his beard and he knocked them away fiercely, his entire demeanor bristling with outrage.

"All but Fenris." He lowered onto the stool.

"Do you think he'll survive the storm?" Dana blinked back tears. If that sweet dog died, she could blame no one but herself. Nor could Morgan.

"Hard to say." But the crease between his eyes had deepened to a chasm. He glanced at the blaze in the fireplace. "At least you stoked the fire."

At least.

Never in her life had Dana felt incompetent. She'd always scorned women who couldn't change a tire, carry wood, or even shovel snow from a walkway. Now she felt an unwelcome sisterhood.

"I'm so sorry." A tear fell over her lower lashes. Twice in one day. Dear Lord, she was even beginning to be as weepy as they were.

"Don't cry," Morgan said sharply. "It won't change anything."

She nodded and sank deeper into her blankets. Her head ached and her stomach rumbled. The storm raging at the cabin walls seemed even harsher than the one before. All was dark outside, and Dana had no idea what time it was. Her stomach growled again, more loudly this time.

"I'll get you some stew soon as I'm done," Morgan said.

"You don't have to wait on me."

He bent to remove his boots, and Dana remembered his frostbitten feet. She threw off the blankets and climbed from the bed.

"I'll heat some water for your feet. I should have done it while you were—"

"That isn't necessary."

"Yes, yes it is. You're a doctor; you should know that." She hurried to the sink and picked up the pan under the dripping pump.

"My feet are fine, Dana."

Ignoring his protests, she bustled to the stove, replaced the venison pot on top of the flickering burner with the water pan, and turned up the heat.

"They're fine, I tell you."

"How could—" She glanced down at his bare foot and gave out a little shriek.

His toes should have been red, even blistering, but they were as pink and healthy as hers.

"That's impossible," she said in a shocked whisper.

"I heal quickly." He hid his foot inside his

141

fleece slipper. "Hunting for the dogs got the blood circulating. My toes stung awhile, that's all." He bared his other foot and shoved it into its slipper with considerable haste.

. . . the act of transforming brings about instant healing.

Dana shook her head.

A husband, a wife, a lover . . .

She shook her head again. What was wrong with her? It was bad enough she might have cost Morgan his dog; she should be glad his feet weren't damaged. Instead, she was having ridiculous thoughts spawned by a stupid book about creatures that didn't exist.

"Uh, good." Feeling a little sheepish, she took the water pan back to the sink, then offered to dish out some stew for Morgan, wanting something, anything, to keep her mind off what she'd just read, just seen.

"I'm not hungry." He stood then and stripped off his jumpsuit. Without another word, he stalked to his bedroom and disappeared inside.

Feeling thoroughly rebuked, Dana lifted the lid of the stew pot, but the normally delicious aroma turned her stomach. Returning to the bed, she bundled up. *The Lycanthropy Reader* lay open next to her, to the page where she'd left off.

It was filling her mind with nonsense, undoubtedly fueled by the fierce storm and relentless darkness, and belonged back on the bookshelf. But despite these thoughts, she picked it up again.

This author prays, dear hunter, that you are not among those who have wept over the coffin of a beloved, slain by your own hand.

The sentence filled Dana with inexplicable sadness, and for the third time that day, her eyes brimmed with tears. She replaced the book on the table, blinking hard, trying to make sense of her feelings. Soon she dozed off.

When the knock came, she'd been dreaming. Someone was shouting "With a huff and a puff," and she felt like a slab of pork about to be devoured. She came awake with a rush of terror, head pivoting, searching the room, trying to make sense of the noise. The sturdy outer door was virtually quivering from the force of the blows from the other side. The tingle she'd come to associate with extreme danger vibrated from her head to her toes.

She ran to Morgan's bedroom and pounded on his door.

"Morgan," she cried. "Someone's here."

His door cracked an inch. "What?"

"Someone's knocking on the door." Her mind whirled with confused thoughts. How could that be? No one could travel in this weather.

Morgan shut the bedroom door in her face. Seconds later, he came barreling through, nearly knocking her over as he headed for the front entrance. He yanked it open to reveal one of the most striking women Dana had ever seen. Shorter than Dana, she was exceedingly slender, with a narrow face and round, tilted dark eyes. She moved out of a swirl of snow and stepped imperiously over the threshold, whipping the skirts of a Cossack-type coat around her legs.

"I wish to speak with you, Morgan." Her voice held chilling self-possession.

A nondescript person, made more so by his contrast with the striking woman, shuffled in from the whirlwind behind them. His eyes were downcast and his shoulders slumped pathetically as he dragged in a snow-caked bundle.

The bundle whimpered.

"Fenris!" Dana dropped to her knees, reached out for the dog's frozen collar, and dragged him to her chest. Ice crystals clung to his poor coat and he quivered against her breast, leaving chilly, wet spots on her thermal shirt. His cold tongue lapped at her cheek.

"Leave him!" the woman commanded. "He's for Morgan."

Dana glowered. "How did you get him?"

The answer came in the form of a feral smile. Although Dana knew it was her imagination, she thought she heard the man growl. She shot him an angry glance and he withdrew, seeming to hide in the woman's skirts.

"For Christ's sake, shut the damned door!" roared Morgan. "Snow's getting all over the floor."

The pathetic man scrambled forward and nearly collapsed in his effort to close the door against the driving wind. But the woman was undaunted.

"I've returned your runt, Morgan. Unwise to leave him roaming about in such weather." She winked, as if there was a secret joke between them.

If there was, Morgan didn't seem to get it. He drew his eyebrows together, deepening the crease between them to a gash. "Is that supposed to earn my gratitude?"

"This we need to discuss." She gave Dana a meaningful and malevolent glance. "Alone."

Morgan looked incensed and apprehensive at the same time. His gaze flickered from Dana to the woman to the man, who huddled near the door. Finally he cocked his head toward his bedroom.

"In there." He took a few threatening steps in the direction of the woman's companion, then glanced down at Dana. "You get my meaning?"

"*Sí, sí,*" the man said obsequiously.

Morgan took the woman's arm and ushered her into his room.

Dana stared at his closed door, fuming. She didn't like that woman's proprietary air toward Morgan one bit! And what was he doing taking the visitor into the room he'd declared off-limits to her? But Fenris was still shivering in her arms and needed her care. She led him to the mat where she told him to sit, then she pulled some towels from beneath the sink. Sitting beside him, she roughed up his soaked gray coat, dislodging the clinging crystals. He wiggled happily beneath her touch and was soon sitting in a puddle on the mat. Dana took him to the fire, instructed him to lie down, then began heating some drinking water for him.

All the while the man followed her movements with cunning dark eyes. Dana wasn't much good at hospitality, especially to such unexpected and unwelcome guests, but supposed she should offer him something.

"I could heat up some cider," she said. "Would you like some?"

"*Sí.*" His sly eyes flickered with momentary gratitude. "It would be, uh, be *bueno.*"

So he spoke very little English. That explained his odd behavior.

A few minutes later, she gave Fenris the warm

water, then handed a steaming cup to the visitor. He took it and began slurping noisily.

"You can sit down if you like." She pointed to one of the chairs by the table and he shuffled over to it. Dana did her best to ignore him while she mopped up the puddles their entrance had left, then headed for her bed where she curled up with the cider she'd poured for herself.

After a few laps from his bowl, Fenris got up and began nervously roaming the room. From his place at the table, the man stared at her over his cup.

Dana stared back, her skin again a mass of prickles.

She wondered just how long Morgan would be.

"The woman for the runt," Lily said sweetly, gliding around the room, touching this, touching that. "It's a fair trade, is it not?"

As her slender hand came to rest upon the shackles bolted to the inside wall, Morgan snarled. She laughed. "And what are these, dear Morgan? Something to help you resist the fullness of the moon? Ah, yes, that night will soon be upon us. Then who do you think will protect the mortal female? Trade her to me now and save yourself the grief."

"There's nothing to trade, Lily. I already have

my dog." They both knew she couldn't harm Fenris anyway.

She frowned delicately. "Poor Jorje was to keep it outside. I must chastise him. Yet he was probably shivering grievously in the storm. He does despise the indignities of the human form." Her hand snaked out, stroked Morgan's beard. "You understand that, don't you? Although, of course, it is the beastly form you despise."

Morgan backed away, repulsed.

"Not just the form. I also despise you for giving it to me."

"I am not as bad as you think. Don't I always spare the children and also keep Jorje from harming them? I am not completely brutal. You think you hate me, but like us, some day you'll come to relish the wolf's life and thank me for bestowing it."

"It's been four years since you tracked me down and I still curse the day we met. Why do you think I'll change?"

She smiled, clearly confident in her ultimate control. "Some, they say, take a decade or more to adjust. I shall wait. Time, dear Morgan, we have in abundance."

"I'll see your bones buried in consecrated ground before I become your mate."

"Sebastian has decreed it!" Lily snarled. "If you do not obey, he will one day come, to your everlasting regret. His chastisements, I assure you, are not as gentle as mine."

Morgan buried one hand in his shaggy hair. Here he was, again debating with a creature completely immersed in brutality and artifice.

He turned his head away.

"How dare you insult me?" she screeched in Lupinese, scraping a threatening foot against the floor.

She darted to his table and swept aside a gas lamp. It crashed to the floor. Fuel spilled, staining the wood, and caught fire. Morgan calmly stamped it out, then turned back to her. In the dimming light from the solar fixture on the wall, he saw her stare at him in outrage. Her silver hair began to bristle and grow. Her fingers, bare beneath the sleeve of her coat, began to splay. With a powerful leap, she landed in front of his dresser, picked up a hairbrush and threw it against the wall. It hit with a sharp smack, then fell to the floor.

"You hopeless fool! That lamp, this brush, that *food* you keep on your silly shelves. These mortal accoutrements do not become you! Nor will they preserve your humanity!"

Then she lunged at the shackles on his inner wall. Growling gutturally and causing a great clatter of chains, she pulled and yanked, clearly trying to tear them from the wall. But her efforts were futile. Morgan had installed them to withstand the full power of his wolf nature, and she could do no more than make them clank.

Frustrated, she turned to his inner door and pounded on it. "Why have you made yourself this cage?" With another roar, she charged at the outside exit, clawing at the metal door. "You've built a fortress, trying to hide from your nature. You fool, you total, utter fool! I gave you a gift, a precious gift, and you reject it!"

As Morgan wearily witnessed her melodrama, he found he couldn't tear his gaze away. How easily she alchemized. No painful spasms. No agonized groans. He despised her with the depth of his soul, but still felt a terrible stab of envy each time he beheld her effortless transformation.

She saw his eyes upon her and her rage disappeared as quickly as it had come. She leaped back to face him. "I have decided to forgive you, my darling. I see your wistfulness. You wish to know my secrets."

Her eyes had sunk into the cranny beneath her emerging brow and were now all pupil and iris. She stared boldly at him and lifted a silvery hand to draw a single claw down the tender skin of his exposed neck. Parting her lips to reveal her deadly fangs, she leaned toward the spot where her claw rested. "Come, darling, let me reveal my secrets to you." Her honeyed tone somehow managed to give sweetness to the bitter sounds of the Lupine tongue. "Slaughter this woman and join me in all our glory. Then you too will know the ease of alchemization. One human kill, Morgan, is all it takes, then the shape shifts without slicing the mortal form with pain."

"Get out, Lily." He deliberately used English, letting her know it was over. He would not participate.

A hum of rage formed deep in her throat. Her eyes narrowed. With a sudden thrust of her head, she clamped her teeth on Morgan's throat. They stood stock-still for an instant, Lily's jaw poised open over his jugular vein.

Her huge head had towered more than a foot above him while she stood upright, and in mortal form Morgan had no defense against her. But her attempt to frighten him into alchemization had no effect. He'd lived as one of her hellish kind long enough to know she would not, could not, harm him. No werewolf had ever killed another. It was a Lupine law Lily would never violate.

Nor could she harm Dana as long as she remained on his land. A werewolf's territory was sacred. But, oh, how she wanted to. He felt her hate, her desire to destroy him for rejecting her so cruelly, felt how badly she wanted to deny the only law she lived by.

"Do it!" he growled. "Put me out of my misery."

He arched his neck, pressing against her sharp fangs. A tooth pricked his skin; blood trickled down his neck.

With a distressed whimper, Lily released her hold and fell back. Her hands flew to cover her mouth, but not before Morgan saw the scarlet drop staining one fang.

His blood. She'd tasted his blood.

The realization filled her eyes with horror. She shuddered, and for a heartbeat Morgan pitied her. Like him, someone had made her what she was. Unlike him, she was too weak to resist her mutant nature. She even relished it.

Then a shutter fell across her face, blocking those feelings. Her fangs and claws faded; the hair disappeared; her brow retreated. When it was done, her eyes were cold and hard. Morgan's pity, too, had vanished.

"Be warned, Morgan," she said. "You are mine. I will not let the woman have you."

With that, she straightened her back with dignity, gathered her Cossack coat around her legs, and stalked out of Morgan's bedroom.

He closed and bolted the door against her,

against the entire nightmare of his life, for all the good it did, and stared at it for a long while. Then he walked to his bedside table, which held a basin. Dipping a cloth into the cool water within, he washed Lily's blood-mixed saliva off his neck.

If only he could wash away his curse so easily.

Chapter Eleven

Dana was still keeping vigilance over the peculiar man at the kitchen table when the woman came bursting through Morgan's door with blazing eyes and streaming hair. For a brief instant, she caught a glimpse of Morgan, who looked angrier than she had yet seen him. Then he slammed the door and bolted it.

"We go, Lily?" asked the man, who apparently was undaunted by the angry display.

"In a moment, Jorje," she replied crossly, fixing Dana with a malevolent stare.

With a toss of her long hair, Lily crouched in front of Dana, leaning forward until their faces were only inches apart. Dana felt the woman's breath burning her skin, felt the hatred stab at her psyche, and couldn't fathom what had provoked it.

"Do not think Morgan is yours, she-whelp. I will be back for him . . . and for you."

"She-whelp?" Dana meant to issue a scoffing challenge, but her question came out like a whimper. Her body vibrated with alarm. Weak, uncoordinated muscles hampered her attempts to put steel in her spine.

"Do not backtalk. And mind what I say."

Lily turned her face away, then rose and gestured to Jorje, who sprang from his chair. Amid another icy flurry, the pair returned to the storm from which they'd come, leaving Dana feeling as if she'd just tumbled into the rabbit's hole.

She let out a heavy sigh and looked around. Except for Fenris, who moved restlessly to the door and sniffed nervously, everything was now as it had been. The stew bubbled on the stove. The fire danced brightly. If not for the puddles on the floor, no one would guess Lily and Jorje had even been there.

Dana followed Fenris's lead and began roaming the cabin, too. She touched the kitchen table, the bed, the door, feeling almost as if she were re-marking her territory after a violation.

Finally, she gave another sigh and went to get the mop.

While cleaning up the second miniflood of the day, her legs unexpectedly turned to jelly. She wobbled to the rocking chair and sat down, trying to catch her now erratic breath. What had she done to earn such animosity? In Dana's admittedly inexpert opinion, Lily's behavior appeared almost psychotic, which probably explained why she seemed so frightening.

Unfortunately, the explanation did nothing to ease Dana's fear. The small room suddenly looked huge and empty. Silly, she knew. After all, everything was light and warm inside, despite the sub-zero fingers scraping at the windows. But the chill from the bizarre couple's unexpected appearance lingered, and she felt it in her bones.

She turned to the fire, rubbed her hands in front of it. Would she ever be warm again? Or away from this windswept, storm-battered place? And how had Lily and Jorje forged their way here? Where had they come from?

Even more frightening was the rapid healing of Morgan's feet. She'd seen frostbite before. It took days, sometimes weeks, to heal, with blood-starved skin peeling off in ugly gray sheets. Maybe she'd blown the damage out of proportion. After all, his feet had been bare only a short time; but when she'd taken them in her hands, they'd been as white and cold and hard as ice cubes. Surely there should have been some aftereffect.

Yet when he'd taken off his boots by the fire—

and she had seen his feet clearly before he'd hidden them in the slippers—even the tips of his toes glowed with perfect health.

Strength began returning to Dana's muscles, but not warmth. Firelight reflected in the small pools of water on the floor, but she went to the bed, collected a blanket, and took it to the rocker. She'd just gathered it around her when a groan permeated the room.

She shivered and sank deeper into the blanket.

How odd could a man's music be?

She laughed bitterly. She'd asked herself that question often lately, always with the same answer.

How odd? It could drive a person mad, that's how odd. God, there was no melody, no harmony, and it sounded like the cries of a doomed soul standing at the gates of hell. She could barely listen without wanting to scream.

All the rumors about Ebony Canyon rushed into her mind. It was, some said, a land lost in time and inhabited by Indians never exposed to society, who performed rituals to conjure up spirits of old to do their bidding. Supposedly, mutant creatures and evolution holdovers roamed free in its rugged, unexplored acres. Unspeakable monsters, invincible specters, bleached bones, lost graves . . .

Her eyes drifted to *The Lycanthropy Reader*. She stared in ghoulish fascination. The best thing she could do for her sanity was to stop reading that book. The supernatural forces and magical powers it described were making her imagination run wild.

She continued staring, drawn like an addict to an obsession, then trudged hypnotically to the bed and picked up the book. Wrapping herself in the bedclothes, as if they could protect her, she opened it.

In creature form, the wer-wolf is impervious to weather. Neither heat nor cold can pierce its lush coat. For hours it can lope through temperatures that soon cause mortal man to perish. Choose your time wisely, brave hunter, choose wisely, lest by the limitations of your own flesh you become fodder for the beast's insatiable hunger.

Was that how Lily and Jorje had forded the storm? By shape-shifting? Could these creatures actually exist?

Dana gasped and swept the book off her lap.

No! She was a scientist, for God's sake. She lived in a real world with known creatures. With reasonable explanations that she needed now.

Only Morgan could provide them.

She glanced at his locked door, then realized she'd so thoroughly blocked out his music she hadn't noticed when it stopped. The quiet behind that fortification now seemed as ominous as the music itself. After hesitating a moment, she put down the book and left the protection of her bed.

Upon reaching Morgan's room, she rapped tentatively, starting when the noise ricocheted through the still room.

"Morgan," she called, frightened even by the echo of her own voice.

When a few seconds passed and he didn't answer, she paused, then rapped a second time.

No response.

She knew that, despite the metal plate, sound traveled in and out of there. Morgan's music always came through clearly enough, and she'd also caught unintelligible snippets of his quarrel with Lily. She leaned against the cool metal, straining to hear signs that he was up and moving around.

"Morgan?" she called, louder.

She heard a shuffle on the other side, a noise that hinted of something scratching. A guttural rasp slid beneath the door. Dana's heart skipped a beat and she jerked back.

"Morgan!"

Still he did not answer, but the sounds subsided.

Dana wanted to dash back to the illusionary

safety of the daybed, but her fear and irrational suspicions angered her. She felt sure that as soon as she talked to Morgan, she'd receive the explanations she needed. Then she heard a latch click. Moving back in relief, she waited for Morgan to come out.

Her wait went unrewarded.

She raised her hand and knocked again, this time hard and long, but still he didn't answer. Soon her eyes began to burn with tears and her throat thickened. She continued to pound ever more frantically.

"Morgan! Morgan! Where are you? Come out!"

The storm outside intensified; the wind hammered at the panes and eaves, nearly drowning out her calls. She fought back by pounding harder, screaming louder. Finally, she could barely lift her arm and her voice gave out. Stumbling to the bed, she collapsed into a huddle and stared blankly at the flames. She hadn't felt so lost, alone, or helpless since . . .

Since just before she'd found her first wolf cub in that vale in Montana. Now her pack was hundreds of miles away and she was alone, all alone, on the brink of hell.

Oh, the smells of the forest, the bite of the fierce wind, the softness of fresh snow beneath his pads. Morgan ran and ran and ran through a swirl of gray and white, devouring miles with his long, powerful legs.

He was running from it all. Lily's ceaseless demands. His guilt over deceiving Dana. His grim half-world existence. He wanted to keep running till he dropped from exhaustion, panting, gasping, dying, leaving every ounce of pain behind.

Which, he knew, was not possible. He was tireless, inexhaustible, invincible. And hungry, always hungry. The need curled in his belly like a snake waiting to strike.

Yet even as he ran, he felt a familiar glory in his mutant state. The subtle variety of colors, the vivid contrasts of light and dark, so intense they were unknown to both humans and wolves. He inhaled the scents, so many, each gloriously different from the next. Sounds of all vibrations caressed his ears. He could actually hear and feel the thrum of Earth turning on its axis, the thrust of plants, growing, reaching up.

New York had emitted different sensations. Myriad lights that assailed his pupils, blurred his vision. The whine of tires on wet pavement, the coos of pigeons perching high, the cacophony of voices, laughing, crying, wailing, cheering. Life's blood, throbbing through veins, emitting a coppery scent that lured him to stalk, to . . .

Kill.

The sheer glut of feeling had almost overwhelmed him. He'd fled the city in terror of his own emotions, his own horrible urges.

As a mortal, he'd hardly noticed the city's activity. He'd grown numb in his plush Fifth Avenue office, listening to privileged people grouse about petty problems, viewing them with a contempt he concealed even from himself.

His mother had died when he was a child, and though he'd always sensed his investment-banker father loved him, the man had been so harried and preoccupied, Morgan never really knew him. His only sister was ten years older than he and had left home before Morgan entered high school. He hadn't seen her since their father's funeral several years before.

After that, Morgan had felt strangely adrift in the world. His personal relationships became distant, ritualistic, mechanical. At night he amused himself with plays and sporting events, parties and unfulfilling sex, and when that paled he'd stare at the city below from the balcony of his luxurious, professionally decorated Central Park apartment and wonder what had happened to the young psychiatrist who'd wanted to eliminate mankind's woes. At these times, he studied books about the awesome possibilities of the human mind and asked himself why no one had reliably tapped into it. He'd dream of one day doing so, then the next morning he'd return to his lackluster practice.

Then a colleague invited him to interview an unusual patient: a Balkan immigrant who'd fled Romania during the breakup of the Soviet Union. The man actually believed he was a werewolf and had rushed into the colleague's office, alarmed at the impending full moon, begging to be locked up for everyone's protection.

Morgan had, of course, been incredulous, but the man's sincere conviction was fascinating, so he'd agreed to take the case. During one late-day appointment, as the city lights began reflecting in the window of Morgan's high-rise office, his attention began to wander. Nearly an hour of hearing about Transylvania and enchanted mountains was stretching his patience.

Lucid, he scribbled onto a yellow legal pad. *Obsessive need for attention.* By this point, he was certain the patient was an unmitigated fake.

"She was a woman of few years," the man was saying. "Her skin still fresh and dewy, tender to the teeth. When she saw me, I could smell the very fear in her. . . . Ah, it was so tantalizing. I could not resist."

"Where was this again, Boris?" Morgan

asked, not really caring, but wanting his notes to be correct.

"In Bucharest, in the rotten heart of the city." The man paused for a moment. "I stalked her for many blocks and she began walking faster, faster, until she nearly stumbled over her own feet. Finally she turned a dark corner. A key was in her hand. I saw my chance. . . ."

Morgan fought back a grimace of disbelief as tears gathered in the corner of his patient's eyes.

"She was at her door . . . safety near, so near. . . . I saw terror . . . terror in her face when she turned to fight me. Then she looked into my eyes and I had her in my will. She fought no more. I said a small prayer for her soul." Another dramatic pause, a poignant hitch in the voice. "I tore out her throat before the scream had left it."

Morgan involuntarily cleared his own throat. "Umm. . . . This is a good time to, uh, address control of the imagination. Can you tell me what occurred before you had this delusion?"

"Delusion?" This was stated sharply. "Are you a fool like the rest, Doctor? A skeptic who will not admit the existence of what you cannot understand?"

"Your *anger* is understandable; let's start with that." Leaning back in his chair, Morgan nibbled on the tip of his pen. "What angered you that day?"

"I was *not* angry!" Boris gave an awkward jerk of his head. "Why can you not believe? It is truth I tell you."

He jerked his head again. His arms and legs began to twitch. Spasms ran through his jaw. Clearly fighting the movements, he arched his neck backward. His mouth snapped opened. A high keening sound arose from his throat, reverberated off the window glass, and filled the room. With a moan, he lurched to the floor and curled up.

Morgan made a quick call for emergency assistance, then rushed to kneel beside the fallen man, whose joints had already swelled to twice their normal size. The man's moans sounded more like whimpers and snarls than human cries of pain, and his wide eyes contained a plea.

Unable to believe what he was seeing, Morgan watched Boris's cranium plate shift. Bones and joints twitched, wobbled, reassembled themselves into larger, sturdier structures. The patient's skin thickened; hair appeared on his gnarled knuckles. His eyes glazed and Morgan sensed he was no longer aware of his surroundings.

Morgan stared in denial and terror as Boris clenched his eyes shut, wrapped himself into a fetal position, and rocked onto his side. His groans grew increasingly agonized, his respiration rapid and shallow. Morgan reached to check his pulse, snatching his hand back when Boris snapped at it.

He called the man's name, but the patient was lost in his own agonized world and didn't hear. His vital signs were getting weak.

Morgan sprang to his feet and yanked open a desk drawer that held a small first-aid kit he'd never had to use. No longer sure what it contained, he fought to still his trembling fingers and scattered the contents of the kit, searching for a paper vial he hoped was there.

While he hunted, he asked himself if Boris's tale might be true. Although the man's body retained human proportions, the changes were irrefutably wolflike.

He refused to believe in such superstitious nonsense, and his studies came back to him. What was at work inside this man that could cause such physical manifestations? Shape-shifting, shamanism, werewolves, and vampires were all nonsense. But who knew what the human mind could do?

Nineteenth-century psychiatric papers suggested that hysterical psychosomatic reactions were once quite common, although few modern psychiatrists had ever witnessed one. Yet even now, people frequently died from psychosomatic illnesses. Could man also use his will to change his body? By harnessing this power, might man finally defeat illness and the inevitable decline of old age? Learn to control thought, thereby eliminating mental and behavioral disorders?

Morgan's fear vanished, but now his heart raced with excitement. The possibilities were limitless.

At that moment, his hand touched the ammonia inhalant. He rushed back and cracked it open beneath Boris's nose, recoiling himself as the heavy, acrid odor filled the room.

When the inhalant reached Boris's lungs, he gasped and choked. A cough rattled in his chest. Tension subsided. He relaxed his arms. Soon his breathing slowed and he straightened his rigidly drawn up legs.

"Boris?"

With a heavy sigh, Boris rolled onto his back and opened his eyes, which were now bloodshot.

"They say the process is easier if you don't fight it," he said, so softly Morgan had to strain to hear the words.

"Who says?"

"The alphas," came the whispered reply.

"Do they tell you to do things, these alphas?"

167

"No one tells me. It's my nature now. And, oh, sweet God, I despise it."

Morgan's mind whirred as he tried to categorize Boris's experience. A disassociative disorder? Schizophrenia, perhaps? He had to know what had brought about these physical changes. But the psychiatrist in him knew he shouldn't probe at this time. Boris needed stabilizing first.

"What thoughts preceded these symptoms?" he asked, ignoring professional protocol to satisfy personal curiosity.

"I told you. The moon is waxing." Then he laughed so bitterly, with such despair, it sent a chill down Morgan's spine. "You had a lucky escape, Doctor. Now lock me up. If I cannot persuade you to do it for your own protection, then do it for mine."

Morgan continued with questions for a while, but got no reasonable answers. When the paramedics arrived, he did as Boris requested and had him committed. For several days he visited the patient, reading reports of physical manifestations similar to those that occurred in his office. Always Boris exhibited extreme pain; always the ammonia inhalant relieved the symptoms; and always he failed to give Morgan a rational explanation.

Late on the night of the full moon, a phone call disturbed Morgan's sleep. Boris had been found hanging by his neck in his room, apparently preferring death to the miserable existence he'd created.

The next morning, Morgan cleared his appointments and booked a flight to Europe, where he hoped to find answers to Boris's anomalous manifestations and disprove his claims of a werewolf curse. A scientific reason existed, and Morgan felt certain it lay in uncovering the power of thought. Perhaps the tragedy of poor Boris's life would help unlock those secrets and provide everlasting benefit.

In Paris, he found the beautiful Lily. Sultry and fey—or so he'd thought at the time—she'd offered to take him to remote villages in the various Balkan mountain ranges where the inhabitants still defended themselves against evil night creatures. Although retaining his skepticism about their beliefs, Morgan hoped to gain insight into the social paradigms that could influence a man's mind enough to cause rapid and profound body changes. The fervor of youthful idealism returned.

Lily assured him he'd find his answers. They met with gypsies and shamans, with village mayors and natural healers, whose fantastic stories disappointed Morgan and failed to give him the desired insight. He asked Lily for more.

Finally, atop a stony mountain bordering the

fabled Transylvania Basin, Lily gave him more than he'd asked for. Much more.

Now, as he raced through the thickening forest above Ebony Canyon, the extent of Lily's betrayal fueled his rage to volcanic proportions. He hated her, hated Boris for precipitating his trip to Europe. Even hated the colleague who'd introduced them. Finally, he hated Dana for putting her life in his untrustworthy hands.

Tightening his flanks, he skidded to a stop, scattering powder with the weight of his enormous body. He sniffed, hoping to catch the scent of some creature cut off from its burrow by the storm. None would be out willingly. Nature's beasts retreated from such inhospitable weather, even the ones that were distant kin to him.

He, of course, was not like them. They fed a hunger of the body, an instinct to sustain themselves. His was a sick and twisted need. Yet he knew his smoldering rage could only be cooled by spilled blood, by the death cry of some living, breathing creature.

Creeping forward, he sniffed the ground and scanned the white-on-white terrain for some subtle hint of shadow that would betray a quarry's presence. His sensitive nose caught the pungent musk of fear and he followed it. The scent grew nearer, stronger, leading him on.

Suddenly, snow flew everywhere. A pale rabbit darted from beneath an exposed tree root, heading for the deeper forest. In one enormous leap Morgan was upon it. His mouth opened above the quivering body, but even before his teeth clamped down, he felt the shudder of escaping life.

He gave the limp form a threatening and useless shake, then dropped it in shame and defeat. The rabbit lay before him, nearly invisible on the white snow.

It had died of fright.

Morgan thought he knew and understood sorrow, but now a piercing despair, unlike any he'd ever experienced, engulfed him. Sinking to his haunches, he lifted his powerful head to the angry sky and let out a long and mournful howl.

Dana! Daa-na, Daa-naa, Daa-naaaaaa!

(

Chapter Twelve

Something wet and cold poked at Dana's face. She brushed it away, but it came back more insistently, and she opened her heavy lids just in time to see a pink tongue dart toward her nose. She dodged too late, then abruptly sat up and wiped off the aftermath of Fenris's affection. Her head ached from the quick movements and she felt a bit stiff, but the debilitating despair with which she'd fallen asleep was gone.

Giving the runt an absent pat on the head, she wondered what time it was. A glance at the window showed a dull light. Apparently it was morning. She threw off the blankets, shivering as she walked over to look outside.

Gray scudding clouds dimmed the sun, the land was covered with boiling windswept white, and she was damned near freezing. She wanted to wail and gnash her teeth and whatever else people did when they were frustrated. Obviously, leaving this place wasn't in the cards this morning, since a new storm was clearly on its way.

The fire sputtered inside the glowing skeletons of logs remaining from the night, and Dana moved to add more firewood. As she stoked the flames to life, she noticed the wood supply was low again.

Warming her backside before the flames while she dressed, she thought about how different everything looked during the day. She couldn't quite fathom why she'd been so badly frightened, and she felt a bit ashamed. After all, she was a wildlife biologist specializing in wolves. She'd explored some of the world's most rugged terrain, often alone, with nothing but her backpack and knowledge to sustain her. She'd faced down bears and cougars, climbed inside wolf dens.

Yet two people emerging mysteriously from a storm and an imaginative book about mythical creatures had turned her into a shuddering mass of phobias. For a brief moment, she toyed with the idea that werewolves did exist. After all, new species were still being discovered. But where would such creatures come from? And how could something that large escape the attention of curious scientists seeking new life forms? This fell in the same category as Bigfoot and the Abominable Snowman. Nothing in her background supported such a wild idea.

But she did know that Ebony Canyon set her nerves on edge. Mission Lobo aside, she wanted to get away from the place as soon as the storm broke again. With or without Morgan's help.

Feeling more herself, she began rummaging through the pantry, discovering some beef jerky behind the canned goods and a cache of pecans and walnuts. Next, she gathered all her stray belongings and shoved them into the duffle bag. With luck, the blizzard would move on during the day, and when it did, she'd head straight back to civilization.

But what about Morgan? The thought evoked a sudden ache in her heart and she placed a hand on her chest to ease it. Would she leave without so much as a thanks? After all, he'd saved her life. Unfortunately, he was rapidly beginning to seem more like a jailer than a savior.

Maybe she'd leave a note, send him some flowers. She tried to smile at the idea of an FTD delivery person attempting to find his remote cabin, but her heartache persisted and she looked for another way to keep busy.

The nearly empty wood rack provided just the task.

A short time later she was standing on the snowy porch, snowshoes in hand, gazing out on the swirling landscape. Although she reminded herself she hated snow, she still felt glad to be out in untouched wilderness.

Feeling more cheerful because of it, she picked up the shovel leaning against the wall and began digging. Her stiff muscles warmed and relaxed. She found herself enjoying the pull of the laden shovel on her back.

Occasionally a bark came from the kennel, and now and then a bird cried, but otherwise she was completely alone. As she threw a final for-good-measure shovelful over the porch railing, she heard wings flapping behind her. She turned to see a large white bird land on the rail. Tilting its head in curiosity, it inspected her with dark eyes.

Birds weren't Dana's specialty, but she was sure this was a hawk. An unusual specimen, to be sure. Totally white, and considerably larger than any she'd seen before.

"My, you're a beauty," she said, leaning the shovel against the wall and moving in for a closer look. The hawk displayed no open fear, but gave a shrill call and hopped back several feet. Dana took another step forward. Again the bird hopped back. They repeated the process several times. Finally Dana gave up. She picked up her snowshoes and started for the steps, giving the bird one final glance over her shoulder. It was gone. When she returned her head back, she gave out a tiny squeal.

A man wearing a fur cloak stood at the base of the stairs. His face was shadowed by a hood shaped like a hawk's head. The beak rested just above his eyes.

"I didn't mean to frighten you." His voice was smooth and rich, and though the words clearly came from his mouth, the beak moved in unison with them, creating an odd illusion.

He tilted his head back and the hood fell to his shoulder. Muted light shone on his heavy dark hair, which was tied at his neck with a thong.

"Where did you come from?" she asked sharply, angling the snowshoes in front of her like a shield, although she wasn't truly afraid. His tanned, angular face clearly showed Native American heritage, and though obviously no more than thirty-five, he reminded Dana of an ancient warrior. She almost felt as if he'd been sent to protect her. "Do you live up here?"

"I came to help you shovel snow. I see I'm too late."

"Who are you?"

"The People call me White Hawk." He

smiled, showing bright, even teeth. "Others just call me Tony."

"Well, Tony," Dana replied, trying to regain her composure. Would mysterious visitors never stop appearing? "You still haven't told me how you got here." She waved her hand toward the clearing. "In case you hadn't noticed, it's been snowing like crazy."

"I noticed. As I said, I thought you could use help. With the wood, perhaps?"

"How did you know I was— Never mind. You probably won't answer that, either."

"Wise woman, but then as much was foretold."

"Do you always speak in riddles?"

"I try to." Again he smiled.

"I thought so."

"How about that wood?" He gestured to the snowshoes. "You'll need to put those on, of course."

The sky was thickening with the approaching storm. Two could haul twice as much as one. She nodded and dropped the snowshoes off the porch, then descended the stairs. When she reached the bottom, she saw he too wore snowshoes, only his were of wood and leather, looked handmade, and rather resembled tennis rackets.

"Those work?" she asked.

177

"You'll see."

While she slipped her feet into the snowshoes, he disappeared around the corner of the cabin, returning shortly with a long sled. "This will make our task easier."

He smiled at her astounded expression.

"You're making me nervous." But she didn't really feel nervous, because she instinctively knew he meant no harm. "I didn't know Morgan had put the sled there. How come you did? For that matter, how did you know I was here?"

"Mysterious powers." He tapped his temple, then laughed. "I ran into Morgan a short while ago. He told me you were visiting."

Dana laughed too. "Don't you people up here know enough to come in from a storm?"

"When you're used to them, they aren't so fearsome. As you'll soon find out." With that, he turned away, pulling the sled behind him. Dana quickly caught up and fell into step with him.

They skimmed through the undulating snow in silence, and loaded the sled with effortless cooperation. Tremendous claps of thunder accompanied their last trip—which was what made it their last trip, since Dana was on a roll and would have preferred stacking the porch with a week's worth of wood.

"One must work in harmony with nature,"

said Tony, when Dana started to venture out again. "To know when enough is enough."

"Umm, sure," Dana said, remembering that her father often gave her similar advice. "But it would be nice to know we won't run out."

"All is cared for by Grandfather Sky," he said. "Your upcoming lesson will teach you that quite thoroughly."

She looked over to see if he was kidding, but found his face entirely serious. "You speak of the future like you know what will happen, but nobody knows that."

"Not all of it. But we can foretell more than you think."

He pulled his hood up, arranging it until the beak was again in the middle of his forehead. His earlier playfulness disappeared. In the distance Dana thought she heard drums beating, but decided it was thunder. Still, she grew uneasy.

"A giant woman shall emerge from the storm on a red steed and tame the wild beast." Tony spread his arms. "So it was told; so it shall be."

This time Dana would have sworn his words did come from the beak. To relieve her edginess, she feigned offense. "I know I'm tall for a woman, but giant? That's a stretch."

Tony's expression softened for an instant. "Some meanings are unclear. Giant in spirit, perhaps. Nonetheless, Dana, you are here for a purpose. Destiny cannot be denied." He reached somewhere inside his cloak, coming out with his hand curled around something. "I brought gifts to ensure your success."

He lifted Dana's hand and dropped several paper capsules onto her open palm.

"Smelling salts?" She giggled stupidly. Still, although she had no idea why, she stuck the capsules in a pocket. "I'm supposed to tame a beast with smelling salts?"

Tony's hood fell back; his seriousness fell away with it. "An old-fashioned term. I think they're now called ammonia inhalants. But you know what Shakespeare said about the rose."

"Tony, I do believe you're nuts."

"You may very well be right." He chucked her beneath the chin. "Hang on to those, anyway. They might come in handy when you least expect it."

Then he turned and glided across the snow with immense grace, especially considering his crude shoes. Dana watched him until his cloaked form began melding with the snowscape, then she gathered up a pile of wood and carried it inside.

When she came back for a second load, she saw a white bird soaring against the thunderheads.

*   *   *

Will Schumacher, esteemed captain of the Arizona Highway Patrol, was beginning to think he'd lost control of his men. Several of them had jumped visibly at the last clap of thunder, and the young officer examining the half-buried Ranger had even let out a yelp.

Unlike his skittish officers, Schumacher wasn't afraid. Although he couldn't deny that finding the mutilated body had given him the willies—hell, that much carnage would have rattled even Rambo—he was only shivering because of the cold.

"Just get on with it!" he yelled impatiently to the man by the vehicle, who was now muttering curses and rubbernecking at the sky.

"I need you to look at something first."

"This better be goddam good." Schumacher stomped over, ready to read him the riot act if he'd been summoned for a trivial reason.

"The snowbank completely covered this car when it collapsed," said the officer, pointing at the driver's door of the four-by-four. "And it's unlikely the occupant could have forced the door open though that much snow." He turned and sketched a ninety-degree radius around the vehicle with his finger. "See those clumps?"

"Yeah, yeah. What about them?"

"I'll bet my badge they came from here."

"You must be going nuts. Some of those clumps are over fifty yards away."

"I know. But there's no other explanation. Someone dug the occupant out from this side and the snow had to go somewhere. I didn't want to open the door until you saw the situation for yourself." A befuddled look crossed the officer's face. "Must've been some bull of a man to throw snow that far."

Schumacher bent and examined the vehicle. Small chunks of snow still clung to the window ledge and mirror, and several deep scratches marred the red paint. A cliff of sheared-off snow hung precariously in front of the driver's-side mirror, resuming at the midpoint of the rear door. Beneath the body of the vehicle ran a horizontal ridge that had clearly been lopped off by an opening door.

Beyond, in the area pointed out by his officer, were scattered mounds of snow. A solid chunk of ice here, a broken-up clump there. Further out, probably a hundred yards by his estimate, were a number of smaller pieces. The captain didn't even want to consider that they also came from this source. Still, his officer was right. There wasn't any other explanation.

"Wouldn't want to meet that guy in a dark alley." He tightened the neck fastenings of his jacket against the cold. "I hope he's on our side."

"Yes, sir." For a second, the two just stood and looked at each other. Schumacher remembered the bits and pieces remaining of Deek Kowalski, but he couldn't say what his officer was thinking.

"Should, er, should I open her up now, sir?"

"Yeah, I guess," he mumbled, then remembered who he was, what he stood for—the best of the Arizona Highway Patrol. "Look, kid," he said harshly. "Don't go sissy on me. We're here to rid this forest of those killers, or die trying. So buck up, do your job, and report as soon as you have an ID on the vehicle. Got that?"

"Yessir!" Yet Schumacher still saw poorly disguised terror in the younger man's eyes.

The remaining officers had fanned out in all directions, searching for the missing occupant or occupants. Two were on a snowmobile, traversing a large meadow. Another man had just entered a snow-clogged path leading up the mountain.

"Anything yet?" he called as he approached the sergeant in charge.

"No, sir."

"Well, step it up! We don't have all day!"

"Yes sir." The sergeant turned away and delved into the dark, thick forest. Schumacher stared after him until he disappeared. Soon he heard the plop of falling snow, **whi**ch was followed by a curse. Obviously a tree had dropped a load of snow on the man's head. Another time the captain might have smiled, but not now.

He didn't like this place.

True, they were miles from those goddam black fingers and that shredded body, but even the base of the mountain seemed to have the same dead feel. It wasn't in Schumacher's frame of reference to call it cursed, yet if he'd searched the depths of his soul with any kind of rare honesty, he would have admitted he felt just that.

It was so cold here. A deep, piercing cold that reached a man's marrow. He stomped his feet to get more blood flowing and moved into the sunnier meadow. Here the snow billowed constantly in the ceaseless wind, so even the sun failed to warm him.

The officer assigned to the vehicle came running up, waving a piece of paper. "This does belong to the missing biologist, Captain." He handed over the Ranger's registration, which Schumacher saw was from New Mexico. It listed the owner as Dr. Dana Gibbs.

"Should we step up the search, sir?"

Schumacher hesitated. The public was screaming bloody murder about the wolf slaughters. This was, after all, Mission Lobo. Yet to leave a well-known scientist to fend for herself in this horrendous weather wouldn't exactly garner good press either. Still, he only had so many men to spare. Which choice would be best for his career?

"Captain!"

The call came from somewhere in the trees and pushed the dilemma from the captain's mind. The officer at his side started racing toward the darkest part of the forest, but Schumacher hesitated for the space of several quick heartbeats. Then, because he knew his duty, he moved forward.

"Here, Captain," someone called from inside the forest. "Over here."

Concentrating on not tripping, he wended his way through the many twisted roots. Jesus, it was dark in here. The boggy ground sucked at his boots like it wanted to swallow him, and he was regretting the thirty extra pounds he'd added over the years.

"Captain!" came another panic-filled cry.

Schumacher forced himself on. As his eyes grew used to the dark, he saw the officer who'd given him the registration. Then the sergeant came into focus. Both men were gawking at the ground.

"Jesus Christ!" the captain exclaimed. "Jesus H. Christ!"

"What the hell do you think made those?" asked the sergeant.

Yeti. Bigfoot. A fucking five-hundred-pound wolf. "I don't know," choked Schumacher. "I don't know. . . . But it's nothing I've ever seen before."

Uncomfortably aware of the quaver in his voice, he collected his emotions into a tight little ball and scowled at the men. "Don't give me any of this lily-livered stuff," he barked. "You don't see me trembling in my boots. Our job is to track this thing down, and that's what we're going to do. So get to it!"

In response, he received a pair of blank stares aimed at his hands. Slowly dropping his gaze, he saw they were shaking like leaves in the wind.

"It's the cold," he rasped, deepening his scowl. Then, ordering the men to make casts of the prints, he walked away, aching to return to the sunlight.

Chapter Thirteen

Dana found some potatoes. Although they were old, soft, and wrinkled, she figured they'd add variety to the stew, so she peeled them and cut them up. As she was adding them to the pot, Morgan's door opened.

She looked over to see him watching her. His disheveled hair and tangled, wild beard gave him a frazzled appearance, and his eyes were almost bleeding with pain. What had gone on between him and Lily? He'd seemed almost happy before that woman showed up.

She felt a sudden stab of jealousy and resentment, then remembered that his brief burst of good humor had ended with the helicopter incident and Fenris's escape. Had she been the one who'd disappointed him? It wouldn't be the first time she'd disappointed someone, usually with dire results. A long time ago she'd lost someone dear because she'd failed to act responsibly. She'd only been a child then, but—

"I'm sorry about Fenris." She dropped the last potato into the stew.

"He survived. That's all that's important." Morgan walked to the hearth and squatted beside the dog, who rolled onto his back and begged Morgan for a scratch.

"We need to take him back to the kennel," he said, attending to the dog's tummy.

"Now? It's going to storm again."

"They have shelter."

"But he almost froze out there, and— Oh, please, Morgan, let him stay."

He regarded her sternly. "I told you, he isn't a pet, Dana. If this keeps up, you're going to turn him into one."

She started to protest, but then thought better of it. Fenris whined and licked Morgan's hand. Thunder cracked outside, shaking the windowpanes.

"It's going to be a bad one," said Dana.

Another span of silence. Another crack of thunder.

"All right. But just tonight."

He got up, walked over to the stew pot, and looked down suspiciously. "What are you doing to it?"

"I added a few potatoes. It's a little monotonous eating the same thing all the time, don't you think?"

"Loses my dog, changes my diet," he said, smiling weakly. "What a woman."

Dana took the comment as a white flag. "So beat me," she said, smiling back.

"It crossed my mind."

He meandered around the room, looked at the replenished log supply a second, went to the peg rack and rearranged the hanging garments, wandered back to the stove.

"How long till the potatoes are done?"

"Half an hour or so."

"I guess I won't starve."

Morgan wondered what Dana would do if she learned how much truth his remark about starving contained, or of what he'd done during his absence. Would she run in horror? Scoff in disbelief? Or would she tend to him as lovingly as she had the runt?

The maiden must willingly perform the rituals, love filling her heart. . . .

Love? A whole and giving woman such as Dana love the likes of him? The idea was ludicrous.

Lord, where was Morgan Wilder, society psychiatrist and one of New York's most eligible bachelors, now that he needed him? Him, Dana might love. But a shape-shifter? A slavering night creature? Not even a Harlem hooker would love him.

"I could trim your hair and beard while we wait," Dana offered out of the blue.

"Can I trust you with scissors near my throat?"

She laughed. "It's a risk you'll have to take."

Morgan touched his beard, then ran a hand through his hair. Until she'd arrived, he hadn't realized how wild and unkempt he must look. He supposed he could more easily win her affections without a ton of hair on his head. "Go for it. I'm braver than you give me credit for."

"Oh, I give you credit all right." She plucked a pair of scissors from a butcher-block slab on the counter. "Not exactly hairdresser quality, but I suppose they'll do. Have a seat."

A few minutes later, Morgan cringed as mounds of his hair hit the floor. Delilah shearing Samson of his strength. But how right it felt, sitting in front of her, listening to the scissors go *snip-snip-snip*. Like a regular working guy letting his wife cut his hair so they could save a few bucks to put toward a house. He'd never led that kind of life. His had been privileged since birth. Everything came easily. Now, in cruel contrast, he schemed desperately to win a woman's heart, with the stakes his own humanity.

"Morgan, who were those people?"

He'd known the question would come eventually, had already formulated a reasonable answer. "Neighbors, loosely speaking. They live about midmountain."

"How did they get here? For that matter, how do any of you get around in these blizzards?"

"You're barraging me with questions, Dana. Which do you want answered first?"

"God, I don't know. How *do* you travel in the storms? I know you were out there, too."

"Oh?" That took him by surprise. "What makes you think so?"

"A friend of yours came by. Tony. You know him, don't you?"

Morgan nodded.

"He said he'd just seen you a little while before."

"White Hawk told you that?"

"Yes, while he helped me carry in the wood."

"Why were you getting wood?"

"Because we were almost—" She blew out an exasperated breath. "For heaven's sake, Morgan, answer my question. How do you people do it? I mean, the weather was awful when you left."

"Nothing mysterious," he said, making it up as he went along. "Dress warm. Wear snowshoes. Pretty soon, you learn where to find shelter."

"Not in my experience, and I was raised in some of the most rugged—"

"I *know*, Dana. You've told me several times. But this is Arizona, not Minnesota, and—"

"Montana."

"Not Montana. Storms don't last for weeks—or even whole days, for that matter." Morgan was feeling pressured; his ire was rising. "I like storms. Okay?"

"So does everyone else up here, it seems. Hold still, I need to get this straggling bit of hair."

Morgan felt a second's gratitude for that stray lock, because it let him tame his anger. Strong emotions weren't welcome here. He might have wondered how she'd react if he revealed his true self, but he wasn't yet prepared to have her freak out over additional stray locks sprouting on his hands.

She must vanquish her horror of her loved one's bestiality. . . . Shadow of Venus, p 147, or so he would once have written in the citation of some learned paper.

And probably sacrifice her life in the process. What woman would do that, even for the human and urbane Morgan Wilder? Besides, when did he plan to reveal himself? Time wasn't exactly on his side. The full moon would arrive whether he was prepared or not.

"So many strange things are happening, Morgan." He heard a small tremor in her voice. "I have so many questions. This sounds crazy, I know. . . ." Then she blurted it out. "How did your feet heal so quickly?"

He'd been prepared for that one, too. "I keep some salve that White Hawk gave me in the dogs' supply shed. I put it on my feet and—well, you saw."

By the little shimmy in the scissors, he felt her nod.

"Herbs, probably," she said musingly. "Do wild Indians really live up here?"

Morgan chuckled.

"Sit still," she instructed crossly. "Do they?"

"I doubt they'd call themselves wild, but they do keep to themselves. Most of them have never been out of the canyon. They see the occasional hiker, of course, but they avoid them."

"Tony seems friendly enough."

"Yeah, well, his story is a little different."

"Tell me about it."

"He's a private man. You'll have to ask him yourself."

Dana sighed so loudly, Morgan knew it was for his benefit. "That's another thing. Nobody gives me straight answers."

193

He turned his head to look at her, but she put her hands on the sides of his head and stopped him.

"I'm going to start on your beard."

She moved in front and gave him a thorough inspection, occasionally tugging his beard. Morgan almost laughed at his inner cringing. If he were still practicing psychiatry, he'd have diagnosed an extreme lack of self-esteem. Probably have prescribed a few sessions, a couple self-help books, maybe a support group. Then he would have sent himself on his way—happy, confident, alive again—physician having healed himself.

If only it were that easy.

"A bit uneven on the left," Dana remarked as she started trimming. After a quiet moment, she asked, "So tell me how Lily and Jorje hiked halfway up a mountain."

"I suppose they came by sled. They have dogs, too." Morgan instantly realized he had left himself open for Dana to renew her request to leave, so he ad-libbed a disclaimer. "Lily's crazy enough to try anything, despite the danger. Not a move I'd recommend, let me tell you."

"Stop talking. It makes your chin move."

"Then don't ask questions. Tell me about your childhood instead."

"What do you want to know?" Dana stopped

cutting and gave Morgan's beard a once-over. "Good. I didn't cut too deep."

"How you learned to cut hair, for instance."

"I used to cut my dad's. We were miles from a barbershop, you know."

"Did you always live in the Minnesota boonies?"

"Montana, Morgan. I lived in Montana."

"Right."

"Shh." She bent again, and he saw firelight dancing in her green eyes. The professional side of him noted that her pupils were normally dilated, but another part just drank in the fascinating shade. Fate had sent a woman to redeem him, and he appreciated the fact that he was also beautiful.

"Since you asked." A tiny grin played around her mouth. "I lived there as long as I can remember. Mom and Dad said we stayed in a commune for a while, but they got tired of all the rules and decided to homestead by themselves." Her grin widened.

"The first thing I remember . . . oh, I must have been three or four . . . I was sitting on the porch, playing with a rag doll my mother made me, while my dad chopped down a tree. All of a sudden, I looked up and a wolf was standing at the edge of the forest. It knew I saw him, but it stayed there for a while anyway, looking back at me. I felt this, I don't know, I didn't think of it that way then, but I suppose you'd call it a sense of kinship.

"I waved, and it kind of nodded its head before turning to walk away. Then Dad caught sight of it. He freaked. He dropped that ax, ran to the porch, and hustled me right inside." She laughed softly. "Dad would never do that now. But back then they were city people trying to live out a dream they didn't have the skills for. Mother is a poet, You might have heard of her."

Morgan searched his memory.

"Johanna Gibbs?"

"Morgan, you aren't supposed to talk," she said with feigned sternness. She tugged one side of his beard, then the other. "Yeah, that's her. Dad is a sculptor, but he never made it as big as Mother. He has a small following, but— They're divorced now. . . . There," she said, stepping back with a satisfied look. "You look quite presentable, Doctor."

Morgan felt disappointed. He'd been enjoying her story. Even more, he'd been enjoying her closeness. The heat, the soap-and-water scent, the quick touches of her fingers, even the clip of the scissors. Now she would stop, move away, eventually return to the daybed and put all those feet of floor between them.

"Do you have a mirror?" she asked, still looking pleased at her results.

Morgan shook his head.

"No clocks. No mirrors. Don't you ever want to know the time or look at yourself?"

"At this face? You must be kidding."

"Actually, you're quite handsome."

Morgan felt a stupid urge to chortle. He got up abruptly, finding himself standing chest to breast with Dana. "Here," she said. "You've got a few loose hairs."

The brush of her fingertips shot through his cheek like an electric current. Without quite meaning to, he touched her curls and bent his head lower.

Dana tilted hers back.

It felt like slow motion, that gradual lessening of the space between their mouths, and when he met her lips an eternity later, Morgan felt the kiss with every cell of his body. Soft lips, warm and sweet, parting for him, inviting him to explore. But not yet. Not yet. He skimmed his mouth across hers, gently, tentatively, nearly overwhelmed by the sweetness of the moment.

Five long years since he'd touched a mortal woman. Five years in which he feared the passion such a touch might arouse. In secret fantasies, men often dreamed of devouring their

197

woman, but for him such fantasies could become all too horribly real.

Until now, Dana hadn't truly comprehended the simmering tension that always seemed present when she and Morgan were together. Suddenly, she understood completely. She wanted him . . . the way a woman wants a man. She had felt this hunger almost from their first meeting. Everything about him called to that secret female place within her. His feral ways, his mercurial moods, his wry and unpredictable sense of humor. She yearned to deepen their chaste and tentative kiss into a violent clash of tongues and lips, to bring out the fierceness she knew lay hidden inside him.

Yet his kiss contained such reverence, as though he cherished her beyond her wildest dreams. Rushing it risked shattering the magic.

These needs, these wants, warred within her, creating unbearably pleasurable sensations. How long since she'd been with a man in this physical way? So long, she could hardly remember.

She felt his fingers moving in her hair, stroking the locks. His beard softly grazed the corners of her mouth. Their breaths mingled into one long sigh.

Time passed.

Then one of Morgan's knees gave. He lurched

forward and steadied himself against Dana's shoulder.

"Sorry," he mumbled, gazing at the floor. "Fenris bumped into my leg."

The dog stood by the table, looked up at them imploringly, then darted for the stove, where he whimpered at the stewpot.

"He's hungry again." She couldn't quite meet Morgan's eye. She'd never been good with romantic situations and didn't know what to say. Should she mention the kiss? Pretend it never happened? What?

"There's plenty for the three of us." Morgan moved to the cupboard, took down three bowls, then began to fill one. After placing it by the hearth for Fenris, he went back to the stove and finally looked at Dana. "How hungry are you?"

Up until a short while ago, she'd been famished. Now she barely had an appetite. "Just a little," she said. When he dished in a scoop, she moved to take the bowl from his hand.

"That's all? You sure?"

She nodded, collected a spoon, then headed for the bed.

"There's more than one chair, you know," said Morgan.

She knew she could make up some kind of excuse, but she only nodded again and went to the table. Morgan pulled up the chair he'd occupied earlier and placed his bowl on the table. Although he showed little enthusiasm, he slowly began to eat.

Dana only stared at her bowl. Outside, the storm began to pick up steam. The windows rattled, the chimney howled. The noise was nearly deafening, but it didn't distract her thoughts from their kiss. Why didn't he say something? Was easing this awkwardness supposed to be left up to her? Getting no answers, she dipped her spoon into the stew and took a bite.

It turned out to be quite good, so she took another one. As she swallowed her third mouthful, she caught Morgan smiling at her.

"You must be hungrier than you thought."

"I guess." She began to relax. "Maybe tomorrow I can bake some bread."

"What a woman." He was still smiling.

Dana smiled back, then got up to refill her bowl. As she fished through the stew, searching for more potatoes, she remembered her plans.

Bake bread? Who was she kidding? First thing in the morning, weather permitting, she'd be hiking down the mountain on her way back to her job. Her lingering smile instantly disappeared and she guessed it didn't matter if they talked about the kiss.

After all, she'd never see Morgan Wilder again.

☾

Chapter Fourteen

Schumacher's teeth chattered. He'd wrenched the last degree of heat from the generator on the motor home he was using as headquarters, and he was still freezing. Wondering if he'd ever be warm again, he disgustedly dropped the report he'd been reading and got up to pour a cup of stale coffee—at least it was hot and would warm his innards—then radioed the communications unit. "Which van is Fish—er, that is, Rutherford in?"

"Unit nine-aught-three, sir."

"Send someone to tell him I want to see him."

"Right away. Also, sir, thought you'd want to know the forensic report on Deek Kowalski came over the fax just before the storm took up again."

"Watch out for man-eating ghouls," joked someone else in the radio unit.

"What's that, officer?" snapped Schumacher.

"Nothing, sir." All other sounds at that end of the radio immediately ceased. "Nothing at all."

"That's what I thought. Keep it that way. And send that autopsy over with Rutherford."

"Yessir!"

Schumacher glanced back at the report he'd left on his desk. Charlie Lonetree was obviously suffering from more than shock. He'd gone completely psychotic, raving about Indian legends, arising beasts, sacrifices to the Great Spirit. What really rankled, though, was how that sorry fool Fishman seemed to have taken Charlie seriously enough to write a recommendation: Cancel Mission Lobo; concentrate all further efforts on finding a serial killer.

Insanity! The autopsies of the other victims clearly showed that animals had killed them. The little they'd found left of Deek Kowalski in that mountain clearing didn't contradict that conclusion.

A rap sounded on the door, and Schumacher got up to let Rutherford step inside. After hastily slamming the door on a frigid blast of air, the captain gestured to a chair. Rutherford unzipped his down vest, took his time settling down, then pulled a folded paper from an inside pocket.

"The forensic report."

The captain was about to ask what happened to "sir," then remembered that Rutherford didn't work for his agency. He took the paper, tossed it on his desk, and picked up the report he'd been reading earlier.

"I want to talk about this." He waved the report just inches from Rutherford's nose. "What kind of bullshit are you pulling here?"

"I'm not pulling anything, Captain. I interviewed Charlie before the medics coptered him out and that's what he told me."

"Clearly he was delirious."

Rutherford nodded gravely. "He did appear to have fact and fantasy confused. Not unusual, considering he'd just found his close friend brutally murdered and barely escaped death himself. But his description is indisputable. Whoever killed Deek and chased Charlie walked on two legs."

"And was covered with fur. Didn't that make you wonder about the rest of it?"

"It was dark up there, Captain. Charlie was scared out of his wits. Maybe the assailant was wearing a fur coat. There are a number of explanations."

"Look, Rutherford, you can't con me." Schumacher rattled the report again. "You'll do anything to get this wolf hunt called off. Even make up a cock-and-bull story like this one."

"With all due respect . . ." Rutherford paused, cleared his throat. "It sounds like you're buying into those old legends about the canyon as much as Charlie has. My conclusion is the only reasonable one."

"B-buying in?" Schumacher sputtered. "Buying in! You read the other forensic reports, didn't you?"

"Yes, I did and—"

"*And*, based on the ravings of a half-crazy man, you want us to change the thrust of our investigation? That's outrageous!"

"As I was saying, Captain, the carnage has never been consistent with known wolf behavior."

"Then what? There's some cannibalistic serial killer running amok in the canyon?"

"Ever heard of Jeffrey Dahmer?" Rutherford interjected.

"Know what I think, Rutherford?" Schumacher leaned over, went nearly nose-to-nose with the man. "I think you know there really is a pack of wild wolves back there, and you're so damned scared they'll rip you up like they did Kowalski, you'll do anything to get out of hunting them."

"We're getting off track here, Captain."

Rutherford's cool demeanor fueled Schumacher's anger. Glaring, he wiggled the report inches from Rutherford's face and spoke through clenched teeth. "I'm telling you, mister, if you file this report, I'll go directly to your superiors and have your job before you can say 'What the hell did I do?' You got that?"

Rutherford stood up. "I can see we aren't getting anywhere." He walked to the door, then hesitated before putting his hand on the knob. "I'm just doing my job, Captain Schumacher. If you think you're right, then I advise you to do yours. I'll let the dice fall where they may."

Then with another blast of frigid air, he left.

Schumacher stared into space for a while, fuming over the encounter. Cowards. Just his luck to be surrounded by a pack of cowards. It was almost more than a man could bear. But being nothing if not practical, he soon decided he was wasting time. The forensic report was waiting. He opened it and began to read.

Tears consistent with animal bites . . .

There, he thought, feeling vindicated. No matter what Rutherford said, wolves had killed Kowalski.

. . . bones crushed and wrenched apart . . .

He shifted uneasily in his chair, not wanting to remember Kowalski's butchered body.

. . . a puzzling aspect . . . the animal perpetrating

these injuries had a jaw span of at least twenty inches.

The captain's mouth dropped open. Did any land-dwelling mammal have a mouth that wide? He didn't think so. With an unsteady hand, he reached for a rough plaster rectangle that had resulted from his order to make a casting of the print in the forest. When the final product had arrived on his desk, he'd given it mere seconds of attention before slamming it facedown and deciding it would make a suitable paperweight.

Now, he slowly turned it and stared at the markings in horrified fascination. He'd seen these prints, then had vehemently denied the evidence of his own eyes. No animal he knew of left such monstrously large tracks.

As he ran his fingers over the textured backside of the mold, the motor home rocked on its tires. Beneath the roar of the gale, Schumacher thought he heard a beast howling.

His teeth began chattering again.

Dana woke up with a start. It took a minute before she realized what was wrong. The room was too quiet. She'd grown used to the ceaseless roar of wind, but now it had finally stopped.

She leaped up an rushed to the window. Moonlight reflected off a calm sheet of snow.

The storm was over. She could leave in the morning and be back to her life before nightfall.

Familiar sounds from Morgan's room broke her moment of joy. How long would those horrible noises he called music last this time? Mercifully, it soon stopped, and seconds later a door creaked, a latch opened, then clicked closed. Dana yearned to follow him and find out where he went during his excursions, but knew it was a foolish waste of energy. She must stay fresh for the long hike ahead. The mystery surrounding Morgan Wilder would remain unsolved.

So why had she let him kiss her?

Let him? That kind of dishonesty just wasn't in her. It had felt so right, as if she'd waited for that moment all her life. No, she'd welcomed that kiss and deeply regretted its untimely interruption. She wondered exactly how far she would have let it go if Fenris hadn't saved the day, so to speak.

Morgan, in many ways, reminded her of wolves. That same untamed quality simmered beneath the surface of his civilized veneer. Also like them, he seldom talked unless he had something to say. She felt he would choose his partner carefully, too, and commit for life. Standard wolf behavior, but not necessarily true for the human male.

Yet he was also a loner, which wasn't common among wolves, those very survival depended on pack cooperation. It wasn't even common among humankind.

How had a city psychiatrist come to live in such solitude? What horrible loss had he suffered to make him leave everything behind?

She would never know.

Trying to deny her sorrow, she drifted back to bed, but found she could only toss and turn. As she sat up to straighten the tangled covers, she again heard music.

Not Morgan's usual listening tastes. Drums beat steadily, rhythmically. A flute, its high, sweet notes calling to something deep in her soul. She listened for a time, transfixed, then realized the melody wasn't coming from the bedroom.

Then, from afar, she heard barking. Fenris, who'd been snoozing by the fire, jumped to his feet and loped to the door, where he gave several yips before darting to Dana. He nudged her hand, whined, hurried back to the door and stared at her imploringly. When Dana failed to move, he again rushed to her side, still whining. The dogs continued barking.

Something was wrong at the kennel!

Dana jumped up and grabbed the jumpsuit from the rack, then pulled it on. Moments later she was in her boots, gloves and snowshoes in hand.

When she yanked the front door open, snow again fell across the threshold. She paused, trying to decide if she should take time to shovel it away. But the barks outside were becoming frantic yowls. Dana stepped over the wall of snow and tried to kick enough away to allow the door to close.

Fenris knocked her aside, then squeezed through the crack, leaped from the porch, and rushed toward his teammates.

"Fenris!" Dana called. "Fenris!"

But he was already just a dark streak on the moonlit snow.

Giving the door a pull that finally closed it, she tossed down the snowshoes and quickly donned them. As she began plodding after the disobedient runt, she slid her gloves over her rapidly numbing hands.

By the time she reached the smokehouse, Fenris was throwing himself at the kennel fence. When he saw her, he whirled, lunged several yards in her direction, whirled again, then stared into the distance.

A large white canine loped along the rim of the canyon.

Aphrodite had escaped!

Dana called her name, but she continued running.

The team was now milling around the pen, some baying, some leaping at the fence, and when Dana got there she saw Aphrodite darting along the perimeter of the enclosure.

Then what was . . . ?

Her heart skipped a beat, but she immediately recovered. No, Morgan was right. Her dream of finding wolves was simply that—a dream. More likely, that dog belonged to Lily and Jorje.

Just then the distant dog stopped, turned to look at them, and let out a chilling yowl. Fenris broke into a frenzy of barking, and the other dogs joined in.

Dana stared in dismay. Should she try to run the dog down and return it? As she turned to grab a harness and leash from a small shed beside the gate, Fenris gave an angry snarl, then lunged through the churning snow after the white dog, which spun and took off along the ridge of the canyon.

Oh, God! Morgan would kill her if she lost his dog again!

She started clumsily after him, leash in hand. The two dogs loped along the canyon, Fenris several hundred yards behind the white animal. They sank and rose in the swirling snow, their forms silhouetted against the sky like the undulating humps of a sea serpent. Crystalline flakes pelted Dana's face as she forged on, head bowed against the wind. After what seemed a long period of time, the white dog neared the forest that intersected the canyon lip.

Dana struggled to move faster. If she didn't catch Fenris immediately, he'd disappear into the thick woods. Not only that, a thick cloud was now drifting toward the moon. If it moved over it, she wouldn't be able to see a thing.

She shouted Fenris's name. He turned, and looked at her briefly, then continued after the white dog. The cloud covered the moon. All was black.

Dana stopped. In her alarm, she'd given no thought to her own safety. Now her body hummed, and she realized she was alone in a place where people had been brutally murdered, without even Fenris to protect her.

The music was still playing, coming from somewhere off to her left. The drumbeat quickened, the flute notes almost danced, and the melody grew even more beautiful.

A sheep bleated pitifully. Not pastoral baas, but the cries of an animal frightened out of its wits. Dana's body vibrated like the strings of a harp and she struggled to retain her wits.

Mercifully, the moon reappeared. Dana peered through its silvery light, searching for

Fenris. She let out a wail of despair. Where had he gone? She had to find him!

Here the snow had grown crusty. Giving a frustrated scrape of her snowshoes, Dana began skating closer to the canyon's edge, calling Fenris's name. When she neared the lip, she hesitated, cautiously moving forward. Her eyes followed a glimmer of moonlight reflecting on smooth rocks, and she saw a path that led to a clearing below.

Huge stone towers jutted from man-high snow clusters, but otherwise the clearing was oddly bare of snow. Dana assumed the canyon walls either protected the location or it was so windswept that snow blew off immediately. Regardless, she found the results more ominous than pleasing.

A fire blazed down there, and Dana crawled forward to get a closer look. A band of men sat around the flames. They had been making the music, Dana saw, and it was now growing more passionate with every note.

One of the men got up to throw several more logs on the fire. It flared, allowing Dana to see the sheep tethered just feet from the edge of the stone-rimmed pit. Although not as frightened as before, it still skittered nervously within the confines of the rope. Streaks of vivid blues, oranges, and reds stained its wool, looking like hieroglyphics.

The man picked up a long-stemmed pipe and raised it high over his head. He wore a thick fur cloak with a hood fashioned from the head of a mountain lion. The lion's mouth was open; fangs glimmered in the firelight. Dana scanned the circle and saw the others were similarly dressed. Some wore simple cloaks and head-bands, while others had on elaborate head-dresses decorated with fur or feathers, beaks or claws or fangs. Several men pounded on crude drums, while another held a reed flute to his mouth.

The standing man brought the pipe to his mouth. A second later he exhaled a rising stream of smoke circles. He then took the pipe to another man and sat down. More puffs of smoke rose to the sky.

Some kind of Native American ceremony, thought Dana, watching as they passed the pipe from man to man. Were these the Indians Morgan spoke of, or simply Native Americans from the surrounding reservations trying to restore the old ways?

Regardless, she didn't care at the moment. She'd already seen more unexplainable occur-rences, met more eccentric people, than she'd ever cared to. All she could think of was finding

213

Ferris. Had he gone down there? She squinted, searching the shadows, but saw him nowhere.

When the howl came, Dana jumped like something had hit her.

The sheep bleated in panic and lunged against its tether. The men shot to their feet. In a whir of activity, they gathered their instruments. Before Dana could collect her thoughts, the entire band had disappeared into the trees.

Another howl came, chillingly near. Then all was quiet again except for the squeals of the lunging sheep.

The sounds had chilled Dana's heart just like the ones she'd heard at the base of the mountain had. This was no ordinary wolf howl. Had the men made those noises? She'd been sure they'd come from the forest.

And Fenris was still out there somewhere!

Although her skin prickled like she'd fallen in a cactus patch, Dana knew what she had to do. She took off her snowshoes and dropped them and the dog leash on the ground. Then, although she was almost too scared to breathe, she inched her way down the rocky crevasse. By the time she got to the clearing, the sheep was screeching in terror, fighting its tether until it fell, then scrambling up to try again.

She looked at it in pity, but Fenris was foremost in her mind. Hollering as loud as she could, she traversed the clearing, seeking the runt, praying he was all right. Each echo of her voice sent her blood racing, and after a while she gave up.

Still the sheep bellowed and struggled to be free.

For just an instant, Dana wondered why the Indians had left it there. Then it came to her.

However unnatural those howls sounded, they did come from wolves. The men had left the sheep to keep the wolves away from themselves. Had she been less frightened, she would have shaken her head at their misguided efforts. Wolves were hunters, and providing such easy prey dulled their skills so much that they sought more of the same.

Like Fenris.

She glanced back at the sheep. If she freed it, might it then draw the pack away from anything else roaming in the forest? She thought so, and moved closer.

Unwilling to risk a kick from those sharp hooves, she picked up a stick, then inched her way to the fire pit and shoved it in the flames. Soon she had a torch, which she held in front of her as she approached the sheep. Caught between two foes, it froze. Dana cautiously bent to release its tether.

The stake went deep; the thick rope was

braided from many strands of leather. With one hand holding the torch and the other covered with a heavy glove, her dexterity was poor, and she found untying the rope very rough going.

Another howl echoed through the canyon.

Dana trembled and continued working. She heard another howl, louder, nearer. Then another.

Her breathing got heavy. Her heart skittered.

Finally the tether broke free. The quailing sheep almost collapsed in fear. For a moment it simply stared at her with wide, darting eyes.

"Shoo!" she shouted, waving the torch near its face.

With a last piercing bleat, the sheep spun and ran into the woods.

Feeling weak with relief, Dana turned toward the path. When she was just feet from the crevasse, she heard the sheep cry out again, its voice rising to a shriek that was cut off by a sickening sputter. She felt a moment's regret, then told herself it was the way of nature. At least the pack would be feeding for a while, giving Fenris a chance for survival.

She cried his name again and waited, hoping beyond hope he would show up. When he didn't, she started for the trail.

Just then leaves rustled in the underbrush. She broke into a run, knowing even as she did that it was no use. As fit as she was, she couldn't outrun hungry wolves. Their keen noses would sniff her out instantly. She needed a small place to hide, too small for them to enter.

She scanned the clearing, searching . . . searching. The rustling became a deafening rattle. Her skin burned. Slowly, she backed up toward the crevasse, wielding the torch.

Something burst from the forest wall.

(

Chapter Fifteen

Dana almost dropped the torch.

A figure charged out of the woods, rapidly gobbling up the rocky span with long, two-legged strides. It was taller than the door to Morgan's cabin and covered in silver-white fur. Moonlight gleamed red in its deep-set eyes and reflected off its sharp teeth. Garbled inhuman snarls streamed from its pointed snout, which was open a staggering width.

Dana's scientific side noted that the creature had both canine and primate physiology, but her fragile, human side simply gaped in astonished terror.

Grandmother, what big teeth you have, she thought giddily as the creature drew so near she could see saliva dripping from its fangs.

She bolted for the crevasse.

A clawed hand clamped down on her shoulder, creating searing pain. She tripped. Her tumbling body slipped from the creature's grasp and she rolled over, waiting for the pounce that would end her life. Instead, the attacker regarded her for a heartbeat, then lifted its head and let out a sound.

To Dana's fear-crazed mind, the noise resembled laughter, but she took no time to figure it out. She inched as deep into the crevasse as possible, then hurled the torch.

With a shriek, the creature clawed at a singed ear, batted at the falling torch. The stench of burning hair filled Dana's lungs. She coughed and scooted further up the path.

. . . come in handy when you least expect it.

As the creature screamed and stomped above her, Dana shoved a gloved hand in the pocket of her jumpsuit, seeking the smelling salts that Tony's comment referred to. But the fabric was pulled tight by the weight of her fallen body, and the vials were deep inside. She twisted and squirmed, trying to gain access.

Just as her fingers touched paper, her attacker recovered. Arching like a cat, it raised its hairy arms and let out a chilling howl. Dana's heart pounded. Blood roared in her ears. She shoved her hand deeper into the pocket.

Snagging a vial between two fingers, she

yanked it out, snapped the paper like a matchstick, then threw it. The acrid fumes spread instantly and she buried her nose in her sleeve.

With a gasp, the creature staggered away, its body wavering strangely. Fur seemed to be melting right off its fearsome form. For a crazy moment, Dana caught a glimpse of white skin, a human toe. She blinked, certain she was hallucinating.

Then the creature gave a mighty kick. The vial soared into the air, flying, flying, flying, until Dana could see it no more. Now looking more dangerous, more monstrous than ever before, the creature closed in, open jaws dripping, ruby-specked eyes gleaming malevolently. Dana shut her eyes and prepared to die.

A furious cry resounded from the trees.

Her eyes snapped open to see a larger, darker figure coming rapidly toward them. It snarled threateningly, and the white creature turned to face it, screaming back.

The sounds were both bestial and human, and unlike any Dana had heard before. They chilled her heart so thoroughly she curled into a ball, barely able to look at the monsters facing off above her.

"Get away from her, Lily!" Morgan commanded in the Lupine language.

"Keep back, Morgan. The woman is mine."

Morgan leaped in front of Lily, bared his fangs, dug at the ground with a foot. "Did you forget she belongs to me?"

"Then slay her! Slay her." Lily straightened, put her long-fingered hands on her hips, and cast a disdainful glance at Dana. "Look how that foul wretch cringes. Smell that noxious stink she brings with her. Can you abide her living presence even one moment longer?"

At Lily's words, Morgan recognized the fumes, which still lingered in the clearing. He tried to stifle a sniff, failed, and recoiled as the essence entered his lungs. For a moment he felt light-headed, then it passed along with the odor.

In the meantime, Lily stepped forward. She stroked his head seductively, waving her other hand in Dana's direction. "When you take your first human, Morgan, nothing compares. Their blood is rich and fragrant; it tastes like honey on the tongue. Not at all like the rabbits and squirrels and farm animals you prey upon."

While Lily's voice crooned in his ears, Morgan stared at Dana in rapt fascination. Her pulse beat rapidly in her throat; terror filled her eyes.

"I give her to you as a mating gift. Take her, my darling foolish Morgan. Take her. She's yours."

He inhaled the thrilling musk of her fear. An

insatiable lust rose from his viscera, nearly over-whelming him. He crouched and salivated. His breaths grew shallow.

Then Dana whimpered.

"Never!"

Morgan rose to full height and clamped his enormous hand around Lily's wrist. "If you hurt her, I'll kill you!"

Lily's dark eyes narrowed.

"You would not do that. The Law forbids it."

"Don't test me."

An owl, undaunted by the sounds of quarreling beasts, hooted from a tree. Water plunked from the canyon walls; Dana whimpered on the ground. Through it all, Morgan and Lily locked their eyes in mutual challenge.

Finally, Lily turned her head away. "You stupid omega whelp," she said in disgust. "I never should have made you. You are unworthy."

"You made me too well." Tightening his hold on her wrist, he stepped forward, widened his jaw, and feinted a move toward Lily's throat.

"Imagine," he jeered. "An alpha slain by an omega. How humiliating."

"No-o-o!" Lily threw back her head and yanked, straining to break Morgan's grip. Although she was strong, he was stronger, and she knew it. He sank his claws deeper into her wrist. She flinched, then spit at Morgan's face.

She missed her mark, but he wouldn't have cared had it been otherwise. He had no use for Lupine law or protocol. All he cared about was Dana.

If he'd arrived just seconds later . . .

So great was the pain, he couldn't bear to think of it. And this snarling bitch who'd tempted him so cruelly filled him with such hate he could joyfully take her life. With a burst of rage, he reached out and closed his jaw around her throat.

"Ki-yi-yi-yi!"

Lily pawed at him with her free hand and twisted her body, battling to drive a powerful leg into Morgan's soft underbelly. One of her claws caught his cheekbone. He felt it pierce and split hair and skin. Still holding her neck in his mouth, Morgan snaked his leg around her thigh and jerked.

Caught off-balance, Lily toppled, pulling Morgan with her. They fell amid a cloud of scattering dirt and gravel, with Lily on her back. Morgan's massive shoulders pinned down her heaving chest. His knees were between her legs, his teeth still at her neck.

Kill her! he thought. *Kill her now!*

He felt her shudder beneath him, heard heavy panting in his ears.

"Copulate with me, Morgan," she urged. "You know you want it as much as I."

A wave of revulsion swept over him. He pressed his teeth deeper into the soft, loose folds at her neck. A single sharp bite could slice her jugular vein, spill her blood like those of the countless mortals she had slain. She lifted a hand, drew it languorously down his back. Her legs opened wider and he fell deeper between then. "Now, Morgan!" she panted urgently. "Here! On this sacred ground!"

Suddenly his revulsion got lost in a burst of pity. He'd been on the verge of snuffing out her life, yet she wanted him so badly. . . .

Praying he wouldn't regret his decision later, Morgan released Lily's throat and climbed to his feet.

"I'll never be your mate, Lily," he snarled, yanking her up to face him. "Never in a thousand Lupine lifetimes!"

"You cur-r-r," she snarled back. "You mortal-loving cur."

"Your insults have no effect," Morgan replied wearily.

With a firm grip on her arm, he dragged Lily toward the forest. She strained and struggled, yowled and cursed, but couldn't free herself. When they reached the edge, Morgan shoved her inside the trees, then looked back to the cringing Dana.

"Run!" he cried in the mortal tongue.

* * *

Dana had wrapped herself into a tiny, shivering ball, but that single word spurred her to action. She sprang to her feet and raced up the path. The white creature's yowls and cries continued ringing in the forest, driving her on. By the time she reached the top, she was out of breath, her shoulder ached, and her legs felt weak and trembly.

Too terrified to stop, she swept down to scoop up her dropped gear, then continued running until the snow turned into impassable powder. She paused only long enough to get into the snowshoes.

Her mind whirled throughout the seemingly endless journey, trying to make sense of what had happened. Everything she'd been reading over the last few days told her she'd been attacked by a werewolf—and also saved by one. At the same time, she knew her conclusion was impossible.

But what, then? That creature was no animal she'd ever seen. And the dark one had spoken to her in plain English. Could they have been humans dressed in animal skins? Perhaps from the Indian tribe?

Or even more sinister, could the men be part of some kind of cult that lured people in for sacrifice? Had she stumbled on the secret Mission Lobo had been sent to uncover?

But one of them had defended her. What was more, that didn't explain the fangs and claws. Maybe, she thought wearily, she'd seen fetishes hanging from their cloaks, and in her fear, imagined them to be real.

Each answer spawned a new question. Soon her mind grew as tired as her body.

The cabin came into view at last. Although she hadn't set the dogs to barking as she'd feared, as she got nearer a few of them began whining excitedly. Even those small sounds set Dana's battered nerves afire. She veered off, coming closer to the shadows of the woods than she preferred.

Her shoulder ached and she felt sure it was bleeding. Her legs felt like weights of steel. To make matters worse, feathers kept blowing into her face from the tear in her jumpsuit. Just a few more yards, she told herself. A few more. Then she'd be at the cabin door.

Just a few more yards.

A dark shape stepped out of the forest. A large hand wrapped around her wrist.

She let out a shriek.

"Dammit, Dana! What are you doing out here?"

"M-M-Morgan." Which was all she could say

before speech escaped her. But her mind continued racing, and she could only think that she'd now have to tell him she'd lost Fenris.

"I distinctly ordered you to stay inside at night." Morgan let go of her wrist, shoving his hands into his hair. It was so dark where they were standing, she could hardly see his face, but she could certainly feel his anger. "Lord, what am I to do? I can't watch you every second. Why in damnation can't you honor my simplest request?"

He grabbed her arms and shook her, causing her teeth to chatter even more and sending sparks of pain through her injured shoulder. A cinder of helpless rage had been smoldering beneath her terror and now ignited and snapped her mute streak.

"What the hell are you doing? Let go!" She slapped Morgan's hands away and backed up a few steps. "Don't ever, ever do that again!"

"Where have you been?" He didn't sound the least bit contrite.

"Where have *I* been? Where have *you* been? Why are you always roaming around out here at night?"

Just then, something whined and darted around their feet.

Dana's sudden rush of relief weakened her legs.

"Fenris," she cried, taking the runt's paws in her hands and making glad cooing noises. She looked up at Morgan's shadowed face and saw a deep scratch that she hadn't noticed before. "Where did you find him?"

"Answer my question. After all my warnings, why were you out of the cabin again?"

She let go of Fenris, but kept a hand on his shoulder as she tried to explain.

"The dogs . . . they were barking up a storm. I've never heard them act like that before. Then I saw a dog along the ridge. At first I thought Aphrodite had escaped again. But she hadn't." She put her hands on her temples. Her head injury throbbed nearly as much as her shoulder, and her legs still felt weak. Glancing up at Morgan, trying to decide where to begin, she vaguely noticed that he seemed even taller than usual; then she worked at collecting her thoughts.

As briefly as possible, she told him about Fenris darting from the cabin, then chasing after the other dog. How she'd followed them along the rim, only to lose them near the forest.

"Do you know those Indians, Morgan?" she asked accusingly, after she'd mentioned seeing them. By this time, she'd already discarded the cult idea and convinced herself that one of the men attacked her because she'd released the sheep. The second one simply hadn't approved of his method and had come to her rescue.

"Yes, but what does that have to do with anything? None of this is any excuse for—"

"I'm gaining evidence that wolves *are* up here. That tribe's doing some kind of appeasement ceremony by leaving sheep out to feed them. It's not right! And it's making killers out of natural predators. What do you know about it?"

"Hear me, Dana, and hear me well," Morgan said coldly. "Don't meddle with things you don't understand."

"Understand? I'm just beginning to understand." But suddenly she wasn't sure she believed a word of what she was saying. The full horror of what had happened rushed back. Dropping her head to her hands, she whispered, "Someone attacked me down there, Morgan."

"I kno—"

Dana's head snapped up. "What?"

"I know you believe there are wolves in the canyon." Although the words were heated, Dana heard pain in Morgan's voice. "You're dead wrong. And if you're not careful, you'll just be plain dead. Those aren't ordinary Indians. Keep away from them. Stay in the cabin at night." He turned then and put a hand on her shoulder. "Come, let's go inside."

It was an order, not a request. Dana considered protesting, but inside was where she wanted to be anyway. She also wanted to be with Morgan. True, he was angry with her, rightfully so. But his presence still made the terror of that canyon seem further away. She could think more clearly, put it all into perspective. Without another word, she went along.

They entered the cabin, stepping into a puddle of water so deep it reflected the gaslight lamps.

Dana groaned.

"I'll mop it up," Morgan offered dourly. "Just get those wet things off and go to bed."

Another order. Again Dana obeyed. She didn't know how much longer her legs would hold up anyway. Her wounds throbbed. Wearily, she leaned the snowshoes against the wall, then went to the stool and removed her boots. By the time she was down to her thermal shirt and sweatpants, Morgan had finished mopping and had added logs to the fire.

As she started to hang the jumpsuit on its peg, he edged in front of her. Startled, she glanced up. His forehead was creased with annoyance. The hair and beard she'd so carefully trimmed somehow still managed to look ragged and wild.

"I'll relieve you of that." He reached over her

and removed the rest of the outdoor gear from the rack, draping the garments over his arm.

"You can't do that," she protested. "That parka is mine."

"I just did." He turned away, his eyes grazing her shoulder. Gently, he reached out and touched her.

"You're injured."

She lowered her gaze to his hand and saw a large patch of drying blood on her thermal shirt.

"Oh, great!" she grumbled. "Now I'll have to sleep with this mess."

"Let me bandage it." He lifted the thin fabric, started to peer underneath.

"I can take care of it!" Dana snapped, pushing his hand away. "Just tell me where the supplies are."

"Suit yourself." He walked to the cupboards, took out a small kit and tossed it on the bed, where it landed with a thud. Then he returned to circling the room, picking up Dana's boots, gloves, and hat, piling them on top of the other items.

"What are you doing?"

"Buying insurance."

Dana watched warily as he snuffed the lamps one by one, noticing that the scratch on his cheek had nearly vanished. Even though the fire blazed hot, she shivered apprehensively.

"You're taking them in there?" she asked through the flickering darkness.

"Yes."

The fire popped; a log cracked and fell. Fenris snored softly. Dana felt a surge of sheer terror.

"Am I your prisoner, then?"

"If you choose to see it that way." He put his hand on the doorknob. "In the meantime, I need some sleep. This appears to be the only way I can get it. Don't forget to disinfect that wound."

Then he entered his bedroom and slammed the door.

Trapped. High above the sinister canyon with an unfathomable man. Her one opportunity to escape now locked in Morgan's forbidden room. She tried to devise an alternate plan, but the looming shadows cast by the flames made her jump each time they flickered in the corners of her eyes. Fenris's deep breaths brought back memories of the beast's snarls.

She timidly made her way to the rocker to gain the only light left in the room and began to tend her wounds. As the disinfectant stung the deep gashes that only a claw could have caused, she found it hard to remain sensible or to deny she'd seen a monster.

Chapter Sixteen

Morgan had risen unusually early that morning, and Dana groggily heard him milling around the kitchen just as sun started streaking through the window. Soon she smelled the aromas of perking coffee and bubbling oatmeal, but her night had been a bad one, full of uneasy dreams that she only vaguely remembered. She was finally enjoying a block of peaceful slumber and didn't much care about food or sunlight.

Suddenly, she sprang to a sitting position. Good God, a sunny morning. Nothing could keep her here any longer. She could leave this cursed place.

"Where are my clothes?"

Morgan, who'd been pouring coffee, turned at the sound of her voice. Without answering, he walked over and handed Dana a cup. Although it was a kindly gesture, his hard face didn't look kind at all.

Dana didn't much care. She flounced out of bed, nearly spilling her drink in her haste, grabbed her duffel bag, and went into the bathroom. She came out fully dressed and again asked Morgan for her outerwear.

"After we eat," he said in a tone that left no room for argument. At least not from someone who felt as battered as she did.

"I demand you take me back to my car," Dana stated firmly, over her bowl of oatmeal. "The storm is over. There's no reason to wait."

"Mmm." Morgan shoveled another spoonful into his mouth.

Dana waited impatiently until he swallowed. "Well?"

"Tomorrow." He dished up another load of cereal.

"No! Today!"

"The passes will still be blocked. They need another day to melt."

She got up irately and took the bowl to the sink, where she swished it in a sudsy basin, rinsed it in another, then picked up a towel and dried the dish.

"Can't the dogs pull us over the snow?" She put the bowl in the cupboard and walked back to the table.

Morgan washed down a last bite with a gulp of coffee, then slowly lowered the cup back to the table. "The sled isn't for passengers, it's for supplies."

"But couldn't it carry passengers?"

Morgan looked at her sternly. "I'm not going to risk injuring the dogs just because you're in a hurry to save some nonexistent wolves."

"Then give me back my damned clothes and I'll hike down myself!"

Morgan slammed his fist on the table and rose so abruptly he sent his chair clattering backwards. Dana flinched, more from surprise than fear.

"You'll leave when I'm ready to take you, Dana! Accept that!"

He whirled and stormed into his forbidden bedroom. Fenris darted after him. The door slammed shut. A few seconds later Dana heard a second slam.

Every memory of the previous night returned. Small things, like the colorful hieroglyphics on the sheep. Large things, like the vicious fangs of her attacker. And with the memories came confusion. How could she deny what she'd seen with her own eyes? Those creatures quarreling over her shivering bones weren't men. Things evil and monstrous lived in that canyon, and she wanted to get as far away from them as possible.

Morgan must be aware of what went on down there. Surely he'd heard the Indians' music at night. Or was his so loud it drowned out all the other sound?

Even as these thoughts raced through her head, other ones popped up as well. By now Morgan must know this place scared her out of her wits, yet he'd walked out on her anyway.

She sank onto the daybed, furious about the tears streaming down her face. What did she expect? People left when you made them angry. She'd learned that lesson early in life. Hadn't her mother left after Dana broke her favorite bowl? If her own mother would leave over something so small, why would Morgan stick around?

Even Dad had sent her to boarding school. For her own good, so she'd become socialized— or so he'd said, adding that he thought she spent far too much time with wolves. But she always suspected he'd offered her as a sacrifice to get Mother to return.

Then there was Ron. He'd asked her to marry him during her second year at Berkeley, had wooed and seduced her into intimacy, then run off in the night with Cynthia Shaffer.

She continued with this line of thinking for

quite a while, until her sobs eventually subsided. As they did, she began rationalizing. Of course Mother hadn't left over a broken bowl. She just couldn't stand the isolation of the wilderness anymore. Her father had only wanted to give her a better education than he could provide with home-schooling. She'd had nothing in common with Ron anyway. And Morgan?

Well, he'd merely gone for a walk to cool off. He'd soon be back.

Her sorrow vanished in a sudden flash of realization. She hadn't heard the lock engage after Morgan had stalked into his bedroom. Had he forgotten about it?

Fear returned. Dark, formless fear. Whatever she felt about Morgan, she couldn't remain on this mountain. Escape might be in her grasp. All she had to do was check to see if the door was locked.

She walked cautiously to the door, pressed her ear against it, and listened for a sound, any sound at all. Hearing nothing, she tentatively turned the knob.

Morgan stood at the edge of the canyon, watching his dogs leap on one another and roll in the snow. After a while, he turned his gaze toward the west and took in the rocky path that led straight to the scene of last night's horror.

From this high place, the fire pit looked vaguely like a stale doughnut carelessly tossed on the rocky ground, and the bright morning sun made the black stones seem like tasteful statuary.

Above it all, the setting moon hung like a decorative plate, barely visible against the bleached sky. It looked palely beautiful and harmless, but Morgan knew its power.

Fenris nudged his hand, begging for attention. After staying inside only two nights, he was becoming a regular house pet. Still, it wasn't so bad, and Morgan gave him an absent-minded pat before gazing back at the fading moon.

Venus, misty planet of love, would join it in the fifth house, which also governed love, on the following night. He smiled wryly. The Morgan Wilder of yesteryear would have labeled this momentous event as utter gibberish. Movements of faraway planets had nothing to do with anything.

But now, in the underworld where he dwelled, he knew astrology played a major role in a person's life. Lily couldn't have cursed him without the blessings of malevolent Pluto. Since then, he'd educated himself, had studied planetary influences, pored over his birth chart, learned that his own planets' positions had aided Lily.

Now they would aid him. But only if he won Dana's love.

Was he meant to love her, too? The Book didn't say, and somehow he doubted it. How could a man put the woman he loved at such mortal risk?

Morgan lowered his head, wanting to pray, but knew there was no mercy for an abomination such as him. God had deserted him long ago, high in that Balkan mountain.

Fenris nosed at his hand again, pulling Morgan's eyes from the moon. As his gaze drifted down, he caught sight of the ragged rocks on the canyon floor. Ignoring the dog's entreaties, he stepped closer.

Sharp down there. Cruel, hard, unforgiving. A man's body would be speared on those rocks, torn to shreds so rapidly no supernatural power could stop it. A few small steps would end his misery forever.

And leave Dana defenseless against Lily and her mewling lapdog.

That gave him a moment's hesitation. Then he remembered the helicopter. True, it hadn't seen her, but surely people were searching. She had friends, family, had already been missing over three days. And he had locked away her winter gear. Without it, even she wouldn't attempt the hike down nor venture out in the cold night.

239

Soon someone would come. In fact, he was the only one who truly threatened her safety.

With a deep fortifying breath, Morgan took another step toward the lip of Ebony Canyon.

Dana squinted into the gloom, then hastily back-stepped as the heavy door began swinging closed. Just the idea of being trapped in that black cave sent her raw nerves into spasms.

Why had Morgan built his bedroom without windows? What's more, how could he abandon the warm, comfortable main room to spend time in that barren cell? While she pondered these questions, she got a chair from the kitchen and dragged it over to prop open the door. It took a few minutes to find a position in which the heavy door couldn't push it away, and still she couldn't fathom Morgan's choices.

By the time she'd finally wedged the chair between the door and its frame, her hands had grown sweaty and she was thinking about how soon he might return.

Wiping her damp palms on her pant legs, she went in. Her eyes needed time to adjust to the dimness, so she hugged the wall and began inching along. She'd taken but a few steps when she felt a crunch beneath her feet. Something glowed in the diffused light and, as her night vision grew keener, she saw shards of glass, the skeleton of a lantern.

Now she knew what she'd heard crash against the wall when Lily was in the room with Morgan. She wondered why he hadn't replaced it, how he saw in here without it, but she had no time for dwelling on that.

She gazed around, able to see more clearly now, and took in a crude bed with a lumpy-looking mattress. An equally crude table sat beside it. She'd half hoped Morgan had simply dumped her clothes over his footboard, but the bed didn't even have one.

So where were they? She scanned the room, finally coming across a freestanding wardrobe. Her nerves getting more ragged by the minute, she glanced over her shoulder to check for Morgan. Reassured, she pulled the wardrobe's handles.

The doors opened with a creak.

After a skittish jump, she peered inside. Flannel shirts and denim pants hung from the rod, but she saw no jumpsuits or parkas. She looked down. On the floor of the wardrobe, shoved against one corner, was a pile of garments. She picked one up, pleased to find a jumpsuit, knowing her parka and boots had to be underneath. Kneeling, she pawed through the pile. Her hand touched the toe of a boot.

Just then, a shuffling sound came from outside the cabin. She twisted toward the noise.

The other door! She'd been so busy keeping an eye on the front one, she'd completely forgotten about it. The jumpsuit slipped from her hand. Springing up, she closed the wardrobe as quietly as her clumsy fingers allowed, then raced out of the bedroom, nearly stumbling as she shoved the chair away and pulled the door behind her.

Just as it shut, she heard a lock turn.

Chapter Seventeen

Morgan propped open the door with a large rock, trying to get a hold on his murderous thoughts about Lily, but his loathing intensified, rising from deep within. The hair on his body bristled. A moan formed low in his throat.

He sagged against the doorjamb as aches mounted in his body, combining with his raw emotions until he felt nearly overwhelmed. Gradually he willed his feelings away. His unwelcome alchemization ceased.

Weakened by his efforts, Morgan staggered toward his bed and reached to ignite the lamp, then remembered it was no longer there. The broken pieces still lay where he'd swept them. One more reason to hate Lily.

The solar power had finally failed, so he didn't even have that feeble light. Since the cold air was easier to bear than total darkness, he left the door propped open and flopped onto the bed to gaze forlornly at the water-stained ceiling. These women were driving him mad. Lily, with her ceaseless pursuit. Dana, with her continual defiance.

One more step, that's all. One more, and he would have been plummeting toward the rocks of Ebony Canyon. But he'd remembered the unlocked door and knew Dana would eventually try it if he failed to return.

He had stared into the canyon for quite a while after that, hearing it sing promises of release, knowing if he heeded them he'd be delivering Dana into mortal danger. Finally he'd wrenched himself away and called his dogs.

Now his sigh of longing filled the shadows of his room. By returning, he'd fixed his fate—and Dana's. He couldn't continue to live this way, doomed to wander the nighttime forests, slithering on his belly through mud in search of some poor creature to destroy. Before Dana, he had managed to eke out a balance between his humanity and his beasthood, but since he'd kissed her . . .

To again feel the half-remembered tenderness of a woman's touch had been too much. Now he couldn't abide another minute of this existence, much less seven more years.

The Book foretold of a woman who would love him, redeem him, give him hope, the most terrifying emotion of all. But—as he'd asked himself so many times before—was Dana that one?

He rocked abruptly upright and pulled two sheets of paper from his bedside stand.

It was all there, delineated by arcane symbols inside page-sized circles divided into twelve sections. Her birth moon conjoined his own moon in Libra—sat right on top of it, in fact. Less than one degree away, her Venus conjoined both their moons. Unless she'd given him the wrong birth time, there could be no mistake. Heaven had sent her.

May heaven also protect her.

He sadly returned the charts to the drawer and fell back on the bed, idly wondering how it was that sorrow and remorse never triggered alchemization.

Would he be feeling this way had he not grown to love her? It was a possibility. If her chart was false, she wouldn't last the night. The same physician's creed that prevented him from ever making his first kill might have also made him reluctant to risk her life.

Loving made it worse. How easily he could reveal his true nature if she hadn't touched his heart. Instead he feared seeing revulsion in her eyes, having her turn away.

His restless thoughts had him tossing on the lumpy bed, rolling right, rolling left. He tucked a pillow under his head, trying to get comfortable. His gaze drifted to the floor, wandering aimlessly, then coming to rest on a fallen article.

A jumpsuit.

He stared a moment, wondering how it got there, then rose and went to the wardrobe. When he opened the doors, he saw objects scattered across the entire bottom.

So Dana had already been in his room. He'd probably surprised her before she'd been able to complete her task. He should have guessed she wouldn't simply sit around and let someone else decide her fate.

The corners of his mouth curved up. If anyone could survive the Shadow of Venus, it was Dana. Even when she'd faced Lily, she'd continued fighting until all was obviously lost.

Venus had sent the right woman.

Her intrusion now gave him a perfect opportunity to reveal himself. When he left tonight, he'd leave the door unlocked again. Dana would come in. He was sure of it.

For a brief instant, he let himself imagine how it would be, kissing her again, putting his lips on that long, slender neck, slowly disrobing her strong, slim body.

No, he couldn't. Not only might he alchemize, but such intimate passion was meant for another time.

In the meantime, he'd treat her like a queen. His romantic skills were rusty, but he supposed he still knew how. If she felt anything for him at all, anything, she'd find no reason to refuse him when this day was done.

Almost dreamily, Morgan's hands came to rest on a large square box stored on the overhead shelf of the wardrobe. He lifted it down, carried it to the bed, and opened it.

Yards of gauzy white billowed inside. He pulled out the dress, smoothing the folds as they fell. He could picture how Dana would look, her lithe body silhouetted by firelight inside the almost transparent fabric. She'd seem like Venus herself, rising on a seashell from the froth, reborn only to redeem him.

Protected by love, they would endure the horrible and treacherous night. Morgan's bonds would be broken forever and Dana would be his.

Unless . . .

Unless, her chart was incorrect. Or, even worse, she turned from him in horror to run back and speak of his hideous secret.

It was the one part of The Law he couldn't defy.

No mortal could ever live to tell about them.

To Dana's surprise, Morgan came out of his room a changed and cheerful man. She'd grown used to the way he filled a doorway, so all she saw was the way the trim she'd given his hair and beard had altered his appearance. Gone was the raggedness of the night before. Now his dark waves fell softly to his collar, his beard was neat and tidy. She wondered if this was how he'd looked when he lived in the city, and though the change was pleasing, she also missed his wildness.

Feeling suddenly self-conscious, sitting there while he smiled at her from the doorway, she became annoyed. How could he act as if nothing had happened?

"The walk must have done you good," she said dryly. "Too bad I had no way to do the same."

"It did." He wagged some clothing, which she'd previously noticed but had given scant attention to.

"Your things." Pulling the door shut behind him, he walked to the daybed and deposited the items on the rail. "I owe you an apology." He gestured at the bed. "Do you mind?"

"Go ahead." But her voice held little warmth.

He sat beside her, leaving only inches of wrinkled blankets between them. She felt an irritating urge to move over, close the gap. Successfully ignoring it, she gave Morgan a blank gaze. "You were saying?"

"You scared me last night. What if you'd been hurt or"—he flinched almost imperceptibly— "killed? I was angry and I didn't explain my reasons very clearly."

Dana raised an eyebrow, rather enjoying his groveling. "*Very* clearly? You didn't explain them at all."

"Sure, I di— Look, Dana, the first day after a storm stops is the most dangerous. The snow is unstable, avalanches are common—"

"I know that! I was raised . . ." Dana grinned sheepishly. "I'm beginning to get repetitive, aren't I?"

He returned the smile, sparking gold-green flashes in his eyes. Dana's peevishness melted, along with all desire to punish him.

"I'll take you tomorrow, okay?" He reached over and stroked her cheek. "I only want to keep you safe."

His eyes were so huge and beautiful. And they held such sincerity. How could she have doubted him? Since the moment he'd found her buried in the snowbank, he'd shown nothing but kindness and asked little in return. Just that she remain inside at night. Their few bad moments had been all her fault.

Why hadn't she honored his request?

"Okay." She leaned into his hand. It felt warm against her cheek, slightly rough and scratchy, and she savored even that. A long-denied need coiled low in her belly, wanting release.

"You have such a sweet side." He touched one of her curls.

"Sweet!" She pulled back. "No one's called me sweet since I was six years old!"

He let his eyes flicker briefly down her body, then looked up with a grin. "In case you haven't noticed, you've grown up. What's wrong with being sweet?"

"I, uh, I don't know." She turned her face away. Too much of Morgan's dazzling smile was, well, too much. "It's so . . . so insipid."

Morgan let out a bellow of a laugh and Dana stared in astonishment. He'd never behaved this way before. So hearty—and bold! Except for that one tender kiss, he'd kept his sexuality well under wraps.

"Insipid?" He laughed again. "Never fear, Dana, if there's anyone who doesn't fit that word, it's you."

He took her hands and stood, pulling her up

with him. Dana's heart skipped a beat, her belly tightened in anticipation.

"Come on," he said. "Let's exercise the dogs."

As he turned to hand over the jumpsuit, Dana tried to tell herself she wasn't disappointed.

Glad to be free of the wind and blowing snow, the team romped on the frost-hardened snow, eagerly chasing the bones that Morgan had gotten from the smokehouse. Occasionally, one of them hit a soft patch, sank down, then scrambled back up, emerging, with a snow-covered head that made it look like it was wearing a cap. Each occurrence brought shared laughter, and Dana found she enjoyed Morgan's rare laugh more than she enjoyed her own.

As she made yet another throw, Odin bumped her, causing the bone to fly straight up in the air. Simultaneously, Odin and Aphrodite leaped for it, and collided, falling right on top of her. Aphrodite's weight hit Dana's shoulder full force and she staggered back.

"Whoa!" Morgan tried to catch her as she fell, but they both tumbled to the ground, along with the dogs. The four of them ended up rolling in the snow, which was wet and squishy and cold. Some of it crept into the gap at Dana's wrist and some seeped down her neck.

"Oh, that's cold," she complained as the dogs

251

climbed to their feet and vied for possession of the bone. She scraped snow off the wristband of a glove, then looked up at Morgan, who was angled across her legs, grinning like crazy.

"You think that's funny?" With a giggle, Dana grabbed a wad of sow and shoved it in Morgan's face.

He raised his thick eyebrows and slowly wiped the snow away. "You shouldn't have done that. Big mistake. Big."

Dana lunged for his hands, but too late. He'd already armed himself, and he pitched a huge snowball directly at her head. It bounced off, leaving crystal pebbles in her hair.

"Playing rough, are you?" She dug out a two-handed scoop, shot it back.

Somehow Morgan had found an arsenal, and his fresh ball struck her just as her own weapon started to fly. She tried to roll and scoop an armful, but Morgan grabbed her legs. Their shrieks of laughter filled the air.

Morgan didn't know when he'd had a better time. He felt mortal again, alive and happy with the woman he loved. A momentary remembrance of what would come nibbled at his joy, but he successfully pushed it away. He'd have this day, if nothing else. This one day.

Dana wiggled in his arms, trying to escape,

pelting him with snow. Still laughing, he moved his grip up. Now he had her around the waist.

Ice hit his neck. Melting rivulets immediately ran into the collar of his suit.

"No fair," he said in a fake whine. "I'm getting wet."

"Oh, I'm sorry. I was just—"

He shoved a snowball into her mouth. It crumbled, fell away from her lips.

"Oh," she squealed. "You brute. You cheated!"

She scrambled for more snow and Morgan slid further up her body, grabbing at her hands. Her bucking hips shoved repeatedly at his belly. Suddenly he felt a tightening of his jeans. He knew he should let her go before it was too late, but his joy was greater than his fear.

He had her wrist now, had pinned her down with his larger chest, could feel her soft breasts give beneath his weight. The thick suits between them felt like armor and he ached to strip them off.

He stopped laughing.

So did Dana.

He looked down, saw excited color in her cheeks, a sudden darkening of her green eyes. God, they glittered like emeralds, and her open lips were moist, inviting.

Still staring, he let go of her wrist. She

253

touched her gloved hand against his cheek. It was cold, yet warm and thrilling, too.

"Morgan?"

She arched her neck, brought her mouth closer to his.

He'd sworn to himself he wouldn't take this risk, but a plea was in her eyes and her body softened beneath him in subtle invitation.

With a groan of despair, Morgan claimed her lips. She opened her mouth for him eagerly, taking his tongue, holding it. He rose to his knees, slid his arms beneath her body, and lifted her from the ground.

And in the deep woods, a pair of dark eyes burned with jealousy as they watched Morgan stumble toward the cabin, never parting his lips from those of the woman in his arms.

Chapter Eighteen

"Move, move," the captain shouted. "Hurry up! Hurry up! Hurry up!"

His officers dashed here, dashed there, throwing weapons in the backs of vans, heaving tents and cookware, heaters and lamps. All the while Schumacher bellowed orders, knowing every man jack of them would mutiny if they had it in them.

Damn! They were only hunting wolves, not Jack the Ripper. Why couldn't he get that through their heads. He despised the look of fear he saw on their faces, despised it thoroughly and wished he had a way to wipe it off.

But when the commander suggested they bivouac at the clearing where Kowalski met his maker, Schumacher knew his crew couldn't spend a single night in that godforsaken place without bolting. So, for their sakes, he'd convinced the commander that a meadow near the spot of the abandoned Fish and Game van was more accessible. They could go by road, then fan out in pairs and search that entire hellhole of a mountain, acre by acre.

"Do we really need the bazooka?" called out Rutherford, who was leaning against his already packed van, looking cool and composed.

"You read the M.E.'s report," retorted the captain.

"Seems to fall into the 'better safe than sorry' category, if you ask me."

"I didn't." Schumacher accompanied this with a baleful stare. In return, Rutherford grinned knowingly. The captain turned away.

"Move it, folks. We've got wolves to hunt down before sunset! Move it! Move it!" The loading went faster than he'd hoped, although slower than he'd demanded, and soon all was in readiness.

He turned to his unit, ready to wax eloquent about duty, and saw leaden resignation in their eyes. For just an instant his voice failed him. A moment later he got it back.

"Get some steel in those backbones," he bellowed, hoping to wipe out their fears with the mere force of his words. "It's just a pack of dumb animals. Keep your chins up, your eyes sharp, your weapons loaded. Now, let's go!''

He tromped to his motor home, which traditionally led such a party, and started it. Sometimes being captain was a burden, but it was his job and he would do it.

With quivering hand, he engaged the gears and started leading his convoy up the mountain.

Dana shivered violently inside the fire-warmed cabin, her skin a mass of goosebumps. But not from cold. No, not from cold. Her blood boiled from a lust she'd never known, a heat that coursed between her legs.

Morgan pressed his body so tightly to hers that even air couldn't pass between them, but still he wasn't close enough. Eyes shut, she arched her neck, ran her hands across the smooth, steely muscles of his arms and shoulders. Quickly at first, then slowly, languorously, wanting to feel each ridge of his biceps. They seemed to swell beneath her touch in the same way his deep groans swelled in her ears.

She'd never known such hunger. There was a need inside her that demanded fulfilling. She took his lips, nibbled upon the fullness of the lower, thrust her tongue inside and tasted him.

Passion flowed between them like the milk

and honey of Nirvana. His teeth were sharp against her tongue; one careless bite could—

Danger! Oh, yes, so dangerous. And thrilling! To open her moist secret place, pull him in and tighten around his hot erection, let him probe and thrust above her weak and willing body.

This was the most thrilling of all.

Although reluctant to cause even a small separation between their bodies, she was eager to remove their clothing. Still holding his lips, she reached between them and tugged at the fastenings of his jeans.

Morgan moaned, both from pain and from delight. Alchemization had started. His bones felt torn apart, his joints burned, made worse by his attempts to hold it back. This was not how he'd intended to reveal himself, and his fear for Dana curled within his passion, creating intensely mixed and pleasurable sensations.

She trembled like a frightened lamb, yet he knew she did not fear him. Her need seeped into the small spaces her hands were creating between their bodies, spaces that cried to be filled. But his bones were alchemizing faster now. Soon his teeth would change and hair would grow, covering him completely. This was not the time, not here in broad daylight where he'd be revealed in all his horror. He must pull away, pull away . . . pull away.

With a jerk, he grabbed her hands.

"We need to talk, Dana."

"Talk?" she asked, with a breathless giggle. "Now?"

"Yes, now." It pained him terribly, but he rolled away, brought his feet around and put them on the floor. His back was to Dana, but he heard her heavy breath, tried to block it out. With weak legs, he rose and padded barefoot to the fireplace, where he added a log to the flames.

The cabin was uncustomarily filled with dogs. Zeus and Odin were sniffing at the pantry shelves. Persephone lolled under the dining table, while Fenris and Aphrodite tussled quietly beside the fireplace. Through the cabin door, which they'd left ajar in their haste, Morgan could see Shakti and Freya milling around.

Garments lay strewn all over the cabin's wood floor. A dingy gray wad of nylon here, another there. Boots and socks and gloves. The red and green of plaid flannel, the soft blue of Dana's camp shirt.

Even as he glanced at the results of their passion, his body changes began to ebb. It pained his soul, but he'd made the right decision.

"Why?" Her voice trembled. Morgan turned, almost afraid to look at her.

She was gazing up from beneath her dark lashes, and a sudden shock electrified Morgan's body. Could she see into his heart with those torrid and discerning eyes? Did she recognize the beast inside him?

Dana's mind whirled in confusion as she met Morgan's suddenly widened eyes. He stood, legs spread, in front of the hearth, the poker still in his hand. Without his shirt, she saw he was slimmer and more sinuous than his lumberjack clothing had suggested; but had he been less than that, she wouldn't have found his body any less glorious.

Was she only imagining the regret she saw? And if he felt it, why had he stopped? A million jumbled questions filled her mind, but somehow she felt at a loss for words.

"What is so important we have to talk now?" she finally asked, plucking at the waffled fabric of her twisted undershirt.

He put down the poker and walked back to the daybed, sitting down beside her. She leaned against his shoulder, and felt his muscles quiver beneath her cheek.

"What?" she breathed insistently.

He kissed her forehead, easing her painful feelings of rejection.

"Would you stay here with me, Dana?"

The question sent her bolting upright. Swinging her legs, she brought her feet to the floor, leaned forward, and grabbed the metal frame of the bed with both hands.

"Here?" She looked around wildly, heart suddenly pounding as she faced an unbearable choice.

"Here?" she squeaked again.

Morgan sighed and lowered his head to his hands. "I guess you've given your answer."

"Oh, Morgan. I don't . . . Something . . ." She stroked the bare skin above the line of his beard, wishing she felt differently. "Something's not right up here. I can't explain it, but I feel it." She tapped her heart.

"This is my home," he said sadly, lifting his head back up. "You love the wilderness. Why isn't this place as good as any where else?"

The pain that so touched her heart had returned to his eyes. Suddenly feeling chilled, she got up and went to retrieve her camp shirt. As she put it on, *The Lycanthropy Reader* came into her line of vision. She walked over to the bedside table, picked it up, and clutched it to her breasts.

"Do you believe in werewolves, Morgan?"

"Werewolves!" A startled expression crossed his face. "Isn't that a bit of a non sequitur?"

"This book is yours, isn't it?"

"A kooky friend gave it to me." He glanced away momentarily. Then, in a faraway tone, he added, "A long time ago."

"Yeah," she said. "Well, it's beginning to seem pretty current to me."

Abruptly, she sat beside him, looked earnestly into his eyes, all the while tapping the book's cover. "The *thing* that attacked me . . . I know this sounds nutty, but, Morgan, it looked just like the creature this book describes."

"Come on, Dana," he said, after a brief hesitation. "Your imagination's running away with you. You had a run-in with a bear—or possibly it was an angry Indian. But a werewolf?"

"I know, I know." So many things were still unexplained. And for the first time, she realized that Morgan had never displayed any deep alarm about her attack. Oh, he'd been concerned enough about her injury, but had never once suggested tracking down her assailant or reporting it to the authorities. Was it possible that Morgan was part of it all?

She shook her head hard, trying to knock the cobwebs loose. It ached dully, and their snowball fight had aggravated her shoulder, which now throbbed like the devil.

"Evil," she whispered, half afraid the very word would summon whatever attacked her.

"What did you say?"

"Something evil lives in Ebony Canyon." This time she spoke more firmly. Then she knew what her next words would be, and even thinking about them broke her heart into a thousand pieces. "I don't understand it, but I do know I can't stay here any longer."

Morgan shot to his feet and glowered down at her.

"First you're sure there are wolves here. Of course, they haven't killed anyone. Then, because you saw some Indians with a sheep, you think maybe they *are* killing people. Or maybe the Indians themselves are doing it. Now it's werewolves. What's going on? You know better. For Christ's sake, you're a biologist!"

Dana looked at Morgan in dismay, knowing his reaction stemmed more from hurt than from anger. She also knew he asked the impossible. Stay in Ebony Canyon?

She couldn't.

Something clanked in the kitchen. Morgan turned and saw Aphrodite with her paws on the stove, nosing the stewpot. He felt a huge wave of relief at the interruption, and when he ordered the dog to get down his voice held more praise than reprimand.

"I, uh, I'll take the dogs back to the kennel," he said. "They're already getting into mischief." As if to illustrate his point, one of the dogs yelped. Immediately afterward, the shovel fell across the open doorway and clattered onto the porch.

Dana nodded, her eyes containing the same

relief Morgan had felt about the opportunity to delay this conversation for just a little longer.

He dressed quickly, called the dogs together, and led them back to the kennels. During the trip his mind was consumed with his dilemma.

Should he tell Dana the truth?

His response had been pure knee-jerk, he knew that. But the subject of werewolves had come out of the blue, was so unexpected, he'd had no time to reflect.

Should he tell her?

He wanted to turn around now, take her in his arms, and spill out the whole horrible truth. But what if she viewed his confession the same way she viewed the canyon?

Evil, she'd said. *Evil.*

Wasn't that also true of him?

Dana was still sitting, turning *The Lycanthropy Reader* over and over in her hands, when Morgan reentered the cabin. He stood in the open door a minute, regarding her intently, then turned and began moving about the clothes-littered room. First he picked up the jumpsuits, then her boots and gloves.

It wasn't until Morgan's hand was poised above the doorknob of his room that Dana realized what he was doing. She felt the shock to the soles of her cold, bare feet.

"Are you going to lock up my things again?" she asked, over a faint tremor in her lower lip.

In typical Morgan fashion, he didn't answer right away.

"Well! Are you?"

He nodded slowly, sending a strand of hair into his eyes. "For your own good."

"For my—my own good!" Oh God, her voice was trembling. She took a deep breath. "Who the hell are you to decide what's good for me?"

"The man who loves you."

"You love me?" Dana felt a burst of joy that was immediately smothered by the reality of the moment. "But you're keeping me a prisoner. That's not love."

Her accusation sent a spear right into Morgan's heart. This, he thought, was a new and deeper experience of pain. Was this what love meant? Exposing oneself to agonies so intense you might never recover? He'd survived all the other barbs from fate, had almost found peace with his curse, had even learned to deal with Lily. But love?

Could he survive that?

"I thought . . ." He faltered for a second. "I thought after . . . Well, I'd hoped you would stay. I see now you can't, and I'm afraid you'll leave impulsively. That's too dangerous, Dana."

Her shimmering eyes widened. "Does that mean you aren't taking me down in the morning?"

The spear went deeper. Morgan swallowed a pained sigh. "You still want to go, even knowing I love you?"

"Please try to understand."

"You'll come back?"

She nodded furiously, but he saw doubt in her eyes.

He'd hoped, prayed, that his declaration of love would evoke a similar one from her, and had held on to that hope on his walk back from the kennels. But it hadn't.

Now he knew he couldn't risk telling the truth. She might flee in terror, and as much as he wanted to believe he was thinking only of her safety, he couldn't deceive himself. If she left before the full moon, she'd take his only chance for redemption with her. He couldn't let her go.

A stifled sob hiccuped in her chest, broke loose. A tear rolled down her cheek.

"Don't cry, Dana." Morgan moved to her, reached out and blotted off the tear. Another followed and spilled over his thumb. "Please . . . I'll take you in the morning. Soon as the sun rises. I promise."

He gazed into her eyes, saw disbelief, and knew it was deserved. When the sun rose, he'd find another justification for delay.

"In the morning . . ." she repeated with a hitch in her voice that sounded like a question.

"I promised, didn't I?"

Then he turned and carried her clothing into his bedroom. As the door fell shut behind him, he thought that no one deserved living in darkness more than he.

Never forget, brave hunter, how prodigious is the werewolf's psychic power. Nay, do not, and this point cannot be emphasized too excessively, do not permit your eyes to meet the beast's. One long gaze, and only one, will immediately draw you under its spell. Your feet shall bond to the very ground beneath them. You shall be unable to lift your arms. Only your dying scream will betray the fear still within you.

Dana was consoling herself by indulging in what she'd come to think of as her secret vice. She couldn't truly blame Morgan for getting angry when she'd offered up this nonsense to him. But even as she ridiculed the words she read, she remembered her paralysis under the eyes of her attacker. Twice, for a brief instant, she'd simply resigned herself to death.

The chapter ended and she turned to one entitled "The Nature of Man and Beast Revealed." The words immediately drew her in.

Remember, dear hunter, that man is not by necessity evil. Neither is the beast. Each in natural form has both nobility and villainy. Each seeks to fulfill its instinct to survive. But mingle the brutality of the wolf with the self-interested cunning of man and here we have a creature more deadly than all others.

Slaughter is not the sole methodology for defeating it. This abomination was made by ritual and by ritual shall it be redeemed, albeit this is not a course for the faint of heart.

Now the pages went into a mass of astrological lore that Dana barely comprehended, and the ache in her heart returned. Morgan had said he loved her, had asked her to stay. Now she was reading a book that inflamed the fear that caused her to refuse. Did she love him, too? She thought she did.

But . . . from the first time she'd set foot on the base of Ebony Mountain, she'd suffered tingles of apprehension that only stopped when Morgan was around. Was she confusing security with love?

She didn't know. Fear and isolation created strange bedfellows. What remained clear, however, was that nothing, not even love, could persuade her to stay.

Would Morgan come with her? He'd said this was his home with such depth of feeling that she felt certain he would not. She put her hand over her heart, although it did little to ease the ache, and returned to the pages, hoping to lose herself in them.

Her eyes stopped short when she hit on a particularly dramatic passage in a book she already deemed to be full of excessive drama.

When pure love of a kind that transforms sour hearts and clears jaded eyes combines with the Shadow of Venus, nothing can withstand its power. The beast's fangs dissolve, its claws withdraw and soon the clear, untroubled face of a mortal stands revealed.

Do not scoff at such purity of heart, dear hunter, for if you do, you shall surely perish in the fires of your own blasphemy. The Shadow of Venus is your ally. Diligently search the skies for it, although it comes but once these seven years. Pore over your ephemeris. Search, dear hunter, search. Venus shall not, indeed cannot, disappoint you.

What on earth was an ephemeris?

Continued reading implied it was a book that foretold planetary positions, and with every reference came new ones to the Shadow of Venus. Holding a finger at her place, Dana turned to the table of contents. Most of the chapters had stagy names such as "Beastly Powers," "Loved One All," and "Nay, the Silver Bullet," but the title she hunted for simply said "Shadow of Venus."

Avidly, she leafed through the volume, hunting for the designated page. When she got there, she let out a sigh that contained all the pain she'd been ignoring.

The whole section had been pulled from the binding.

This filled her with unaccountable despair.

She put the book down, told herself she'd been reading it too much. Morgan had insisted that Fenris stay in the pen now that the weather had broken, and she missed him.

Getting up, she wandered to the window, seeking a glimpse of the kennels. The sinking sun was casting brilliant highlights on the thick woods outside. Soon it would again be black out there, except for the moon. A night into which she'd never venture again.

Nothing seemed so bad in the daylight, however, and with the sun to keep her company, she let herself again question the improbable. What if there really were werewolves? How would one know? *The Lycanthropy Reader* contained plenty of clues, some of which, unfortunately, had already been borne out in reality.

She recalled Morgan's miraculously healed feet, the here one minute, gone the next scratch on his cheek, the horrid cries seeping from his room, which now seemed chillingly reminiscent of those described in *The Lycanthropy Reader*.

How about Lily and Jorje's sudden appearance in the midst of the blizzard? That thought brought a brief flash of the beast's white fur, a shade eerily similar to Lily's hair color.

Even Morgan's explanations seemed suspect. Miracle salve provided by Tony? And she doubted even the strongest dog team could travel through that fierce storm.

With a shudder, she recalled the inhuman sounds of the specters as they quarreled above her. Their noises appeared to have a meaning they both understood. Had they been speaking in the Lupinese language the book mentioned?

Once more, she tried to convince herself she'd only seen men wearing animal pelts. When this failed, she considered the possibility it had been a bear, as Morgan suggested. She even dabbled in the notion that a twisted cult of devil-worshipers ran amok down there, performing brutal sacrifices.

Whichever way she went, she found herself torn between the wildly incredible evidence of her own eyes and the natural logic of her mind. A fictional character—Sherlock Holmes, she believed—had said that once you eliminated all possibilities, whatever is left, no matter how improbable, must be the logical conclusion.

Yet this conclusion told her that Lily was a werewolf. That Morgan was one also.

Dana stepped closer to the window, let the sun warm her face. She wanted to laugh, and wasn't sure if the urge came from amusement or hysteria.

Morgan a werewolf?

If so, why was she still alive? She'd been his

unwilling guest for nearly four days now, plenty of time for him to destroy her. Yet it had been the white one who'd seemed bent on killing her. The other, so much darker and larger, had come to her defense. Should that be true, why had he defended her? Was he keeping her for some other reason?

Slowly, she turned from the window and stared across the room at the open book lying facedown on the bed. "The Shadow of Venus." Was that it?

Her thoughts turned into a baffled whirl. None of it made sense. But something evil did live in that murky night. Frightened Indians, frightful cultists, or fearsome monsters? She didn't even want to know.

In her bones, she felt the canyon was cursed. She also knew that Morgan would break his promise, would never let her leave until she'd served his purposes, whatever they might be. It was up to her to escape.

She turned her gaze to his closed door. He'd left it unlocked that morning. It was probably too much to hope that he might do it again. But as soon as he went out that night—and she knew he would—she had to try. It was her last hope.

(Chapter Nineteen

Night had fallen. Although he was in his already dark room, Morgan knew it by the need that curled within him, the approaching signs of change he couldn't ignore. He heard the nocturnal forest rousing from its slumber, smelled the distinctive perfume of the midnight hours.

When his torturous alchemization had finished, he gathered up his enormous jumpsuit, built large enough for a fullback, and put it on. He wore it only when he expected to encounter mortals. The clothing bound his limbs unnaturally, but if his looking more human than monster eased Dana's terror, it was a small price to pay.

With one more glance—for with his werewolf eyes, the room was alive with light—he checked to be sure he hadn't inadvertently locked his door. Reassured, he opened the outer one. Slowly, very slowly, making sure it squeaked more loudly than usual.

Even as he left the cabin, drums pounded on his eardrums, the flute sounded painfully shrill. Maybe the tribe would put out another sheep. He needed a kill tonight, not just to satisfy his need, but to keep him from dwelling on his indecision.

If all went as hoped, in a few hours Dana would agree to play her role in the fearsome ritual. The Book had sworn she would, even though he was forbidden to use his hypnotic powers to persuade her. His fear about her birth time still haunted him. Many people thought they knew when they were born, then later learned they'd been misinformed.

Without Venus's protection, she'd never last the night.

He wouldn't think of it. He'd hunt for a while, give Dana time to build the courage to try his door again. He had to trust The Book, trust the planets, and even more, he had to trust her love.

Dana gave a small gasp of surprise when the door actually opened. For several hours she'd kept a sharp ear, cringing only mildly when Morgan's music started, and listening carefully for the click of the outer door. As soon as it closed, she'd shot to her feet.

Now that her hopes had been realized, she grabbed a chair and shoved it between the door and the jamb, then slipped inside.

It seemed darker than she remembered, and she waited a few minutes until her vision adjusted before hurrying to the wardrobe.

The items were scattered on the floor where she'd left them, and she knelt, quickly rummaged through them, and came out with her parka, gloves, and boots, all of which she tossed through the open door. Then she groped for a jumpsuit. Her hand finally contacted slippery nylon, and she pulled to free the garment from the rest of the pile. Feathers flew from the tear at the shoulder, tickling her nose. She waited for a sneeze that didn't come, then she threw the heavy down-filled garment over her shoulder and headed for the door.

As she tried to climb over the chair, it got in her way, so she dropped the suit on the seat and went into the main room for the items she'd thrown out of the bedroom.

These she shoved under the daybed. Unless Morgan crawled on the floor, he'd never see them.

With that thought, she sadly wondered when she'd begun to consider him the enemy. For a while there, she'd almost convinced herself he was a werewolf. Then she shook her head impatiently. After she got back to civilization, she'd decide what to do. How she could go on without him, she didn't quite know, but it wasn't as if he were going anywhere. She knew where to find him when she made up her mind.

When she stood up to go for the jumpsuit, her eyes fell on *The Lycanthropy Reader*. She paused.

The missing chapter . . .

Could it be in Morgan's room? She wanted to read it with an urgency she hardly understood. He hadn't been gone long. His excursions usually lasted most of the night. Surely she had time to look.

Purposefully, she walked toward his room and climbed cautiously over the chair and jumpsuit. As her feet hit the inside floor, she teetered slightly and steadied herself against the wall. Something brushed her arms. She gave a small jump, then looked up.

A garment hung from a hook on the wall. It appeared to be a robe of some sort, or maybe a woman's dress. Dana touched it. Soft, rather like gauze, but silkier, more pleasing to the fingers. Curious, she took it off the hook.

This was far too small for Morgan.

Did the gown belong to that woman? Dana experienced a rush of pure jealousy, which quickly drowned in a wave of sorrow. What did it matter? She couldn't continue kidding herself. Once she left Ebony Canyon, she'd never be back. If Morgan had some kind of relationship with that obviously sick woman, she had no right to resent it.

But she did. Her sorrow mingled with malice and turned into a push-pull of emotions. Heart aching, she hugged the soft fabric, felt it caress her cheek, smelled a faint scent of lavender.

Thus absorbed, she failed to heed a warning creak until a stream of moonlight cast an enormous silhouette on the floor.

Foggily, she looked up.

A scream swelled in her throat and she opened her mouth, emitting only a pitiful squeak. Something pinned her feet to the floor. She couldn't move.

The silhouette ducked its enormous head under the doorframe and slowly moved closer, one furred and long-fingered hand extended. Light glistened off the pointed claws.

Terrifying memories of the white beast flashed through her mind. *Don't look into its eyes*, screamed a voice deep within her, and she ducked her chin into her shoulder. But she couldn't keep from looking. Mesmerized, horrified, still unable to move, she was fascinated nonetheless.

Her senses heightened. Each strand of the fabric in her hands felt separate from the next. She heard every subtle sigh of floorboards sagging beneath the monster's weight. She saw the long woolen jacket falling from shoulder to knee, the shiny nylon covering its legs, but though it wore human clothing, she knew it wasn't a man.

This was a werewolf.

Her mind grew strangely clear and calm, and she found herself observing it with a clinical detachment and thinking it was actually quite handsome. Highlights gleamed off the bared parts of its sleek dark coat, and its narrow wolflike face was nearly human. A swath of full hair swept from its jutting brow down to its neck, and its eyes sparkled gold.

It would kill her, of course, and she was helpless to prevent it. Had she not been so terrified and awestruck, she might have laughed at the irony. In seconds she would become prey to a version of the animal she'd worked so hard to protect.

Now it was close. So close she could feel its breath, hear the faint sounds as it inhaled and exhaled. She licked her lips, tasted tears she hadn't known were flowing, and backed against the wall. Metal hit her injured shoulder. She flinched, heard a clank, jerked her head.

Omigod! Chains. They were touching her, falling across her shoulders. Huge mawing manacles dangled just inches from her arms. She hugged the gown more tightly, wondering if the thing would hang her from the wall and torture her into insensibility.

A hand reached out; silky fur grazed her cheek.

"Please," said the creature with incredible gentleness.

The imploring word broke Dana's paralysis. Strength returned to her legs. Her scream erupted, high and shrill. She dropped the gown and spun away from the thing, diving for the propped-open door.

A hand gripped her arm, then slipped away. Dana tumbled. Time dragged as the floor rushed up to meet her. She felt every whirl of her flailing arms, every lurch of her airborne legs, and she reached for the chair, hoping to halt her fall.

Her hand came upon a wad of spongy nylon, closed around it as if it alone could save her. A shoulder crashed into a chair leg, struck the floor. She felt her wound tear open; something trickled down her skin. Rolling, she ignored the spark of pain. The chair wobbled, then fell and clattered on the floor of the other room.

The inner door swung shut, leaving only the moon to light the room. The creature loomed above her, blocking even that.

Dana curled her fingers into the downy nylon and encountered a small, hard cylinder. At the most visceral level, she knew she had little chance of surviving, but she wasn't going easily. She scooted back, strained into a sitting position, and dug frantically for what she knew was in the pocket.

She came out with the paper vial just as her back hit the wall. Snapping it open, she threw it, then brought the jumpsuit to her face.

The beast gasped and choked, then fell back with a shudder, but didn't paw or attempt to bat the capsule away. It fell to the floor, filling the room with its acrid scent.

Just as it had happened with the white beast, this one's fur melted in front of Dana's eyes. In seconds, the jutting brow receded, the golden eyes grew closer. Height diminished. Soon, Dana saw a beard, thick dark eyebrows with a deepening crease between them.

"Morgan?" She hardly realized she'd called his name.

He inclined his head gravely, picked up the broken capsule, and threw it out the door. Even as he turned back, his height increased, fur returned, eyes receded. All the while he groaned, nearly doubling up, as if in great pain.

Shielding herself behind the jumpsuit, Dana stared up and pulled her legs to her chest.

Someone whimpered. Something roared like a river. She heard it clearly, but it came from so far away. Then she knew. Her own cries. Her own racing pulse.

Oh, to die at Morgan's hand. The greatest irony of all.

Then his groans ceased. He straightened, and Dana saw the full extent of his size. His head almost touched the ceiling. A squeeze of one clawed hand would crush her skull.

Now he was above her, gazing down, head tilted. Something reflected in the moonlight beneath his eyes.

He was crying.

Dana looked into his sorrowful eyes and knew then, with absolute clarity, that no matter what he did, she did love him and would continue to do so for eternity. A huge sob gathered in her chest and burst forth into soul-racking tears.

He bent over. Dana prepared herself to die.

The blow didn't come. Instead, a powerful arm slipped beneath her knees. Another moved behind her back. The floor receded and she felt herself pulled against a scratchy wool-covered chest. The rough fabric felt oddly normal, and Dana huddled against it, heard his strong heart thrumming in her ears.

He took her to the bed, laid her gently down, then went to close the door.

Night-blind now and totally without defense, Dana wrapped into a rigid ball. Soft footfalls approached the bed, and she sensed his presence just above her. Fabric rustled against fabric; several faint plops resounded on the floor.

"Perhaps," he said in a pained voice, "you won't find me as repulsive in the dark."

One of Dana's hands slipped off her knees; the tension in her body eased a bit.

Repulsive?

Terrible and beautiful, yes. Majestically fearsome. A being like no other, combining qualities of both the species she adored. But never, not once through this entire nightmare, had she thought him repulsive.

But all she could do was stutter, "N-n-no."

For Morgan, the room had plentiful light. It seeped under the doors, fell from minute cracks in the ceiling. And in that light, he gazed upon Dana and wondered exactly what she meant.

He wished he could see into her soul as clearly as he saw her trembling body. According to Lily, this was a werewolf's shining moment, when at last a human cringed in fear below him. Sweet and fulfilling, she had promised. But he now knew that wasn't true.

And he wished with all his heart that he

hadn't learned it by terrorizing Dana. Carefully, he lowered himself to the bed. His weight was a dangerous thing. If he sat too quickly, he might throw Dana onto the floor.

"Do you?" he asked.

"W-w-hat?"

"Think I'm repulsive."

The silence lay heavy in the dark room and nearly broke his heart. He felt a whimper roil in his throat, swallowed it.

"You . . . you frighten me."

"If I'd intended to hurt you . . ." Mindful of his sharp claws, he ran a hand along her rigid shoulder. Her shudder caused another hurtful stab. "Relax, Dana," he crooned, giving his heartache no attention. "You're safe with me, always safe."

She started sobbing again.

With all the tenderness he possessed, Morgan took her hand and pulled it to his body.

"Stroke me, Dana." He knew she had no idea of the courage he'd drawn on to make that request.

Dana tugged futilely against his hold. Although he didn't force her closer, he also didn't release his grip. Soon she stopped struggling, put a tentative hand on his thigh. Morgan sighed.

She let her hand rest there for a long while,

saying nothing, sobbing occasionally. Then, with obvious caution, she moved her fingers slowly down his leg.

"Soft," she said, wonder evident in her tearful voice. "Soft and silky."

She backtracked, let her fingers dwell on the curve of his thigh, stroking with loving tenderness. Then her hand reached the vee of his thighs. A finger touched his testicles, brushed against his stirring erection.

"You're just like a man," she said in a startled voice.

"In that way, yes."

Her hand lingered momentarily, then moved on. His heartbeat quickened, a deep breath left his lungs. As much as he feared the answer, he must ask the question.

"Now that you know my true self, can you love me, Dana?"

He sensed her hesitation as she lifted her hand from his leg.

"I don't . . . know."

Morgan let out an involuntary groan.

She sat up abruptly, groping in the dark. He saw the tiny half-moons of her nails, the dusting of fine hair on her arm. Then her fingers reached his cheek, stopped, rested.

"You're crying. . . . Oh, Morgan, I'm so sorry."

She dropped her hand, brought it to her mouth, and licked his tears from her fingers.

"Salty, just like mine," she said.

"I am so much like you, sweet Dana. You cannot know." He put his hands on her shoulders and pressed her slowly back to the bed. She didn't resist. "It's more than I could hope for that you'd love a monster like me. But if you can't, please, for this night, let *me* love you."

She shivered so violently he jerked his hands back.

He had failed.

But please, sweet Venus, he pleaded, *if only once, let her hold me, feel her dear body under mine, her touch on the beast I am. By that alone I will be redeemed.*

And in his prayer, he promised to return her to safety the next day, then walk to the edge of Ebony Canyon and assure he'd never harm a single mortal.

"Undress me, Morgan."

Her surprising request startled Morgan and filled him with mixed emotions. He'd schemed for this all along. The ritual could not succeed until they bonded as man and woman. But now, thinking of the danger, his heart quailed.

When he finally touched her, he realized her trembling came from need even greater than his. In awe, he lifted her shirt over her head, drew down her loose fleece pants, her pleasingly silky undergarment. When his claws scraped gently across her skin, she moaned as if in pleasure.

He rolled her to lie on her belly, and she moved pliantly beneath his hands. Little sounds came from her mouth, but these were not from tears or terror.

Dear Venus, protect us both.

When he climbed to straddle her, holding his weight so as not to crush her fragile body, she twisted, snaked an arm around his neck, and pulled his mouth to hers. Hungry noises purred in her throat, she drew her tongue along the edges of his sharp, deadly fangs, almost daring him to draw blood.

For that instant, Morgan gave in to her passion. He suckled her tongue violently, only barely mindful he might harm her. Tasting a faint drop of blood, he started to draw away, but she only whimpered and drove her tongue more deeply into his mouth. He placed his hands on the sides of her legs, bared his claws and began lightly pulling them up her body.

She writhed deliciously beneath him. Then, with a greedy cry that excited Morgan beyond reason, she broke the kiss. Shifting frantically, she pulled her knees beneath her, shoved her perfect little bottom against him, and put a cool hand around his large erection. Only the same strong will he used to restrain unwanted alchemization kept him from exploding at her exquisite touch.

"Oh!" Her tone held surprise and alarm.

"You cannot take me," he said, breathing into the delightful curves of her ear, knowing what provoked her exclamation. He was much larger and fuller than a human male.

She shuddered, whether from desire or fear, Morgan could not tell. Then she spread her knees wider, moving him against the edges of her dilated opening. Moist and smooth it was, and hot, so hot. The contrast between heated womanhood and cool fingers sent electric sensation through Morgan's body.

He reached down to where they touched, felt warm juices flowing between her parted legs, ached so badly to have her, he thought he might die.

With a quick move of her hand and another clever thrust of her hips, she pushed his fingers away, tried to sheath him. But Morgan grabbed her wrists, pinned them to the bed, then pressed himself against her back and rained kisses on her neck.

Now she bucked beneath him, heedless of his power to hurt her, seeking the length of him, striving to engulf him. He straightened, held her hips, refusing to let her have what she sought.

The muscles of her back flexed and fell with her every thrust. Moans of desire came from her mouth.

Exquisite, painfully exquisite, to be between her legs, yet deny what they both so badly wanted. And despite his fear of hurting her, Morgan could barely resist the temptation to give it to her.

Then his earlier question reentered his mind, cooling his passion. He'd sworn an oath to Venus. He must not ask again. If she answered differently this time, fate would be set in motion.

He told himself this—but without success.

"Can you not love me, Dana?"

She stopped moving. He stroked the gentle swell of her bottom, letting his claws graze lightly, oh, so lightly. With another moan, she jutted up and tried to take him again. Once more he stilled her movements.

Then he started moving. Slowly, very slowly. Up and down, sliding himself against her swollen mound. She screamed with pleasure so intense Morgan felt it in his soul.

Convulsions racked her body. He held her hips, bent to kiss the smooth skin of her trembling back, wanting to hear her answer, wanting not to hear it, struggling not to release his own need.

Time passed. Sparks of her climax still convulsed her body. Finally came moments of stillness. Occasionally she circled her hips. Her breathing slowed.

Giving one last satisfied sigh, she spoke.

"Yes, Morgan, I love you."

He felt as if a beam of pure golden light had passed through him, providing him with an inner sense of calm. Suddenly, his teeth lost their jagged edges. Hair melted from his limbs. Fingernails replaced his claws.

Passion, so intense he knew it might never be fulfilled, accompanied his restored humanity. With joyful fury, he drove himself inside her, deep, deep as he could. She was still hot and wet and wanting him, and his violent thrusts renewed her passion. He felt her tighten, and blood engorged him to such fullness as he had never known.

"Dana," he whispered hoarsely. The cry escaping his throat was met by hers. Long and high and joyful, mingling in the night, filling the room with love. Morgan fell onto her trembling body, thinking he'd never heard a sweeter sound.

And also bittersweet.

Because nothing could stop fate now.

((

Chapter Twenty

Morgan smiled lazily and rolled to take Dana in his arms. He hit an empty space. Instantly, he came awake and listened for footsteps in the front room. But all was silent. Daylight streamed through the open bedroom door, and Morgan scanned the room for Dana's clothes. They were gone. So was the jumpsuit.

"Dana."

He got no answer and jumped to his feet, running naked into the main room, looking wildly around. The daybed was made up. A bowl and spoon lay draining near the sink. But Dana wasn't there.

Had she gone to feed the dogs? Get more wood? Surely, after the night before, she hadn't—

The note was lying on the table, a pen on top of it, holding it in place. Morgan slowly moved forward. His hand trembled slightly as he picked up the piece of paper.

Dear Morgan—
I love you and always will, but I haven't the courage to do what you ask.
Forgive me.

She'd signed it with a large wavering scrawl, and he dimly noticed the ink had feathered and blurred. His eyes grew hot, stung bitterly, and he blinked several times before closing his fingers around the paper.

A white-hot ball of frustration burst forth from inside him, followed by the tug of ligaments. Familiar streaks of pain shot through his limbs. A howl rose in his throat, came out in a blast of fury.

With another howl, he threw the crumpled page across the room. It ricocheted off the fireplace screen, then bounced inside. Flames licked at its edges.

With another howl, he rushed over and tossed the screen aside, snatched out the burning sheet and began batting it between his hands. The flames bit at his fingers, but he didn't care. When only a few smoky spirals remained, he pulled the sheet protectively to his chest. It seared his skin. He smelled scorched hair.

But those tiny burns were nothing compared to his splitting heart. He knew he could go after her. With his superior knowledge of the trail, even in human form he'd soon find her. And if he alchemized, he'd catch her in mere minutes.

Then what? Risk her life for his redemption? He had made a vow to Venus to let Dana go free. Even if he hadn't, he loved her too much to expose her to the dangers of the ritual. No, she'd sealed his doom; but at least Ebony Canyon still waited for him.

He smoothed the smoldering note to his naked chest, feeling almost as if he were holding Dana. He couldn't destroy it. Until he died, it was all he had left of her.

At that moment, Dana was thrashing around in a soggy snowbank. Snow was everywhere. Down the neck of her suit, where it ran in frigid rivulets, inside the bindings of her gloves, clinging to her hair. Every foot of the perilous trail had been a challenge. If she wasn't skidding over ice, she was sinking knee-deep in melting snow. She felt foolish and bereft.

And once she finally worked her way out—and she would, of course—she had no idea how much longer she had to go before reaching her four-by-four. She could then look forward to digging *it* out. Night could fall before she finally freed it.

What if she got trapped down there after the sun set? Fortunately, she had no time to give much thought to that possibility. In a twisted sort of way, she welcomed the obstacles of the hike, because they kept her mind off her aching heart, off the terror she'd endured since leaving the cabin.

She'd awakened with a burst of joy, feeling the smooth, taut muscles of Morgan's body against hers. Then memory had quickly returned, inducing a panic that turned her to mush. She'd slipped from Morgan's bed into the darkness and pawed around for her clothes, luckily spying the fallen jumpsuit as she opened the door. Dashing back, she snatched it up, then raced into the living room to dress.

Oddly, birds still sung beneath the rising sun, the fire murmured in the hearth. No one would guess the passion and the hunger she had felt the night before.

By daylight it all seemed so sick. She'd invited a furred creature to mount her like a bitch in heat, had gloried in their fiery joining, loved it with obscene wantonness. Had he seduced her with his hypnotic werewolf powers? Was that why she'd so eagerly allowed his lovemaking?

Yet that direly accurate book spoke only of vicious, murderous impulses. Morgan hadn't been like that. He'd been tender and gentle, so careful not to nip her with his werewolf teeth or tear her skin with those dangerous claws. There wasn't a scratch on her body, and despite what her mind said, she felt only the afterglow of love.

Then, when his wolf form had dissolved above her, when the brush of fur changed to the slick, sweaty feel of an impassioned man . . . oh, the power she'd felt. Not her own, no, not that, but the unleashed power of love. Even now she remembered the pure bliss of his entry. She'd finally felt complete.

Later, he held her lovingly in his arms and explained the Shadow of Venus. The idea of redeeming him initially made her heart soar. Then he'd graphically described the dangers, especially if she'd given him the wrong birth time.

She shuddered against his shoulder and he paused, stroked her hair, told her she didn't have to do it. At that time, she felt she had no choice. Redeem Morgan or leave him. And with his hard, smooth, loving body next to hers, she knew she couldn't leave.

But sunlight usually sharpened the edges of hard reality, and this morning was no different. Even though she loved him, she couldn't face three snarling monsters alone, protected by nothing but a circle. Nor could she live with Morgan as he was—a supernatural creature with animal instincts, who lived in a place so full of evil she could almost smell it in the air.

Yes, he'd made love to her last night. He could just as easily have killed her.

Shivering, she fed the fire, quickly dressed in front of its warmth, then put on the jumpsuit and went to get the rest of her things.

After she pulled the gear from beneath the bed, she looked down at the crumpled blankets, remembering the night she'd first seen Morgan emerge from his room. A telltale thickening came to her throat, and she felt an oddly desperate urge to make the bed.

When she'd done so, her stomach growled. She looked at the covered pans on the unlit stove, deciding she needed to eat before she left. Listlessly, she dished up some cold porridge, which slid tastelessly down her throat.

When she emptied the bowl, she put water on to heat, then gathered up her belongings and put on her boots. Soon the kettle whistled. She poured hot water into the soapy basin.

As she dipped in the bowl and spoon, it occurred to her that Morgan could awake at any minute and surely wouldn't let her leave. Was she hoping he would? She looked toward his room, heard him snoring quietly. With a sigh— whether from relief or disappointment, she couldn't say—she went to pick up her bag.

Then she moved to open the door. All she had to do was pull. The night had been calm; no pile of snow waited to fall inside. A few steps and she'd be free.

Should she leave him a note?

He might wake up.

Should she?

With a small groan, she put her burdens on the floor. A few seconds later, paper and pen in hand, she scribbled a hasty good-bye. As she signed it, a tear dropped on the page. Then another. With an angry sniffle, Dana had wiped away the ones that followed, then walked sadly back to the door.

Now, as she wallowed in cold, squishy snow, she sniffled again. Why had this happened? All she ever wanted was to make sure some gun-crazy highway patrol officers didn't wipe out the last pack of wild wolves in Arizona.

Bracing herself for the cold shock to come, she shoved her arms deep into the slush, trying to lever to her feet. The metal snowshoes, a blessing earlier, only made the job harder. Each time she put weight on them, they slipped on the ice.

She let out a whoof as her bottom hit hard ground.

"That's why my tennis rackets are superior."

Dana ping-ponged her head in search of the

voice, finally spying Tony half-hidden in a stand of pine.

"How long have you been standing there?" she asked crossly.

He laughed and stepped out of the shadows, approached with his hand extended. His crude wood-and-leather shoes, she noticed, had no trouble on the icy patches. The fur cloak he wore the day they met was gathered around him, but the hood was on his shoulders, its eyes and beak hidden in the folds.

She stuck up her own hand. He put a foot over the end of her snowshoes, then swung her out of the drift.

"Thanks." She brushed snow off her suit.

"Nothing to it. Where are you headed?"

"Back to my car." He picked up her bag, held it out for her to take. She thanked him and slung it over her shoulder.

"Mind if I keep you company?"

Mind? Dana tried to hide her relief as she accepted. He said very little at first. Now and then he pointed out a darting animal; occasionally he steadied her when the going got slick. Dana kept looking over at him, wondering exactly what he was all about.

"Have you lived here all your life?" she asked, expecting him to say he had.

"No, I came a while back."

"You did? But the other members—"

"Most have always lived here. But a few of us came from the outside."

"That must have been a big decision."

He smiled at her. "Actually, it wasn't so hard."

"But, I mean, you went to school, had friends, television . . ." She laughed. "Guess that wasn't any sacrifice."

"Mostly I miss computers. That's what I majored in."

"You went to college?"

"Southern Cal, got my master's degree and a lucrative offer from Microsoft." He said this matter-of-factly, without a hint of arrogant pride. "My dad damned near hit the ceiling when I left the reservation and turned away from civilization. That was the hardest thing. Giving up family."

"But, why?" What would impel someone to make such a choice?

He waved a hand. "That's all behind me now." His gaze suddenly became distant, as if he were listening for a subtle sound. "Shh."

He stopped walking. Dana, who was virtually skiing over a particularly icy patch, veed her shoes and looked over her shoulder. She found herself staring blankly into the hawk's eyes.

"Though brave of heart, the woman still

quails at the sight of the beast. Then passion will stir. Thunder and lightning shall clash in their souls. . . ."

"What are you babbling about?" Dana asked nervously, again feeling as though Tony's words came from the beak.

"After their joining she will flee—"

"Tony, you're scaring me." How could he know what had gone on between her and Morgan? But somehow he did.

"—but soon come to see that destiny will not be denied."

Cold chills raced up and down Dana's spine. Not from fear, but from an intuitive knowledge that all Tony said was true.

The trees created a green window behind his cloaked silhouette, through which Dana saw the peak of the mountain. She could almost imagine Morgan's cabin. For a second, Tony drifted out of view.

When she looked back, he was gone.

She stood there for a long while staring at the empty space, then let her eyes move back to the mountain. She thought of the night she'd cut Morgan's hair, of the warmth of the blazing logs, of dear Fenris milling about the cabin.

Until now, Dana had always believed people created their own destiny. Yet what had guided her to that boggy, off-highway road at just this time? Chance?

Maybe.

But Tony's words had struck a chord. Did she really have a destiny, and was it to be fulfilled with Morgan?

After a considerable struggle, both with the snowshoes and her own mixed emotions, she turned her feet on the trail's slick surface and began fighting her way back. Behind her, a bird took flight.

A short time later, she turned a bend and saw Morgan up ahead. She'd never believed a heart could rise and sink all in the same moment, but hers did. She stopped a minute, waiting until he saw her, too.

At first his beautiful eyes seemed to hold a question, then his face exploded into that wondrous smile. Dana spread her arms and, although thrown off-balance by the weight of her bag, did her best to run to him.

When finally his arms were around her, when finally she inhaled the smoke and pine scent of his clothes, she breathed. "I've come back to you, Morgan. Will you have me?"

"Forever," he whispered in return. "If I could."

Then he took her arms and moved back. "But

you must go to your own world now. I've come
to make sure you get there safely."

"You don't understand, Dana. Tonight is the
apex of the moon. Even our love can't protect
you. When the moon rises, I'll have no control
of myself."

Having finally banished the chill from her
bones, Dana was leaning into the crook of Morgan's arm as they rested on the daybed. They
had quarreled heatedly on the trail, and she was
feeling a little smug that she'd won. He was still
doing his best to convince her to leave, but the
fresh warning had done nothing to change her
feelings.

"You didn't hurt me last night. Why should I
be afraid of you now?" She reached up to brush
back a lock of falling hair.

"Haven't you been listening?" He buried his
hands at his temples, and the lock fell forward
again.

"Yes, and I still want to do the ritual. We're
meant to be together, Morgan. Don't you want
that? Haven't you been lonely?"

Morgan laughed bitterly. "Lonely? Oh, yes.
But you don't know the dangers."

"It can't be that bad."

"Can't it?" He got up then, and Dana watched
quizzically as he disappeared inside his bed-

room. Minutes later he came back with a small portfolio, which he dropped in her lap.

"Read," he instructed, turning to the kitchen, where he ignited the burner under the stew. They would need nourishment for the night ahead.

He flinched at his own thought.

There would be no night ahead. Hadn't he already decided? He glanced nervously out the window. The sun was only now reaching its zenith, leaving plenty of time to take her back.

Why had he let her talk him out of escorting her down? Or had he only been kidding himself? Had his true purpose always been to bring her back to the canyon? He'd certainly let her sway him quickly enough.

"Morgan?" Dana sounded puzzled. "What is the Song of Hades?"

"Not that," he growled, annoyed he'd forgotten to remove the section.

She looked stricken.

"The ceremony that made me, and makes all werewolves." He tried to make his voice sound kinder. "You have no need to read it. Move on."

But Dana wasn't one to discourage easily, and he saw her rapidly skimming the pages.

"Move on," he insisted. "That garbage isn't fit for your eyes."

This time she did as he asked, and as he continued preparing their supper, he glanced over at her from time to time. Apparently the contents absorbed her, because her eyes moved continuously, the pages turned frequently.

Finally she looked up. "This is why you kept me here all along, isn't it?"

"Yes." What else was there to say?

"The conjunction with Venus is tonight?"

"Yes."

She nodded as if she understood completely. He knew she didn't. The pages only hinted at the mortal danger.

"One thing." She tilted her head in question. "The first ceremony doesn't take long, yet the redemption ceremony takes all night. Why is that?"

Her startled reaction to Morgan's roar of mirthless laughter was almost comical. Unfortunately, he felt too grim for comedy. "It's kind of like marriage," he said. "Easy to get into, hard to leave."

With another nod, she returned to the pages. A little while later, she gave the portfolio a definitive closing snap and got up.

"No," she said. "It won't do."

"What?" It was his turn to be confused.

She rushed up and took his arms, staring at him earnestly.

"Don't you see, Morgan?" she asked ardently.

"We don't have to risk a ceremony where we both could die."

So she had understood. But fully? He doubted it.

"What makes you say that?" He asked the question cautiously, but was totally unprepared for what she said next.

"You can make me a werewolf, too."

(*Chapter Twenty-one*

Stunned, Morgan backed away.

"You don't know what you're asking."

"But I do!"

She took his arms again, tried to shake his large body.

"I left this morning because I thought we'd always be different. I didn't know a ceremony could make me like you. But now . . . Oh, Morgan. We'd spend centuries together. Mate for life as wolves always do. And be free! Completely free! The sounds, the smells, the sights—" She appeared momentarily let down. "Oh, I forgot. You see in black and white. . . ."

Morgan shook his head. Should he tell her all he really saw? Shadowy netherworld shapes roaming at midnight. Souls lifting from bodies as they gave a last cry.

"You see color? What about your tail? Do you really use it for balance? I've wanted to know these things all my life—"

"Dana!"

She stared at him imploringly, green eyes glittering.

"Morgan. I'd be with you forever."

Her excitement enticed him for a split second, ringing in his ears like a siren song. Forever. He and Dana. Forever.

Forever.

No, the hundreds of years would only seem like forever. Gripping Dana's elbow, he led her to a chair and made her sit.

"I'm going to tell you what hell forever can be."

He started with poor Boris, then spoke about his trip to Europe, about Lily's horrifying ritual and her pursuit of him. How long he'd searched for a place to hide before he found Ebony Canyon, of the animals he stalked, the sheep left by the Indians to appease him, how Lily finally tracked him down.

"She'll never stop pursuing me. Even transforming Jorje didn't end her loneliness."

"We'd never be lonely, Morgan. We'd have each other. And we wouldn't have to kill humans. You don't."

"Listen."

306

She grew silent again.

"You don't know the cost of resisting blood-lust. Every night my disgusting cravings compel me to run through the forest until finally I've wrenched apart some poor creature. During that time, I stay away from the tribe, although many of them are my friends. They perform their night ceremonies, call on spirits, and leave me poor half-dead sheep in hopes that they themselves will live. But I hear their breaths, the beating of their hearts, and yearn to still that breath, tear out those hearts. And when the moon is full—" He stared into her eyes, urgently hoping she'd understand. "Why do you think I have chains in my room?"

"Wolves only hunt to eat!" She leaned forward and spoke with frightening passion. "There's plenty of food here. We don't have to live that way."

"Werewolves are not wolves!" Morgan slammed his fist on the table, but even that didn't dull Dana's excitement. "The melding brings out the worst aspects of our kind, and we're a noxious speck in the eye of God. Can't you understand?"

"Together, we could draw on each other's strength. Be different."

That comment popped Morgan's indecision like a child's balloon. He stood up quietly, went into his bedroom, and locked the door. Seldom did he alchemize during daylight hours. The searing light, the ceaseless noise, the melding scents of man and beast smothered his senses until he barely functioned. But for Dana, he would.

Removing his clothes, he willed himself to alchemize, trying to do so silently, but unable to stifle his cries. Soon Dana pounded on his door, calling his name again and again.

Eventually, his pain disappeared, his vision cleared. Dana's frightened cries merged unpleasantly with her knocks like the instruments in an off-key marching band. The chains on his walls glared repulsively in the thin light.

When he opened the door, Dana's pounding arm came down on his furred chest.

"Are you afraid now?" He enclosed her fist in his hand.

If she was, he couldn't see it in her eyes.

"It never was music . . . all this time. Does it hurt that much?" She reached to stroke his face. He let go of her and moved swiftly away.

"Don't turn from me, Morgan," she pleaded. "I love you just as you are."

"So much you want to be like me?" He picked up her boots and tossed them to her like they were nothing.

"Put those on."

She hesitated, about to argue. He caught her gaze and held it frozen in his.

"Do it. You cannot refuse."

She did as he said, and when her boots were on, he tossed over her parka.

"That too."

She pulled up the zipper, now completely under his control. Walking closer to him, she smiled up saucily, touched the curve of his jaw. God, she was irresistible, standing fearlessly before his monstrous self. An arrow of pure love pierced him so deeply he almost changed his mind. *Could* he make her like him? He'd missed the invulnerability and heightened senses, he knew that, had known it all along. With Dana beside him, maybe this life wouldn't be so bad.

No! Better to risk the Shadow of Venus than to take her into hell with him! But he would do neither.

Steeling himself against temptation, he swept Dana up like a matchstick and slung her over his shoulder.

As he stooped to pass through the door, she shrieked in delight, and for the first time ever in werewolf form, Morgan smiled.

By the time the woods passed blurrily before her eyes, Dana wondered why she'd forgotten about Morgan's hypnotic powers, and was now mad as hell.

"Put me down, Morgan!" She balled her hands and pounded on his back. Although she might as well have beat on a mighty oak, that didn't stop her. She squirmed, wiggled, beat, and shouted, but still Morgan raced down the trail.

"I'm not leaving," she bellowed.

"Stop it!" He tightened his hold around her waist. "You're wasting your energy."

"I won't leave. I won't."

"You have no choice."

Then he started running so fast that the white ground whizzed beneath her eyes like an out-of-control moving sidewalk. She was getting cold. Wind buzzed in her ears. Every fall of his feet forced air from her lungs.

"Please," she whimpered, feeling a bit dizzy. "D-d-don't s-ss-send me a-away."

"It's for your own good," he growled, so sadly and unequivocally Dana knew he wouldn't change his mind.

He was sending her off just like her father had sent her to school. Only this time there'd be no weekend and holiday reunions. She fell into a well of sorrow. Without Morgan, nothing had meaning anymore.

She shouldn't have asked him to make her a werewolf. Her request had clearly stunned and terrified him. She'd seen it in his eyes. Yet he loved her; she knew he did. And she loved him. They were meant to be together.

Which left only one option.

"M-M-Morgan," she stuttered, "I'll d-do it."

He said nothing.

"M-Morgan?"

"Do what?"

He slowed to a light, rhythmic lope and she could breathe again.

"The Shadow of Venus."

Again, he didn't answer, but neither did he quicken his pace. When several miles had passed, Dana decided to take matters into her own hands.

"I think I'm g-going to be sick," she whined, deliberately forcing the stutter back into her voice.

"Sick?" He sounded puzzled.

"I'm getting b-bounced around up here. My—my stomach's queasy."

He stopped. She skidded facedown toward the snow, but he caught her bottom, steadied her, then set her on her feet.

"If you're going to puke," he said hard-heartedly, pointing to a cleft among the trees. "Do it over there."

He'd just given her a perfect opportunity. She nodded docilely, hoping she was only imagining the suspicious glint in his red-flecked eyes, and walked to the spot he'd indicated. He was stronger than she, faster than she—stronger and faster than any human alive—and subterfuge was her only weapon. She moved behind a tree.

"Stay where I can see you," he ordered harshly.

"I'd like some privacy, if you don't mind." She hoped she sounded the epitome of wounded dignity.

"All right," he said grudgingly. "Be quick."

As soon as she was hidden, Dana headed through the trees, lifting her feet high, putting them down flat, just as she'd seen wolves do when stalking prey. Snow was light here, and though slick and muddy, the ground was mostly bare. She moved faster than she'd hoped she could, zigzagging between tall pines and bare birches. Occasionally a twig snagged her parka, but otherwise she moved freely.

This was probably a fool's errand. When Morgan realized she'd gone, he'd be upon her in a heartbeat. But if she succeeded . . .

She'd beat him to the cabin. There, she'd get the white gown, the portfolio with the rules for the ceremony, and harness the dogs. Morgan would know where she'd gone; he'd come for her. He had to. Because if he didn't, Lily surely would.

Dana shuddered and kept on traveling.

☾

Chapter Twenty-two

If the captain had known they'd bivouacked so close to the goddamned clearing he would have chosen another place. But he didn't find out until a couple hours after sunrise, when one of his teams discovered the path to the wretched site and came back to report.

They'd also come across one of Kowalski's shoes, which they handed over to him. Schumacher hoped there wasn't a foot inside. One look at the messengers and he knew the cowards hoped the same thing. Mercifully, the shoe was empty, probably thrown off by the first blow that hit that poor sap, Kowalski.

He gruffly dismissed the officers, telling them they goddam better come up with some wolves pretty soon. That was their job and they better not forget it.

It became increasingly clear that duty required him in the field, and he, unlike his men, never shirked his duty. As the day progressed, several teams found more oversized paw prints, and wanted to cast them in plaster. One team reported fresh snowshoe marks on the ridge above the canyon.

"Didn't we put out a hiker's advisory?" he asked his communicator, receiving an affirmative.

"Guess some damn fool ignored it. As if that crazy wolf woman wasn't enough."

Every time Schumacher turned around yet another damn fool needed him for yet another damn fool errand, but finally he made it out to the site. Now he stood in the clearing among those freaking stone sentinels with several of his officers, who were pointing out their progress. At least the wind had eased up, although he still couldn't seem to get warm enough.

He looked at his watch, saw it was after three o'clock. Off to the west, the descending sun glared cheerlessly. Soon it would disappear behind the mountain, leaving the clearing in shadow. He'd better not leave these pantywaists who called themselves his officers out here after dark—or so he told himself—so he decided to keep up the search for about half an hour, then call it a day.

He was dog-tired and couldn't shake the cold out of his bones. Had hypothermia set in? Maybe they should go back sooner. If only he could get his men to do their jobs, he might find a second to rest.

"Captain."

He turned to see Rutherford hurrying forward.

"I found this near the path, Captain."

A broken paper capsule fell into Schumacher's hand. He clumsily picked it up with his gloved fingers, saw something printed on it in faint letters. *Tiny* faint letters, put there to challenge bifocal wearers.

"Halant?" he asked, trying to puzzle it out.

"Ammonia inhalant," explained Rutherford.

The captain frowned.

"Smelling salts."

"I know what they are! I'm just wondering how this got here."

"Beats me." Rutherford plucked the vial from the captains's fingers. "But it hasn't been here long."

"How can you tell?"

Schumacher got a look that suggested he was an idiot. "It's as white as the snow. After any length of time, it would be smeared with dirt."

"So what do you want me to do about it?"

"Obviously someone's been here recently. We

ought to send someone to search for that backpacker."

"*In the dark?*" Schumacher caught himself, repeated his question more calmly. "In the dark? I won't risk my men for some idiot who doesn't have enough sense to heed advisories."

"Whatever you say."

With that, Rutherford walked away and fell in with the others. Schumacher heard him ask an officer if she'd seen smoke coming up from the canyon's rim.

The woman said she had.

"When are we going to check it out?"

"We aren't. The captain said it wasn't important."

Rutherford turned and stared darkly at Schumacher, who glared back. The wildlife man had no right to question the judgment of a superior officer from another agency.

He'd show the guy who was in charge.

"Listen up, folks," he bellowed. "We search this spot for one more hour, then regroup for the morning. Tomorrow, we'll scour every last acre of these hills, hear? And we're going to find those wolves, wipe that menace out of these mountains! What do you say to that?"

Schumacher supposed he hadn't expected a responding cheer, but all those blank-eyed, nodding heads? With teams like this, no wonder he hadn't fulfilled his mission yet.

Tiring of looking into the face of apathy, he circled toward the dark forest.

He could feel it. Something was out there. Something inhuman.

Morgan squinted into the woods, searching for Dana. Dappled sunlight reflected painfully off the trees, offending his eyes. The warmth of the sun released a host of odors that mingled into a confusing mishmash. He sniffed, trying to pick up Dana's scent, caught a whiff of soap that quickly got lost in a rush of pine, mice droppings, and rotting wood. The sounds of moving insects and animals deafened him.

He called her name. When she didn't answer, he moved forward. He'd respected her modesty too long. If she was going to be sick, she should have done it by now.

"Dana." One last polite warning before dragging her out. He stepped into a cleft between the trees.

She was gone. He stared down for a minute, his eyes relieved by the shade but his soul quaking in fear for her, then threw back his head and let out an angry sound. Birds scattered everywhere. A deer darted onto the snowbound path, then dashed into the woods on the other side.

Why must she always defy him? All God's creatures feared and despised him. Couldn't she have the sense to do the same?

But he was wasting time with this. She couldn't have gone far. He'd find her, put her over his shoulder again, and take her out of harm's way forever.

The going was rough. Although his sight was better in the dimmer light, his large body often wouldn't fit between the trees, and soon he was tearing out branches, pulling up bushes.

Alive in the daylight, the woods were full of frightened scurrying animals. Quail rose from their nests. Rabbits flew to their holes. A porcupine curled into a ball.

Morgan ignored them, hating how their noises and their putrid smells dulled Dana's trail. He breathed deep and long, hunting for the smallest scent of her, then tried to discern her footsteps in the busy forest.

As he was about to change from man-wolf to full wolf form, he saw her running through a snowy clearing, sometimes slipping, always catching her balance just before she fell. A huge pine, surrounded by smaller offspring, blocked his path. With one leap, he scaled the shorter trees. Just a couple more jumps and he'd be upon her.

Then he saw a dark streak along the clearing's

edge. Only a few feet inside the trees, it kept pace with her, slowing when she stumbled, speeding up when she did.

Lily had sent her lapdog out on reconnaissance. The clumsy whelp made a lot of noise that Morgan knew wasn't in Dana's hearing range. She continued wading through the melting snow, one hand clutching her injured shoulder. Morgan smelled blood. Jorje could smell it, too. Orders or not, the scent would incite his hunger.

Would he try to kill Dana? Perhaps Lily had forbidden it. Armed with her cruel sense of justice, she might want to destroy Dana in front of Morgan, so he'd know who'd stolen his chance at redemption.

Just then, the wolfling exploded from the forest. His pads were soft; they made no sound. Dana's back was to him; she'd stumbled yet again.

With a loud warning snarl, Morgan alchemized to four legs, then shot after Jorje, crying Dana's name. She turned toward him with a resigned look, still not seeing the other werewolf coming from behind.

With a powerful thrust, Jorje leaped toward Dana's back.

Morgan tightened his haunches and flew at the lapdog's throat, colliding with him midair.

The smaller werewolf yelped and rolled, then scrambled to his feet. Dana screamed, calling Morgan's name.

"Run for the cabin, Dana," Morgan cried, keeping her in his side vision as he crouched for another attack.

She whirled away, whirled back, her eyes darting between Morgan and the whelp. Behind her, the falling sun cast dizzying kaleidoscopes of light on the snow. Morgan could barely see and was unprepared for the weight that struck his shoulder.

Teeth clamped down. Jorje shook his head, snarling furiously, ripping into Morgan's ear. Blood ran into his eyes, dimming his eyesight further, and his attempts to break free caused greater pain. He steeled himself for the eventual tear that would release him.

The pain got more intense. As his sense of time and place began to fade, he saw a huge branch descend, then heard a loud crack. Jorje screamed and released his hold. Dana stood above them both, holding the branch like a club.

Jorje lunged at her. His balance was off and he missed his mark, fell on his side, then quickly scrambled to his feet.

"Get out of here, goddammit!" Morgan screamed, putting himself between Dana and the other werewolf. "I don't need your help!"

She did run then, slipping and sliding on the snow. Jorje feinted to the right, tried to dash left. Morgan was too quick for him. In an instant, he had the lapdog on its back, his fangs at its throat.

"I have no quarrel with you," Jorje whimpered in the Lupine language. "Just give me the woman."

"She is of my pack and under my protection," Morgan growled, but he backed off anyway.

"Lone wolves have no pack." Jorje spit at him. Rather stupidly, Morgan thought, considering he'd had the cur's jugular between his teeth just seconds before. "I do not know why Lily suffers you to live."

"Go back and tell her the woman will be gone from the mountain by sunset. We will not do the Shadow of Venus tonight." Morgan turned his head away, refusing to keep the lapdog in his sight another second. "As for you, you need not trouble yourself about me any longer. I've found another way to escape."

"You cannot escape. Law is law."

"Yes, and I will abide by it enough not to kill you, worthless whelp that you are." Morgan longed to return to human form. His ear hurt like blazes and the sun was killing his eyes. "Now get out of here before I change my mind!"

Jorje warily backed away, keeping his eyes firmly fixed on Morgan. When he disappeared into the shadows of the trees, Morgan allowed himself to shape-shift. But only long enough to heal.

He couldn't let the wolfling run free with Dana still moving about. But he had time. There was no danger of losing the trail, even with the sensory overload of the daytime forest. A were-wolf's scent was unmistakable.

When Morgan got back to the cabin, he found the door wide open. He paused in dread. Would he find his lovely Dana torn apart in there? After catching up with Jorje, he'd tracked him to the den he shared with Lily and sealed its door shut after him. Had Lily somehow escaped already and made her way to the cabin . . . ?

He lowered his head with impending grief and stepped inside.

Except for the dying fire, all was as he'd left it. Not a speck of blood marked the walls or floors. Dana's bag still sat on the floor. The bed-cover still had the wrinkles their bodies had caused. Water still dripped slowly in the pan under the pump.

Werewolves hadn't been here.

For once, he felt thankful for The Law, and for Lily's abidance of it.

But where had Dana gone?

He inspected the front room thoroughly, searching for missing items, and his eyes came to rest on the pegged rack. The jumpsuit was gone. He also noticed a conspicuous absence on the bedside table. Quickly, he scanned the bookshelves.

The Book and the portfolio were both missing.

Hoping he was incorrectly jumping to conclusions, Morgan entered his bedroom. When he saw the empty hook, he groaned and stumbled to the wardrobe. As he'd suspected, Dana had also taken the fur robes and the holy water. He should never have let her read the portfolio. She'd studied it too quickly and too well.

At least he knew where to find her.

The planets, it seemed, couldn't be thwarted. Whether he willed it or not, the Shadow of Venus would take place that night.

Aphrodite's feet were tangled in her harness straps again. Damn, Dana thought she'd finally gotten it right, but obviously she hadn't. Breathing a curse, she laid the portfolio carefully on top of the burdens on the sled, then climbed off and waded through the slush.

Although her legs and hands weren't trembling as badly as they had during her rush to collect everything, they still were weak and unreliable, and the gown bunched beneath her jumpsuit hindered her mobility. It took quite a bit of fumbling to untangle the poor frustrated dog.

When she was finally freed, Aphrodite lunged forward, pulling the other dogs after her. They weren't prepared, and Fenris tottered, almost fell. Then the team took off, and Dana barely managed to leap on the runners in time to keep the portfolio from slipping off.

She scanned the instructions for the ceremony once again, knowing she had to commit it to memory. Daylight was rapidly slipping away, and she wouldn't get another chance when it was gone.

They reached the rocky trail without further incident, and Dana took note of the lengthening shadows. She knew she should be terrified, but now she felt only icy calm. She called the dogs to a halt, then got off to unleash all seven.

Seven canine servants of man, the text had said, *must witness the soul's redemption. Christen them with holy water, devoted lover, and bestow names of ancient Gods and Goddesses. Thus, the spirits of these deities will strengthen their will to serve.*

Why seven? Dana wondered, but she dared not skip a single step, even if she didn't understand it. She lifted a bundle from the sled and started down the path, calling the team to follow. They tumbled down gleefully.

Dana's heavy cargo slowed her down, and by the time she reached the bottom, the dogs were rolling in the dirt, jumping on one another, completely undaunted by the tall, foreboding obelisks. Fenris raced around one, scattering snow, and Dana sternly told him to heel. Odin started into the forest, and she had to call him back.

She had no idea how to control them all while she went about her business. In frustration, she repeated what she'd read in the text.

"All be still."

As the pages promised, all seven came near the edge of the fire pit, then fanned out in a large circle. Obviously Morgan had prepared them for this night.

Lowering her bundle to the ground, Dana quickly untied it and pulled out a small bottle with a cork stopper and a long string attached to each side. Blessed in the Vatican, the label said.

Bracing herself for the chill to come, she unzipped the jumpsuit and stepped out. The white skirt fell to just above her ankles, and though the breeze was slight, it nonetheless whipped the gauzy folds around her legs. She felt momentarily reverent, as if she wore a wedding gown, and looked down, dismayed to see the ride inside the jumpsuit had crumpled the fabric. Feeling as if she'd committed a kind of blasphemy, she shook her head. What did a few wrinkles matter? They'd soon blow out.

She dropped the string over her neck, let the bottle fall between her breasts, and searched for a suitable stick. When she found one, she began solemnly drawing a circle inside the ring the dogs had formed. Unbroken, she reminded herself, it must be unbroken, and she inspected it nervously as she worked. She mustn't hesitate; she was losing light. After she finished, she skirted the perimeter, spilling drops of holy water every few inches, reciting a spell for protection. If the consequences of this night weren't so potentially disastrous, she would have felt silly.

When that was done, she moved to the dogs, who still sat quietly. First she approached Aphrodite and sprinkled water on her great white head. "Aphrodite, goddess of love. Protect my love and me through the long night."

Aphrodite dipped her head and Dana moved to anoint Zeus. "Oh, great Zeus. Father of the skies, watch over us."

Zeus nodded, too. Dana turned to the namesake of the Norse god Odin, beseeching his wisdom, then next to Freya, asking that she rise on falcon wings and watch over them.

"Queen Persephone," she chanted next, the

water fairly flowing from her fingers now. "Defeat the foul god Pluto, and you, Shakti, bring rebirth to my love."

Finally she got to Fenris. "Oh, Fenris-wolf," she cried, bestowing holy water between his glowing eyes. "Rise and fight all who would oppose our quest."

Instead of dipping his head like the others, Fenris arched back and emitted a long howl. Dana stood in front of him while the cry rebounded on the rock walls and obelisks. Finally it faded.

When all was silent, she returned to the bundle and took out seven split logs, which she carried to the fire pit. The scratchy bark stung her chilled fingertips, making it harder to stack them precisely as directed. One fell away from the complex arrangement and she stifled a curse.

The uncertainty she'd felt since leaving the cabin came back in a rush. Would Morgan come? What if he'd been seriously hurt in his fight with the other wolf? Even killed?

She couldn't let a single doubt intrude. He was bigger and stronger than the other one. As surely as the sun would set, he would come. Holding that thought close to her heart, she reset the final log. Next, she gathered kindling. When she'd arranged it around the logs, she struck a match and dropped it in the pit. The damp twigs and leaves smoldered, went out. She lit and dropped another match. Several attempts later, the logs caught fire and she held her icy hands over the flame, trying to warm them up.

Beyond the trees, rivaling the dancing reds and oranges in the pit, was the sky. Dazzling pinks, incomparable blues, and brilliant silvers streaked through the billowing cloud cover. Then the colors faded and the sky began to dim.

Just then, she heard a terrible roar. A mountainous form came sailing down from the air above her. Dana whirled and leaped into the circle, praying its protection wouldn't fail.

(*Chapter Twenty-three*

The tremendous form thudded to a landing just behind the sitting dogs. Fire reflected in its savage eyes, glinted off a fang. Dana's nerves exploded. She screamed repeatedly. The dogs shuffled, began to whine entreatingly, and still she screamed.

"Quiet, Dana!" The mountainous shape moved closer and stroked Aphrodite's head. Immediately, the pack calmed down. "You're scaring the hell out of the dogs."

Her next cry died painfully in her throat and her knees grew weak. It was only Morgan. He had come. She was safe. She rushed from the circle and wrapped her arms as far as she could around his huge chest, burying her face in his smooth coat.

"Oh, Morgan, you came. I was so afraid you'd been hurt."

"Get back in the circle!"

Stunned by his harshness, Dana stepped back. "Why? There's still daylight left."

Ignoring her protests, Morgan lifted her, then dropped her in the circle so quickly she had to struggle to stay on her feet. He staggered from the ring's perimeter, his body jerking several times. After regaining his footing, he fixed her with a stare.

"Never trust me on a night such as this! And look away."

"But the moon hasn't risen yet."

"A little knowledge is a dangerous thing," he mumbled irritably, bending down for one of the fur robes Dana had carried her things in. He tossed it to her. "Wrap up! Then explain why you must always defy me."

Dana hadn't taken time to imagine Morgan's reaction when he realized she'd prepared for the ceremony, but this certainly wasn't what she'd pictured. Her lower lip began to tremble. She bit it fiercely.

"If you have to ask . . ." She knew she should be terrified, but all she felt was a deep and terrible hurt. If he loved her as she loved him . . . She turned her back, spoke into the empty, darkening night. "So we can be together. I love you, Morgan."

"Dana . . ." The rough timbre left his voice.

Dana glanced up and saw him standing naked in the firelight. He'd alchemized to human form while she'd been staring into the dark, and now looked so gloriously fierce that Dana's love burst anew. She turned, about the leave the circle once more.

Morgan put up a warning hand. "It's because I love you, too, that I tried to prevent this."

He glanced up. Dana's eyes moved in tandem with his and she saw pale twilight overhead. Gloom was nearly upon them.

He shivered and she did, too. "Wrap up," he said again, more kindly, then moved to pick up the second robe. "The cold is bitter."

Pulling the fur close to his neck, he gazed around. Dana saw him take in the carefully laid fire, the precise circle on the ground, the meticulously arranged dogs. Finally his eyes came to rest on the small bottle hanging from her neck.

"You've done well, Dana." He lowered himself agilely near the edge of the circle and sat tailor-fashion. "Now we have to talk."

The crease on his forehead had deepened so much his eyebrows seemed to touch. Dana's heart sank. After all this, he would still send her away. Pulling her skirts into the protection of the fur, she sank to the ground, eyes downcast, dreading what she knew would come.

"If anyone can survive this night," Morgan said, "we can."

Dana jerked her head up and smiled tremulously. "You mean it?"

Morgan's face softened. A small smile played around his lips and he didn't try to smother it. "How can I refuse so brave a lady?" He looked up, saw the sun sinking in the darkening sky. "Our lives are in the hands of Venus."

Dana nodded gravely. Morgan could still see a glimmer of green in her beautiful eyes. But not for long. Soon all would be shades of gray. Even then, though, she would fill his soul with light and color.

"You really do love me," he whispered, so softly he saw she strained to hear.

"With all my heart."

"I love you just as deeply, Dana. Please believe I do."

"I know." Her eyes brimmed with tears. "And love will protect us."

"We can only hope." He reached into the circle and brushed a trickling tear off Dana's cheek. This time he felt no repulsing shock. In human form he could pass through the sanctified line as he wished. But later, thank the heavens, it would keep her safe from him. Unless she failed to . . .

"Some warnings," he said sternly, desperately

wanting Dana to follow every last instruction. "When the moon rises, I'll instinctively alchemize. Although I know I have less control of my impulses during a full moon, I'm not sure how much less. I've chained myself on nights such as this to keep from finding out. Most of the time, I fall into a haze, and when I awake I remember little of what happens."

Pausing briefly, he got lost in watching the firelight dance in Dana's green eyes. He might lose her tonight, and the possibility chilled him so thoroughly, he dared not think about it. Dana waited expectantly until he continued.

"Perhaps I'll have more control than I think I will, but we can't count on it. I may fall into the darkest side of myself. If so, I'll . . ." He looked away. "I'll try to kill you. I know you've read the ceremony, so please remember the most important part. Don't ever meet my eyes. I might beg you to look at me, to invite me into the circle." He drew a hand along the line in the dirt. "It's the only way I can cross."

He went on to remind her not to leave the circle, no matter what happened, describing in graphic terms how capable he was of ripping her to shreds. Darkness fell while he spoke, and soon the fire was their only light. Occasionally it popped or one of the dogs stirred. Otherwise, all was unnaturally quiet.

So was Dana. But more than once he saw her cringe, and he kept up his litany of warnings, wanting to frighten her so badly she wouldn't dare disobey.

Then he asked her to repeat the ceremonial words.

Dana rolled her eyes, but Morgan had seen the terror there and knew her action came from bravado.

"Do you think I'd be here if I didn't already know them?"

"Indulge me."

She made an annoyed sound, then began.

"Yealanay, cawfanay, nayfanay, may. Yealanay, cawfanay, nayfanay, may. The power of love triumphs this day."

Morgan smiled approvingly, and Dana picked up her tempo, moving through the remaining stanzas without once faltering.

"What a woman!"

She laughed weakly. "What a man!"

The moment passed all too soon.

"One more thing." Morgan leaned forward soberly, felt a rock jab at his backside. His knuckles were growing raw from the cold. "I've blocked the opening to Lily and Jorje's den, but I'm sure they have a second exit. Maybe the whelp believed me when I said we wouldn't do the ceremony, but Lily surely won't. They'll come." He paused, intentionally being dramatic. "Whatever happens, don't pull a trick like you did up there in the meadow. You cannot defeat a werewolf. Don't even try."

"What if they hurt you?"

"They won't. At least not mortally." He stood up. "Trust me on this, Dana, for once. Never forget that I am your greatest enemy tonight. The love that protects us also makes you vulnerable."

She stared into the flames. "I'm afraid, Morgan."

"So am I."

The wind picked up, blowing under the edges of his fur blanket like a freezer blast. Morgan's testicles retreated deep into his body; gooseflesh rose on his legs. But the discomfort would soon be over, for him at least.

"The moon is rising," he said ominously, seeing the pale disk peek over the canyon wall. His muscles flexed, stretched, screamed from the effort. Hair appeared on his arms. He plucked the cloak from his shoulders and tossed it into the ring.

"Put it on," he ordered in a thickening voice. "The night will be long and cold."

"But, Morgan, the book says I'm to have only one."

"It will do us little good if you freeze to death before morning."

He turned and fixed his gaze on her. She turned away, but still picked up the fur and obediently draped it over her head.

"And Dana?" Morgan could scarcely see her answering nod through his glazing eyes. "The ritual has begun. Remember, I'm your enemy. Don't meet my eyes again."

Then he fell to the dirt and rolled into a ball of pain.

"Yealanay, cawfanay, nayfanay, may," Dana cried, stretching her arms to the moon. She was supposed to repeat this until his alchemization was over, wasn't she? Dear God, she'd memorized it so completely she thought she could never forget.

But now, with Morgan writhing in the dirt, hearing his screams, seeing his skin actually split apart, her mind had turned to mush. She drove her hands deep into her windswept curls, pressing them against her skull, willing memory to return.

"Yealanay, cawfanay, nayfanay, may. Yealanay, cawfanay, nayfanay, may."

The moon moved up, deepening in color. Dana reached higher, repeating the phrase over and over until her tongue grew numb, her mouth grew stiff. The wind heightened, howling around her, whipping tendrils of hair into her eyes. The dogs arched their necks and let out endless howls. And still Dana chanted.

What horrors he had endured through all these years. She'd heard him cry in pain, of course, but never in her wildest dreams had she imagined such tearing and renting of bone and sinew and muscle. His screams tore her heart like his changes tore his body. And to think she'd begged to be like him. What a fool he must have thought her.

For just a heartbeat, she thought to rush outside the circle, drop beside him, and hold him to her heaving breasts until his agony passed. Then reason returned. Not self-preservation, but the knowledge that if she weakened, she would doom Morgan to suffer this forevermore.

Her head cleared. The words came back. She continued chanting. Soon Morgan's pained moans diminished. He lifted his head, leered at her with wolfish avarice.

"Da-a-na-a-a," he crooned. "Please he-el-lp me. Let me in."

Dana shook her head furiously, kept her eyes fixed firmly on the craters of the moon. She was supposed to say the next line now. What was it? Dear heaven, what was it?

"The power of love will triumph this night."

She sensed more than saw Morgan's head drop. The sound of terrible weeping reached her ears. She must not look. Oh, she must not look.

The next stanza . . . please, let the words come. . . .

> *"Lady moon in her great fullness*
> *trines sweet Venus now.*
> *Yet fickle Lady waits for none*
> *and soon moves on."*

A howl sounded in the distance, different from the one the dogs had been endlessly repeating. Another followed, deep and baleful and horrible. Dana shuddered. Still, the words flowed from her tongue.

> *"Oh, spirits of transcendent love arise*
> *and heed my cry.*
> *We need your light to vanquish those dark foes*
> *who curse this man."*

Time passed. She completed the verse, began again.

"Yealanay, cawfanay, nayfanay, may . . ."

The dogs howled more furiously. Morgan scrambled to his feet, hunkered over, gaping savagely at Dana. His arms were bent and lifted, curled fingers dripping with long claws. He drooled and snarled, and several times Dana's eyes drifted down. He'd never looked more abhorrent. For a moment, her love quavered.

"Let she who loves him . . ."

I love him, thought Dana. Love him more than I love my own life.

She tore her eyes from Morgan, reached higher for the moon, wanting to also touch benevolent Venus, who she prayed would fulfill her promise.

"Let she who loves him plead for grace this night.
  Show mercy, please, oh, Venus.
  Restore my love's humanity.
  Erase his fangs, his claws, his wolfish strength.
  Oh, make him pure again."

The forest rattled as if a steamroller were smashing it down. Branches snapped, roots groaned and screeched, seemed pulled from their very ground by passing hands. Garbled utterances mingled with these horrible noises, and Dana shivered with the dreadful realization that she'd heard those same sounds on the night she freed the sheep.

Lily had arrived.

Morgan was lost in a haze of bloodlust. Horrifying and cruelly satisfying images filled his mind's eye. He saw Dana under him, eyes wide in mortal terror, his slavering jaws lowering to her tender throat. Blood flowed, rich and fragrant. He salivated, preparing to feast.

No-o-o-o! Never!

Reality lurched into focus. How long they'd been there, he couldn't say. The muted thuds of werewolf footpads reached his ears. He felt the forest quiver, heard Lily's shrill voice even over the baying of his dogs.

"You stupid omega fool," she shrieked in the guttural werewolf tongue. "Did you really believe they would not do the ritual?"

"But, Lily," whined her companion. "Morgan—"

"Blocked us in our den, all because you led him to us."

"Fast, fast, fast, sweet powers of love," cried Dana, drowning out Jorje's response.

Morgan then heard the pair skid to a stop, almost saw Lily putting up one arm. "Listen! Listen, you stupid pup. The vile female chants the words even as we move."

"How can we stop them now? The h-holy water . . ." Dread filled Jorje's young voice.

"I have ways," said Lily slyly. "Oh, I have ways."

Then their pads fell again upon the pine-covered earth.

As they neared, the dogs spun to face away from the circle, and Morgan felt a moment's pride. He'd trained them well. Then the moon tugged at him again. He looked up, fell beneath its spell. Huge now, round, and glowing yellow-orange, its man face called to him. Foul images rose up. Instrument of Death, they cried, move swiftly. His hunger erupted with a howl that rent the air.

Lily and Jorje burst from the forest. The dogs bayed more furiously. Dana's chants increased in volume.

Morgan fell into a mindless fog, and just before it enveloped him he heard the whir of flapping wings. A bird alighted on the stone edge of the fire pit, cocking its head watchfully, the crimson flames reflecting darkly on its white feathers.

Its outline quickly blurred, replaced in Morgan's mind by images of bloody slaughters and screaming deaths.

☾

Chapter Twenty-four

"Okay, men and women," Schumacher blustered, pacing back and forth before his troops. "Come sunrise, I want every man jack of you in uniform, armed and ready to march. We're wiping this wolf scourge off the mountain by sundown."

A low murmur ran through the troops. Schumacher scowled and it immediately ceased.

"I know these things seem fearful, but they're just a pack of wild dogs, that's all."

"*Canine lupis*," muttered Rutherford.

Ignoring him, the captain went on. "Stiffen your backbones, folks. Shake off those willies, and start hunting in earnest. I expect nothing but the best from all of you. Hear that? Nothing but the best." He put on his most inspiring smile. "You can do it! I know you can!"

When he dismissed the unit, they wandered listlessly off, convincing Schumacher he'd been wasting his breath.

"Quite a speech," said a now-familiar voice from behind him, in a tone that suggested it wasn't a compliment, and the captain turned to see Rutherford, who was wearing a wry smile.

"Don't put the troops down," the captain said. "Most of them are young. Can't blame them for being scared."

"Oh, I wasn't putting *them* down."

Deciding to ignore the implication, Schumacher started to walk away. But Rutherford stopped him with a restraining hand on the shoulder.

"Do you really believe we'll find wolves out there?"

Schumacher stared at the man's hand. Rutherford finally dropped it. But he took his time doing it.

"You saw those plaster casts," he continued. "Can you honestly say they belong to a wolf?"

"Obviously, you don't think so. Just as obviously, you're going to give me your opinion whether I want it or not. So shoot."

"A clever man is trying to throw us off by disguising his tracks, that's what I think. What I don't quite get is why you aren't changing the focus of this mission."

Schumacher's blood began boiling, making him warm for the first time in days. "Look, you goddam wienie," he growled. "I'm fed up with you trying to get this wolf hunt called off. This unit's going out tomorrow, and we're coming back with a load of carcasses! If you know what's good for you, you'll stay outta my way!"

"A waste of time," Rutherford stated definitively. "But suit yourself."

The captain whirled awkwardly, then stalked back to his motor home. Sunrise would arrive soon enough, and he needed his sleep.

A short while later, an elephant began battering at his door. An enormous beast, with padded feet like a wolf, its trunk a long, undulating tentacle covered with gaping suckers that wanted to draw him in, absorb his essence. The ramming intensified. Soon the beast would break through. He was helpless to prevent himself from becoming fodder—

"Captain! Captain Schumacher!" Each word was punctuated by a slam on the door. The captain shot straight up in his bed, gripping his covers tightly around him.

Dragging a blanket with him, he got up and moved to the door. He still trembled from the aftermath of his nightmare, so he ignored the insistent knocking for a minute until he regained control.

Finally—and slowly—he opened up. The cold chill of predawn greeted him as he gazed into Fishman's face.

"Don't you hear that?" Rutherford asked, waving excitedly into the distance. "It's been going on for hours."

"What?" Then it came to his ears. Bloodcurdling sounds that brought back the horror of his nightmare. Howls and yowls, screeches and screams. His first thought was to whirl and climb under his bed.

He couldn't. Steeling himself, he asked where the sounds were coming from.

"We think from the clearing in Ebony Canyon," replied Rutherford, stepping inside and pulling the door shut behind him.

The captain stared speechlessly into Rutherford's pale face. He could see the man was frightened, too, but his shoulders were resolutely squared and he was fully dressed, clearly prepared to face the horror happening just a few hundred yards from where they were. If the captain had been a better man, Rutherford's courage would have shamed him.

"Your people are ready, Captain. We need to move quickly if we want to save that hiker."

"Who ordered that?" Schumacher asked sharply.

"I did, sir." Rutherford shuffled, then planted

his feet firmly on the ground. Schumacher could tell he was waiting for the ensuing challenge, so he didn't disappoint him.

"On what authority?"

"Officially, your sergeant ordered the mobilization. We couldn't wake you, Captain. We've been trying for several hours."

Schumacher couldn't hide his shudder. "It's been going on that long?"

"The first report came shortly after midnight. We have to hurry, Captain."

The captain nodded numbly. But he knew his job, if nothing else, and he hurried to pull on his clothes. Now his professional side was taking over, and as he zipped up his parka, he glanced at the clock. Five in the morning. The sun would be rising soon.

He turned back to Rutherford. "Order a helicopter. Tell them to be heavily armed."

"I already did. They'll come at first light. The rest of us are meeting at the trailhead in five minutes."

With that, Rutherford returned to the screaming darkness.

The heinous sounds swept inside along with the frigid, whining wind and beat at Schumacher's ears. He slapped his hands against his head and rammed the door shut with his shoulder. But the cries continued, rising and falling, falling and rising, and he pressed his hands ever more tightly. His lobes stung in protest and still he pressed.

He couldn't face it. He just couldn't. Couldn't. Stumbling to his bed, he fell and rolled into the blankets, seeking warmth to melt his frozen bones. But warmth didn't come. His teeth chattered. His body quivered violently, and even his hands couldn't block out those chilling sounds.

A few minutes later the elephant returned to his door, and he scrunched deeper into the blankets. No matter what, he wouldn't answer. Maybe it would go away.

Finally he heard a voice—imagined it came from a hungry sucker.

"Maybe he's already down there."

Another voice agreed and the elephant retreated.

Schumacher wept in relief and soon his trembling eased. He looked up, realized what he had done.

He was ruined.

But at least he was still alive.

"Look at me, look at me, look at me, look."

Lily's singsong carried above the heads of the dogs and rang in Dana's ears. Steadfast, Dana kept her eyes on the sinking, fading moon and called the next stanza. Her arms ached from reaching up, her wounded shoulder throbbed, and cold tears streaked down her frozen face. Her robes had long ago fallen to the ground and her teeth chattered. She was growing weak.

"Speed, speed, speed," she ordered. "Oh, blissful love."

Was it any use? Some time before, Morgan had changed completely to a wolf. No trace of humanity remained. He lay on his side, halfway between his howling dogs and the edge of the circle, body convulsing horribly. His whimpers tore into Dana's soul. Soon the sun would rise. She'd be trapped in this glen with these lethal creatures. Nothing between her and them but a few drops of holy water and seven dogs.

"The Lady rolls on," she mouthed, although each movement of her chapped lips was excruciating.

"Da-na-a-a," trilled Lily. "I see into your heart and can give you its desires. Come out and I shall make you one of us."

"Time grows short," said Dana, trying to quell her rush of alarm. How had Lily known she'd once wanted to be one of them?

"Da-na-a-a," Lily repeated seductively. "I'll give you everything you've ever dreamed of."

Involuntarily, Dana's eyes drifted lower. She saw her tempter's coat shining silver in the fading firelight. Behind her, Jorje paced in agitation.

Suddenly, Lily jerked her head, caught Dana's gaze and held it.

"I know you're tired, Dana. So tired. Cease your struggles now and come to me."

Dana lowered her arms. Lily was right. Her every muscle ached with fatigue. It wouldn't be so bad being one of them. Not so bad at all.

"Meet us in haste. Meet us in haste," she intoned automatically. "Time grows short; meet us in haste."

With each word, she took a step forward, coming ever closer to the protecting line.

"Yealanay, cawfanay, nayfanay, may."

"Cease that loathsome babbling!" screamed Lily.

At that very moment, Dana stumbled. She looked down, breaking Lily's hold on her eyes, and saw a heap of crumpled fur, then another. Why two? she wondered numbly. The text clearly said there should only be one. Was that why the ritual wasn't working? Her spirits soared with hope. With one swift movement, she bent, snatched up and hurled the robe. It rose in a long furred sheet, then fell to cover Morgan's writhing body.

"Dana." Lily's voice sliced through Dana's surge of will. Although she fought it, she could not stop her head from rising. She saw her reflection in Lily's dark and scheming eyes. Helplessly, she lifted a foot, replaced it on the ground outside the ring.

"Yes," Lily urged, her voice as smooth as honey. "Come forth."

Dana lifted her other foot.

Lily stepped between Fenris and Aphrodite. Abruptly, the dogs stopped howling. The bird screeched a shrill alarm.

Rutherford looked through the formation of men and women lining up at the trailhead and searched for the captain, but found him nowhere. The yowls had stopped, at least for the moment, but that only scared him more than ever. He thought then of Charlie Lonetree's horrifying interpretation of his attacker and of Schumacher's half-hidden but still transparent fears.

"I think we should start without him," he advised the sergeant standing next to him, wishing like hell he hadn't said it.

"Yes," replied the officer, who then marched to the front of the line, shouting, "Let's go! Let's go!"

As the wilderness expert, Rutherford took a place beside the sergeant. From somewhere in the distance, he thought he heard the motor of an approaching helicopter, but the faint sound grated on his nerves rather than soothing them.

They had thousands of candle-watts of power, what with all the lanterns and flashlights, but it only served to darken the shadows, and make the towering pines look like hulking monsters. The bare-branched birches rattled ominously in the heightened wind.

Still, a hiker was out there, apparently in mortal danger, not from some supernatural creature as Lonetree and the captain would insist, but most likely from some human monster he'd prefer to avoid. Rutherford took a step onto the trailhead and two dozen men and women began to move behind him. Would they make it in time? Judging by the deadly silence that now cloaked the night, he didn't think so.

They set a pace that left Rutherford a bit winded. He was a hiker, not a runner. They moved quietly, with very little talking. Suddenly, the sergeant stopped.

"Did you hear that?" he croaked.

Rutherford only nodded, too terrorized to speak. The night was again alive with snarls and howls and yelps, sending the wilderness creatures into flight. He fervently wished he had the luxury of obeying those same instincts.

Behind him rasped the labored breathing of the others; an occasional murmur traveled down the line.

"Tell your people to ready their weapons,"

Rutherford finally said. Although he really didn't want to talk at all, they couldn't go unarmed into whatever carnage those wretched cries foretold.

The sergeant's order echoed down the line. It was all Rutherford could do not to jump out of his skin as he heard cartridges clicking into place.

Almost too soon, they were again creeping through the light fog wafting from the predawn ground. From their previous explorations, he knew they'd arrive at the scene of those horrible cries in less than ten minutes.

Except for the screams, everything was deathly still.

(

Chapter Twenty-five

The robe settled like a balm onto Morgan's pain-racked form. Soon he stopped jerking and twitching. He lifted his aching neck, keeping his eyes from the offending firelight, and struggled onto his paws.

Something wasn't right, he sensed it keenly, but gruesome images still blurred his vision. Then he saw Dana stepping from the ring.

"Don't!" The word came out in Lupinese.

Yet she wouldn't have heard it. She walked toward Lily in a dream state, going to her death without a hint of fear. Passing through the circle of dogs, Lily reached out greedily. Morgan saw triumph shining in her eyes.

He flew between them. Sprang with a menacing roar and sank his teeth into Lily's outstretched hand. She screamed in rage, and tried

354

to tear away. Morgan's fangs went deeper; blood poured from the wound.

At that moment, the dogs went wild.

Fenris nipped at Lily's ankles, barking furiously. Aphrodite flew at her shoulder. She tried to shake them off, but screamed in pain as her hand remained in Morgan's clamped teeth.

Dana still stood in a daze outside the circle. Morgan swung his flanks to nudge her back inside. An instant later, she called his name in a voice filled with alarm.

In his concern for Dana, he'd eased his hold on Lily. Now she tore free, swinging both arms wildly. Aphrodite soared through the air. One swift kick sent Fenris *kı-yi-yi-ing* to his leader's side.

"Back away!" Lily towered angrily over Morgan's lupine body. "I will not suffer that she-bitch to live one more night."

"You must kill me first," he challenged in reply.

Her eyes flickered between Morgan and Dana, who had now lifted her arms and resumed chanting. Warily Lily moved closer to the circle, reached out her fingers as if testing for heat, then immediately recoiled. Behind her, Morgan saw his dogs gathering.

Odin flew up. Lily staggered into the circle's edge, shrieked and fell to her knees, clearly stunned. Zeus rushed in and tore at her arm. The rest of the pack followed. Persephone grabbed one of Lily's long toes and pulled, while Shakti nipped at her hindquarters. Aphrodite and Fenris returned, jumping repeatedly at Lily's shoulders. She batted at them like at a swarm of bees. Each time her flailing hand sent one soaring, it regrouped and attacked anew.

With hackles fully raised, Zeus leapt at Lily's jugular.

A loud, deep howl rose from her throat, and Jorje tore into the fray. Gripping Zeus by the scruff, he threw him aside like a used food wrapper. But Zeus landed upright. He whirled and charged again. Jorje lifted a massive foot, prepared to stomp it on the dog's back.

Enraged, Morgan lowered his head and rammed him in the stomach. With an outburst of air, Jorje crashed to the ground. Morgan climbed on top of him. the dogs came forward, surrounded then, snarling, then darting forth to nip.

Lily cried at them to stop. Dana continued chanting.

Jorje's teeth dug into Morgan's leg, tearing hair, splitting skin. Clawed hands scraped at his twisting, struggling body, taking patches of hide. He felt a painful tear just above his eye.

Beneath him, Jorje wasn't faring any better. One of Morgan's bites had taken half his ear. The wound poured blood, and Morgan's powerful legs were digging into his soft underbelly, ripping skin. The relentless dogs took their own toll.

The wolfling started changing into the more agile wolf form, his body wavering in front of Morgan's eyes. With a last effort-filled cry, Jorje succeeded in his transformation. He twisted under Morgan, broke free, and whirled to a four-pawed landing. Morgan tottered, struggled to stay on his paws. He was losing blood at an alarming rate, growing weaker.

"Yealanay, cawfanay, nayfanay, may . . ." came Dana's voice, bringing new strength to Morgan's heart. Fire returned to his eyes.

With lowered heads and bristling guard hairs, the two wolves faced off. Morgan crouched and crept forward. Jorje did the same.

Then he heard a pitiful cry. His head swung around involuntarily.

Lily had scattered the dogs, and now she bit into Fenris's ear, shaking him viciously. Then, screeching with rage, she grabbed one of the runt's legs and spun him around and around. When she let go, he sailed through the air and struck an obelisk. With one final whimper, he collapsed on the ground in a motionless heap.

That diversion was all Jorje needed. The next thing Morgan knew, the wolfling had flipped him on his back and had his forelegs firmly entrenched in Morgan's belly. His gaping jaw was poised hungrily above him.

Like all feral creatures, Morgan stopped struggling and awaited his final moment.

"Stop!" Lily's voice so thoroughly split the air that even the dogs cowered. Jorje jerked his head up.

"Lily . . ." he whimpered pleadingly. "It is an honest kill."

"One of our own?" she asked in horrified outrage. "You would kill one of our own? Have I taught you nothing?"

"Oh, yes; yes, you have." Apparently emboldened by the battle, Jorje twisted his face into a mean snarl. "You've taught me you'll do anything to bring this unworthy one to your side, while I, your faithful companion, get only the leavings of your affection."

Still glaring defiantly at Lily, he let out a protesting howl. "No more!" he cried into its echoes. "I claim this outcast as my rightful rival."

With that, his teeth closed in on Morgan's throat.

A second later, Morgan was free. He flopped weakly to his side, saw Jorje hanging from Lily's

hands. The wolfling gave out one faint yelp before those hands closed and broke his neck with
a single twist. Shuddering slightly, she tossed
his limp body into the forest.

She came to stand above Morgan.

"See how much you mean to me," she said
sadly, then looked up at the brightening sky.
"The moon retreats, taking Venus with her.
Your ceremony has failed."

Morgan's gaze turned to Dana, who was still
chanting. He saw her frightened eyes widen
until they rivaled the size of the circle that protected her. The sounds of crunching underbrush
and tromping boots vaguely reached his ears,
but Lily seemed unaware of them.

"Soon the woman will be mine, dear
Morgan."

His body felt leaden. He couldn't move a paw
or lift his weary head. He tried to protest, but
only a sigh escaped. And when her toe touched
his battered form, he couldn't move away.
"Then you, too, will be mine," she said. "Your
flight from me has ended."

He was losing consciousness. Spots swirled
before his eyes, mercifully blocking Lily from
his sight. From far away, he heard dogs whining
with grief. A bird called out mournfully. A huge
machine whirred somewhere above his head.

An unnatural light filled the sky. He was sinking into a dark chasm, never to return.

"Morgan!" Dana's voice shocked him back. Somehow he managed to lift his head, saw a blur of pure white.

"Come to me," she called. "Come into the ring."

Although a warning pealed inside his head—he mustn't endanger his sweet Dana—he felt powerless to resist. He rolled onto his battered, aching stomach, began slowly crawling, oh, so slowly, to her.

Then Dana's gentle hands were on his forelegs, urging him, pulling him on. Her voice sang sweet words, almost wiping out the foul curses pouring from Lily's mouth. Soon he lay across her lap, his head limply hanging from one of her knees. When he smelled her blood, heard her racing pulse, his hunger rose powerfully inside him.

Like the rabid dog that will not bite its master, he began ripping at his own battered flesh. He heard Dana begging him to stop, felt her tears falling hot and sweet upon his coat. And soon she started to sing again.

"Oh, spirits of transcendent love arise and heed my cry."

Her voice hitched, fresh tears fell on his nose, and all the while she stroked his bloodstained coat. "We need your light to vanquish those dark foes who curse this man. Let she who loves him plead for grace this night."

Morgan's terrible hunger faded. No longer did he need to sever bone and sinew. His pain ebbed. Soon his muscles softened and shifted, melting, transmuting. . . .

"Show mercy, please, oh, Venus," Dana passionately begged. "Restore my love's humanity. Erase his fangs, his claws, his wolfish strength."

Alchemizing.

"Oh, make him pure again."

Humanizing.

"Fast, fast, fast, sweet powers of love. Speed, speed, speed, oh, bliss of love. The Lady rolls on, time grows short. Join us in haste. Join us in haste. Time grows short, join us in haste."

Someone wailed and wept in the distance, but Morgan barely heard it. He only knew it wasn't Dana, because her voice filled his ears, strong and sweet and joyous.

"Yealanay, cawfanay, nayfanay, may. Yealanay, cawfanay, nayfanay, may."

The sun rose in a burst of light that seemed, to Morgan, to come from an angel. He heard the gentle flap of wings. A soft cloak fell about his body. Except for muted faraway sobs, the clearing grew reverently silent.

"The power of love triumphs this day," cried Dana.

Daylight bathed his healthy human form. Nestled in the folds of Dana's pure white gown, Morgan fell into a deep and healing sleep.

Chapter Twenty-six

"Not a mark on him."

The uniformed woman stooped over a nude male body whose brown skin contrasted sharply with the snow. Except for the awkward position of his head, the man appeared to be sleeping.

The clearing was alive with people dressed in tan, whom White Hawk observed from an intersection of the canyon walls and the forest. Many clutched assault rifles nervously to their bellies and swung them back and forth, seeming ready to shoot at anything that moved. Deciding it would be unwise to be discovered, White Hawk moved deeper into the shadows.

From there, he saw a man who had a sergeant's patch on his jacket kneel and put his fingers on the fallen man's neck, as if checking for a pulse.

"Dead."

The woman nodded sagely.

"Stone cold dead, and not a mark on him."

The woman nodded again. "That's what I see."

"His neck appears to be broken," offered a man dressed differently from the others. He wore glasses, which he continually pushed back up the bridge of his nose. "Not long, though. Rigor mortis hasn't set in."

"Hmm." The sergeant slipped his hand under the corpse's neck. The head rolled loosely in the other direction, and all three observers gave a start. "Yeah. Broken, all right."

"Seen many murder victims?" the man asked, again shoving back his slipping glasses.

"Never. Not till we hit this ridge." The sergeant got up, wiped his hands on his uniform with a shudder.

For a time, they all just stood talking among themselves. One of them asked if someone called Schumacher had shown up. Another said he hadn't. After a short pause, the sergeant chuckled, then said, "Probably pissed his pants."

They all laughed, and White Hawk wondered why. He also wondered when they'd hear the woman. She'd been whimpering in the brush for quite some time. He shook his head impatiently.

Obviously, these officials needed help. The woman must survive and face her sins.

He took no care to be silent. Civilized man made so much noise. Between the roaring helicopters, the shouting, and the stomping around, it was a miracle they heard each other. But the woman heard him, and she lifted her head at his approach. Her eyes darted wildly back and forth, then she scooted deeper into the shelter of a bush. All her slick sophistication was gone. Her silver hair was matted, filled with damp leaves. Mud caked her naked body, and the unmistakable blue of impending frostbite streaked her toes and fingertips.

Madness filled her eyes.

She lifted her lips in an ineffectual snarl. A guttural stream of sounds rushed from her mouth.

White Hawk kept moving. When his hand touched her chilled shoulder, she snapped at him. He pulled back, watched as she scrambled onto hands and knees and tried to crawl further into the brush. Calmly, he leaned and grabbed her ankle. She fell onto her belly, rolled to face him, all the while screaming unintelligibly.

Exclamations immediately arose from the clearing. Boots stomped on the forest floor, crushing branches, snapping twigs.

Continuing to scream and babble, the woman

clawed at his hand, but her ragged fingernails failed to scratch his skin. White Hawk reached in, caught her arm, pulled her roughly to her feet. She tried to spit at him, but he twirled her in the opposite direction, sent her stumbling toward the approaching people.

"Your victims shall become your oppressors," White Hawk forewarned, then disappeared into the brush as the man wearing glasses came through a copse of trees.

The woman nearly fell into Rutherford's arms, which he instinctively wrapped around her. She pawed and snapped at him, spewed out angry-sounding foreign words.

"What the hell!" he sputtered, fending off her blows the best he could. "Hey, hey, hey. We're here to help."

"My God, she must be freezing!" someone cried.

Somebody shoved a blanket at him, and Rutherford tried to wrap it around the shivering, fighting woman. She resisted at first, but then warmth fell on her flailing arms. She stopped screaming and clutched the blanket's edge. With frantic, jerky movements she pulled it around her body, held it at her neck, and pressed into the crook of his arm.

"Let's get her into the helicopter," said the sergeant.

With a nod, Rutherford picked her up, mildly surprised when she meekly settled against his chest. Seeking his heat, he supposed. As they started back, the others fell in behind him and talked among themselves.

"Wonder what she saw," asked a bull of a man, who carried one of the weapons.

"Stark-naked," said another. "Where are her clothes?"

"She's acting nuts, if you ask me," said the female officer.

To enter the clearing, they had to pass the body, which hadn't yet been covered. Again the woman came alive. With a powerful twist Rutherford wouldn't have thought possible for someone so small, she flew from his arms and fell on the corpse.

Her blanket dropped away. The blazing morning sun revealed deep scratches on her mud-caked back and legs; white tear marks streaked her dirty face.

"Jorje!" she wailed, running frenzied hands across the man's limp shoulders, apparently unaware she was wallowing knee-deep in snow. When the man didn't respond, she patted his cheeks briskly, like someone trying to revive a patient from a faint. His neck flopped lifelessly back and forth. She whimpered, bent over his head.

When she began licking his tawny face, still murmuring something that sounded like a name, Rutherford stared in astonishment. Then he joined the others in trying to pull her away. She fought them furiously for a time, like the wild thing she appeared to be, her screams almost drowning out the instructions they called to one another.

Finally, the bull of a man yanked her up and shoved her into Rutherford's arms. She shuddered there a second, then threw back her head and let out a keen.

"S-spooky," said the breathless sergeant, who was now standing at Rutherford's elbow.

"Absolutely," he replied, staring in bewilderment at the tiny madwoman howling like a wolf inside the shelter of his arms. "Absofucking-lutely."

Later, when they finally loaded the trembling woman into the helicopter to be evacuated, and Rutherford stared up at the retreating speck, he wondered exactly what madness they were unleashing on society.

Tony White Hawk had a way of turning up when needed, and that morning wasn't any different.

"Thanks." Dana said, taking the miscreant in hand.

"Don't pet her Dana," Morgan said, staring sternly down at Aphrodite, who didn't yet know the wrath her earlier escape had caused. Still, Dana suspected Morgan would go easy on her, considering she was still pretty battle-worn.

"Where did you find her?" she said to Tony.

"Down at . . ." Tony turned his head away. "In the Clearing of the Black Hands. I also found this."

He held out a small bottle, which he put in Dana's hand. "Keep it always. Its return is a good omen."

With a smile, Dana took it and rolled it between her fingers. It was still half-full of holy water. Maybe she and Morgan would use it to christen their children. "Always the cryptic one, aren't you?"

White Hawk laughed, then bent to stroke Fenris, running his finger along the dog's tattered ear. "Your brave pet is faring well."

"He'd do better if he'd stop chewing on his splint," Morgan grumbled.

"Leave him alone," Dana shot back. "Besides, we'll take him to a vet as soon as we get out of here."

Fenris scampered off and joined the other dogs. For a short time, they all stood and watched the dogs play in the sodden meadow, enjoying themselves despite their angry red wounds and missing patches of fur.

"The runt does well on three legs," White Hawk said.

"He should. Any dog with heart enough to attack Lily . . ." Dana let her words drift off. Already, the ritual was becoming a dimly remembered nightmare, and it seemed incredible it all happened only the night before last. Her face darkened, and she turned toward the porch of the cabin where they'd left the backpacks they'd be carrying down.

She heard the men following. When she cleared the top step, she turned and looked at Tony. "We can't thank you enough for all you've done."

He put up his hands. "No need."

"There is," said Morgan. "If you hadn't helped Dana get me out of the clearing . . . She could never have done it without you."

Dana moved forward and gave White Hawk a hug. "I hope we see you again," she said thickly. She stepped back, and Morgan watched her gaze around as if seeing the mesa for the first time. Suddenly, a startled expression crossed her face, and she asked a question, speaking in a horrified whisper. "What about Lily?"

"You didn't know?"

White Hawk's voice contained surprise, something Morgan had never heard from him before. He felt a rush of alarm.

"Know what?" he asked.

"Just as Venus transformed you, my friend, so she transformed Lily."

"You mean she's not a werewolf anymore?" Dana's voice held a host of emotions.

Morgan didn't understand why White Hawk sounded so solemn. This was cause for celebration. Finally, he was free. Lily would never come after him again. "How do you know?"

"I saw her before the officials took her away."

"I wish you could have killed her," Dana said. "She's evil. She . . . deserves to die."

"I felt the temptation. Were it not for the children . . ." White Hawk turned his face away, but not before Morgan saw pain in his eyes.

"Children?" Morgan echoed.

"Lily never killed the children."

"That explains it," Dana remarked. "I became intrigued about the wolf slaughters in the first place because they'd passed over a child. It wasn't typical wolf behavior."

This stirred Morgan's memory of Lily saying she always spared the children. But he still didn't understand.

"Does that suddenly make her a saint?" he asked harshly.

"Not in my book," White Hawk replied. "But some think it makes room for mercy. Regardless, this wasn't for me to act upon. The tribunal will decide."

Then he slipped his hood onto his head.

"Don't do that creepy stuff, Tony," Dana protested.

But already the hawk's eyes peered at them. Morgan awaited the prophecy he knew would issue from the beak.

"Out of the skies will come a warrior. With neither weapon nor shield, he will rein in the white beast and take her to face her victims. Naked and ashamed, she shall gaze upon their anguished faces and quail from the agony in their cries and know what she has done. . . ."

Dana moved closer to Morgan. He reached out. The dogs stopped playing on the mesa and turned toward them.

White Hawk dropped his hood.

"Whoa!" he said. "That *was* pretty creepy."

Dana and Morgan chuckled weakly, then she picked up her backpack. White Hawk secured it for her, and when that was done, he helped Morgan into his.

"So, you're on your way?"

Morgan and Dana nodded simultaneously.

"You sure you don't want the cabin?" Morgan asked.

"It's a kind offer, but the People are simple and we prefer our pueblos." He looked off into the distance. "Besides, your chimney draws the attention of civilized man, and he is already encroaching far too rapidly."

"Then burn it to the ground. Unless, of course, that will draw attention, too." Morgan laughed bitterly. "After what happened, I suspect the legend of Ebony Canyon will keep folks away for a long time."

"No. They will come. The curiosity-seekers, the hunters." Again Morgan thought he looked solemn, but in the next instant he shook it off and smiled. "Not for some time, though."

"There you go again," Dana responded. "Talking in riddles."

They all laughed. Soon they said good-bye, with Dana giving White Hawk another hug. He remained in the meadow while Morgan and Dana collected the dogs, and stood there watching them as they started down the mountain. After a few turns in the wooded road, they could no longer see him.

A long, cold, muddy hike later, Dana and Morgan arrived at the Ranger. A sticker on the windshield instructed the Forest Service to tow it, and Dana gave a sigh of relief that they hadn't gotten around to it yet. Thankfully, the keys were also still in the ignition.

An enormous weight was lifted off her shoulders. They were really leaving Ebony Canyon. She turned to Morgan, smiling. He looked so wonderfully human as he drew his colorful parka around his beardless jaw.

The previous morning had been the end of the nightmare. Tony had come out of nowhere just as the helicopter closed in. Jorje's body lay in a sun-streaked snow cluster by the trees. Lily was nowhere in sight, and the dogs had gathered around Fenris, whimpering. Dana had been holding Morgan's naked body in her lap, unable to rouse him, terrified, and knowing she had no way of explaining the scene to the highway patrol.

Murmuring encouragement, Tony helped Dana get Morgan up the path to the sled, then returned for the fallen dog. The sled was barely big enough for both large forms, and the remaining dogs, tired and hurt, strained to pull it. Tony trotted alongside the entire time, urging the dogs on, soothing Dana.

At the cabin, he put Morgan on the daybed— Dana couldn't face the thought of returning to his dark room—and she'd climbed in beside him, huddled next to his chilled body, and prayed he would wake up.

What if the ritual had been too much? She'd seen the pain he'd endured. Maybe he wouldn't survive. Exhausted and distraught, she eventually fell asleep.

Morgan finally awoke and climbed out of bed in a frenzy. He gathered all his drab clothing, took it to a trash heap near the smokehouse, and burned it. Then he'd insisted that Dana shave his beard.

Now as she gazed at him in the bright blue-and-red parka he'd kept in the rear of the wardrobe but had never worn, she reached up and touched his smooth, handsome face.

"I love you," she said.

He moved forward, put his arms around her. "Not nearly as much as I love you."

"Oh, my love would be hard to beat." She rubbed her cheek against his jaw. "Mmm," she purred.

"Nice." He rubbed back. "I swear I'll never have a beard or wear gray again."

"What a colorful idea." She laughed at her own subtle pun.

"What a woman."

Dana wanted to stay there forever, but the dogs were milling around and they all required a veterinarian.

"The dogs," she said with a sigh.

Morgan sighed, too, released her, and called for them. Then he opened the back of the Ranger and told them to pile in.

As Morgan helped Fenris, who was having a hard time due to his injured leg, Dana's eyes drifted to her vehicle. Red. It was red. A memory stirred.

A giant woman shall emerge from the storm on a red steed and tame the wild beast.

Could a four-by-four be considered a steed? Her eyes drifted to the top of the mountain where they'd last seen Tony.

"Morgan!" Dana cried.

Morgan had been buried in the back, trying to rearrange cargo to make more room for the dogs, and when Dana cried out, he jerked up in alarm.

"Ouch!" He rubbed his head.

"Look!" Dana was pointing to the sky, but the tall trees above the Ranger blocked his view.

"What's so important? You shook me up so bad I hit my head."

"You'll live." Dana wagged her finger urgently. "Look!"

Morgan smiled as he hurried over. This was the woman who'd chanted the Shadow of Venus through the night, the woman he would marry, the woman who would drive him nuts. God, was he a lucky man.

When he reached her side, he put an arm over her shoulder and looked to where she was pointing. His heart skipped a beat.

"What do you think?" he asked.

"Tony burned the cabin."

A huge cloud of smoke covered the northern sky. Dark, thick, swirling, taking the stains on his soul to heaven, or so Morgan felt, leaving him whole and pure and free.

"That's what I think, too." He tightened his embrace and smiled with absolute joy. "Now we'll never have to come back."

Dana didn't say anything, but he knew she understood. She snuggled closer, wrapped her arms around his waist, kissed his cheek. They stood there for a long time, watching the symbol of their horror go up in smoke.

Finally, Dana said, "Let's hit the road."

"Good idea."

They headed for the Ranger arm in arm, ready to leave Ebony Canyon forever.

And above, behind their backs, glided a white bird of prey, wings spread wide against the blackened sky.

It cried shrilly, then soared away.

Dear Readers:

I hope you enjoyed the adventures of courageous Dana Gibbs and enigmatic Morgan Wilder as much as I enjoyed writing about them. This fated couple came alive for me and touched my heart with their story of love taming the beast within. If they did the same for you, then I know I've done my job.

Readers from Arizona may wonder where in blazes they can find Ebony Canyon and the Clearing of the Black Hands. Here's a hint: Don't check your maps. To create a fitting mood for a story about things that go bump in the night, I wanted the mystery of the Superstition Mountains and the remoteness of the Sitgraves National Forest—plus a few other places I've either seen or read about. The result was Ebony Mountain and all its eerie ambience.

I'll be returning to the mountain sometime in the winter of 1997 with a tale about two of the secondary characters who have hopefully intrigued you in *Shadow on the Moon*. I promise you a story as dangerous and exciting as this one.

All my best,

Connie Flynn